THE IMAGINATION'S PROVOCATION:
VOLUME II

To the Students of ICC,
Best Wishes!

Yours,
Scott William Fey

Also by Scott William Foley

The Imagination's Provocation:
Volume I

Souls Triumphant

Visit the author at www.swilliamfoley.com

THE IMAGINATION'S PROVOCATION: VOLUME II

A Collection of Short Stories

Scott William Foley

iUniverse, Inc.
New York Lincoln Shanghai

The Imagination's Provocation: Volume II
A Collection of Short Stories

iUniverse books may be ordered through booksellers or by contacting:

iUniverse
2021 Pine Lake Road, Suite 100
Lincoln, NE 68512
www.iuniverse.com
1-800-Authors (1-800-288-4677)

This is a work of fiction. All of the characters, names, incidents, organizations and dialogue in this novel are either the products of the author's imagination or are used fictitiously.

ISBN-13: 978-0-595-40590-9 (pbk)
ISBN-13: 978-0-595-84956-7 (ebk)
ISBN-10: 0-595-40590-8 (pbk)
ISBN-10: 0-595-84956-3 (ebk)

Printed in the United States of America

Contents

Special Thanks

I want to thank my wife, Kristen, for her constant inspiration and patience with me as I pursue my passion of writing. She is an endless source of motivation and encouragement, and her editing skills continue to prove invaluable.

I'd like to thank my mother, Connie, for taking the time to proofread my work as well. She and my father, Ross, have always supported my dreams and imaginings, and I will forever treasure them as my role models.

Puncher's Paradise

I've got a secret to tell.

I've got to tell someone, otherwise I'm going to go insane. You're the only person I can tell. Because, sure, by the time this thing is over, you're going to know me plenty well. But, I'm never going to know you. I'll never have to look you in the eye. I'll never hear your words of disgust when mentioning me or suffer your righteous glances. I don't want to know you, but I do want you to know *me*.

I love my wife. I adore my kids. I play the dutiful husband and the responsible father. But, truth be told, if you want in on my little secret, I hate my life.

I hate it.

My typical day consists of waking up and getting ready too early for any sane man, putting the dog out, then feeding the dog. I don't mind this so much as I consider him—I call him Ulti-Mutt—my only true friend. I then wake up our ten-year-old, Carole, and our six-year-old, William. I get them cleaned up while my wife, Faye, takes care of Charlotte, our one-year-old. I get breakfast for the older kids before putting them on the bus for school. I next say goodbye to Faye, Charlotte, and Ulti-Mutt and head for work. I put in a full day as a negotiator for a big power company that shall remain nameless, then I leave early to take Carole to ballet and William to soccer. After that I head back to work to finish out my day and try to get caught up, and then it's back out to pick up Carole and William. I take them home, get them cleaned up, put out Ulti-Mutt, let him back in, and commence dealing with the unwavering chaos of children.

Faye gets home about forty-five minutes after I do, under normal circumstances. She's a patent lawyer, and her hours are not as consistent as mine. She's in charge of dropping off and picking up Charlotte from the day-care.

By the time Faye gets home, I've usually prepared dinner for everyone, including Ulti-Mutt.

After that, Faye cleans up and puts Charlotte down, and I make sure the kids have their homework taken care of as well as any chores that require my tending for the night. Most of these responsibilities center around the kids.

Basically repeat this process day in and day out, except add in recitals and games, along with going in to work on the weekends, and you've got my life.

I remember just eleven years ago I was married to an adventurous wife who hit the night scene with me on a regular basis. Clubs, plays, concerts, musicals, museums, weekend getaways, you name it. I never had as much fun in my life as I did in those two years of marriage. Then we had our kids, and all that changed.

Including my wife.

Now, she's basically married to her work and a mother to her children. She nurtures either one or the other at all times.

Most of her co-workers thought she wouldn't be able to balance her work with having children, and she became determined to prove them wrong after Carole was born. At first, I didn't mind. With Faye always focused on either Carole or the work she obsessively brought home, it gave me some free time to catch up on hobbies of my own. I wanted to take up fly-fishing, but that put me away from the house too much, so I went back to my childhood pastime, model trains. Half our basement metamorphosed into one giant landscape with papier-mâché hills, valleys, and railroad tracks. The east side even had a little town I'd erected. For the first few years, it was fun. After we got Carole settled in for the evening, Faye would start working on her things, lasting far into the night, and so I'd head for the basement to do my thing.

After a while, however, I missed the companionship our marriage had once offered. We tried to sort it out; we began scheduling "date nights." Long gone were the days of impulsive passion and lovemaking, now everything had to be penciled in. The result of this new practicum was William, my only boy. He was a welcomed addition to our family, but it certainly didn't free up any time for Faye and me to be together. Now that we were both up to our eyeballs in work and children, I could no longer stay late at the office. I had to meet the needs of Carole while Faye dealt with William.

And, as though we hadn't learned our lesson, those last thirty seconds of spare time were too much of a burden, and so we brought Charlotte into the world. We were actually relieved; it had reached the point where we were going to have to act as husband and wife again rather than as the mother and father of a newborn who required constant care and attention.

So, I am currently a full-time caregiver, and I happen to share a bed with my co-full-time caregiver.

I miss the old days.

And, again, while I love my wife and kids, I hate my life.

I know that sounds harsh, cold, and contradictory. Well, guess what? I'm that messed up. I'd be willing to bet hard cash I'm not the only one, either.

Can I tell my wife any of this? Are you kidding? She would immediately think I wanted a divorce and freak out. I learned long ago there are certain things I just can't talk to her about unless I want to send her into a breakdown. Can I tell any of my friends? Well, I could tell my one friend, but I doubt he'd have much to say on the matter, seeing as how he still enjoys licking his own butt from time to time.

I guess that leaves you, doesn't it?

I don't know you. If I did, I might like you, I might not. But we'll never know, will we? I just need to tell my story. One way or another, it's coming out. If you don't want to hear it, close the book. Nobody's got a gun to your head, do they? If you want to find out just how messed up I really am, keep reading. Makes no difference to me.

Anyway, my name's Cass Morgan. Cass is short for Cassius. My parents were really into Shakespeare. I don't know why they chose that name. He wasn't exactly an inspiring character, as I recall. Whatever. Faye and I were much kinder. Although people think we chose far too formal names for our children, there was a purpose behind it. Charlotte is my mother's name, and Carole and William are Faye's parents' names.

I'm thirty-eight, Faye's thirty-seven. We met in a political science class at Eastern Illinois University. I was nineteen at the time; she was eighteen. We got to know each other, started hanging out. We were just friends at first. It wasn't unusual for us to hook up after partying. We never formally called each other boyfriend or girlfriend, but I would have gone along with such a thing in a heartbeat. She was one of the coolest girls I had ever known, brilliant in discussion and wild in the sack.

Unfortunately, Faye eventually met some guy her senior year who wound up going to the same law school she chose to attend. I heard less and less from her until we eventually broke off all contact.

Then one day, years later, when I was twenty-six and living in Chicago, I got a telephone call from her. She told me she had called my mom to get my number, that she'd been missing me. I was floored! Turned out she lived in Chicago also, so we made plans to meet for a drink after work one day.

We've been together ever since.

But, she's not the same Faye anymore, and I'm not the same Cass. Now we're a lawyer and a negotiator who happen to have three children to bring up. All aspects of our personal selves are gone.

Is this normal? Does this happen to everyone? I just don't know. We long ago lost contact with our friends, most of whom remained childless. I don't know what other parents go through. I'm selfish; I know I'm selfish. I want my old wife back, the one who'd stay out late at a jazz bar drinking martinis with me. I know I'm selfish, but aren't we all?

I love my wife and kids.

I hate my life.

Every year, I have to go to a conference for my company. It happens to be Vegas this year. Last year it was New York City. The year before that, Tampa Bay. I love these excursions. It's what keeps me going. I go with several of the other negotiators, whoever they happen to be that year. We all pretend we're old friends, gambling and drinking together like a bunch of frat boys back in college.

This time three of them weren't much more than frat boys in college, actually, and one of them was a man who had lost his wife to a rare heart disease years ago. Then there was me, the only dad in the crew, just trying to forget about the prison he called home.

The guys all call me "Puncher" because whenever anyone at work asks me how I'm doing, I always return with, "Punchin' the time clock." Truth is, I work on salary, I haven't punched a time clock since I worked for recreation services back in college. They all think it has something to do with work and the stresses thereof. But, since I'm being so honest about everything with you, when I say that little phrase of mine, it's a reference to how I always have to be somewhere, doing something, in regards to my home life. There's always, and I mean always, something that needs to be done.

Dinners to cook, groceries to buy, clothes to wash, a lawn to care for, things to fix, errands to run, and on, and on, and on.

But, in Vegas, none of that existed.

We went to a few meetings, we hobnobbed with some VIPs, and then the rest of the day and night was ours.

Our first night there, Thursday, the guys and I decided to eat at the hotel restaurant and then hit the casinos. I'd love to give you a play by play of how the evening went, but I lost four hundred dollars, and that about sums it up.

I'd like to catch you up on what happened the second night.

The guys and I, and again, we're not really friends so much as accomplices, raided the casino in the early evening. This time, I was up eight hundred dollars. Pretty hard to feel bad about that, huh? Best of all? I could keep playing if I wanted. No obligations, no schedules, no pick-ups or drop-offs to worry about.

It got to be about eight at night when I asked the guys if they wanted to go across the street with me and grab a drink. They'd all been having bad luck, so they instantly agreed. I'd had the bad luck yesterday. When I woke up this morning, though, I knew my luck would change.

Tonight was supposed to be my lucky night.

We headed across the street. It'd been about a year since I had a drink and I'd forgotten how much I occasionally enjoyed it. I started off with a Manhattan, then had a Cosmopolitan, and I was in the middle of a Whisky Sour when a strange woman approached me around nine o'clock.

She was tall, had long dark hair, wore black-rimmed glasses, and appeared a nice mix between quite pale and slightly tanned. I could only assume, judging by her clothes, she was a businesswoman of some sort, perhaps there for a conference as well. Although her skirt went almost down to her knees, it fit her leanness and made her all the more sensual.

"Hi," she said.

I put down my Whiskey Sour and replied, "Hi."

She started giggling before she flirted, "You come here often?"

"No, I'm here on business, in fact. You?"

"Same." She paused to look me over from head to toe. She then grinned seductively, "Where you from?"

"Chicago," I answered promptly. "How about you?"

There she paused for a moment, looking slightly caught off guard. It was as though she didn't know how to answer. I saw her blue eyes dart back and forth, and then she replied, "Tampa Bay. You know, in Florida."

"Right, I've been there on business."

"It's nice, isn't it?"

She took a step and a half closer to me so I could practically feel the heat coming off her breasts. Her perfume was intoxicating. I could feel my head swoosh after the sweet scent of her body mixed with the drinks I'd had. It was euphoric.

"What's your name?" she asked me, her face so close I could feel her breath against my chin.

"Cass."

"That's an interesting name."

"Thanks."

"I'm Faye."

Imagine my surprise.

"You don't say."

"Buy me a drink?" she asked.

I glanced over at the guys standing several paces off from me. They'd seen me talking with a beautiful woman and had decided to give me some space. They knew I was married, but my actions didn't seem to bother them whatsoever. I think I had friends at some point in my life who would have stopped me from doing something like that, but those days are long gone.

After all, these were just co-workers. They hadn't met my wife, who also happened to be named Faye. They didn't even know what she looked like. Of course, I keep a picture of her and the kids on my desk, but no one ever takes the time to look at things like that. That would require a degree of caring that doesn't exist in the workplace any longer, if it ever has.

I love my wife. I love my kids. Of course I keep a picture of them on my desk.

I hate my life.

I kept turning until I faced the bartender. He was a middle-aged guy with thinning hair and a potbelly. He looked like he'd been doing this for a long time, if the bags under his eyes were any indication. Of course, I have matching bags, so I don't know why I'm picking on him. I also have a nice little belly of my own. Hey, at least I still had a full head of hair; that's something, right?

I ordered her drink: "Dry martini."

"My favorite," Faye approved over the loud music, blowing her sumptuously warm breath into my ear. "How'd you know?"

"Gut instinct," I returned, meeting her lustful gaze with my own.

She grinned even wider.

Hours passed, as did many drinks. My co-workers eventually headed back to the casino to lose what little money they had left, hoping to finally get lucky. Way I saw it, I was about to get lucky without taking any sort of chance at all.

I paid my tab to the bartender with Faye standing behind me, her hand riding up the inseam of my pants. Needless to say, I told him to keep the change.

In a slightly drunken stupor, we trotted across the busy street and into my hotel, which was right above the casino wherein my associates were losing a month's salary.

I didn't even bother to turn on the lights when we burst into the room and started peeling off clothing. I wasn't surprised to find Faye wearing a rather provocative piece of lingerie beneath her business clothes. I had a distinct feeling she'd been planning on this little escapade.

We fell into the king bed, clutching each other in our arms, and I spent the rest of the night in paradise.

The next morning, I awoke to find my bed empty, save for the lingerie Faye had been wearing strewn about and a few dark hairs that had come loose upon the pillows in the night's melee.

I got up to take a whiz and found a note on the bathroom counter. It said simply, "See you next year. Love, Faye." She even went so far as to press her newly painted lips against it. I cleaned up and met the guys in the lobby. We had one more meeting to attend before we could head home.

"Hot little number last night, Cass," one of them said to me.

"You don't know the half of it," I replied smugly.

"Score?" one of the younger guys asked outright.

"Yep," I answered.

They all started giving me high fives and fist knocks, telling me my secret was safe with them. I told them I did this every year, no matter what city the annual conference happened to be in, and they could feel free to tell anyone they wanted.

I'd done nothing wrong.

I love my wife. I love my kids.

I hate my life.

That's the only secret I have. That's the only thing I feel ashamed of that I'm sharing with you. By all accounts, I've got everything a man could want. Great wife, awesome kids, a well-paying job, and the most loyal dog a man could ever dream of. But, it's the constant and mundane madness of it all that drives me crazy.

What's wrong with spicing things up every once in a while?

We finished our last, tedious meeting, then hopped a shuttle to the airport. Seeing as it was Saturday and I'd been away from my kids for a few days, I opted to avoid the pile of papers that never stopped multiplying at the office, and headed straight home.

I was excited to see Faye, after all.

When I walked through the door, I dropped my bags and looked for the kids to come running down the stairs or out of the TV room to greet me. The only one that bothered was Ulti-Mutt. He knew enough not to bark anymore; after Carole was born, he'd been scolded enough after waking her on several occasions to be properly conditioned against such outbursts. He did, however, wag his tail madly and suck in and blow out air to the point I thought he might hyperventilate.

I patted, rubbed, and petted him sufficiently as to appease my only pal and then went about the house searching for my family.

Complain as I do, I don't *really* hate my life. That's another secret for you. I told you I was messed up, didn't I?

When I go on those little trips, I realize that the alternative of not having Faye, Carole, William, Charlotte, and Ulti-Mutt would prove unbearable. I hate the constant chaos of my life, but I love my wife and kids. I wouldn't trade my life for anything, as much as I sometimes get annoyed with it.

After all, everything in this house is my paradise.

I'd be a fool to ever give it up.

I picked up my bags and headed up to the bedroom only to find my wife on our king, toiling, as usual, on some paperwork. As soon as I entered she set all of her work on the floor, then sat up on her knees.

"Hi, stranger."

"Hi, baby."

"Good trip in Vegas?" she asked.

"Very good," I said with a smile.

"You didn't screw any women out there, did you?"

"Just one," I replied.

I removed her black-rimmed glasses so I could see those beautiful blue eyes of hers, then pulled her dark hair loose from its ponytail.

"Where are the kids?"

"Charlotte just went down for the night, and Carole and William are both at slumber parties."

"You don't say," I mumbled as I pulled her shirt off.

"Hey," she began, "you didn't happen to grab my lingerie did you? I think I left them in the room."

"Yeah, I got them," I answered.

And then we revisited paradise once more.

Actually, twice more, and then we woke up Charlotte. This was shortly followed by a call from William, who'd gotten scared and wanted to come home.

The chaos resumed.

Paradise.

The House Hunters

"This is the one."

"You sure this'll be easy?"

"Have I been wrong before?"

"Today?"

"Funny, Bunny. Let's go."

Hannibal turned off the Rendezvous. He and Bunny sauntered along the walk to the front door of the exquisite house. Though run-down, it was still probably worth more than all the houses on the block combined. And in this neighborhood, that was saying something.

"Ring the doorbell."

Bunny reached out with a meticulously manicured finger and pushed. They were met with a tired, deep bellow. She looked at Hannibal and grinned; her straight white teeth beamed in the spring sun.

"Nervous?"

Hannibal chuckled. "We do this too often to get nervous anymore."

"We'll settle down one day."

"Promises, promises."

This time Bunny chuckled.

She nearly pressed the doorbell again when they detected slow, shuffling steps moving towards them. The stained glass door painfully creaked open. Before seeing a face, they were met with Beethoven's *Für Elise* playing loudly over what could only be an ancient record player.

"Can I help you?" a feeble voice offered.

Hannibal spoke above his normal volume in order to be heard. "Hello, sir. My name is Hannibal Lopate. This is my wife, Bunny. We were passing by and saw your gorgeous home, and, well, we know this is quite bold of us, but we were hoping you wouldn't mind giving us a tour."

A gray-headed, emaciated man poked one eye out from behind the door. Contradicting the decrepit skin hanging loosely around his viewable face, the couple grew stunned by the preternatural vitality they perceived ravaging within the greenness of his only visible eye.

"You say you want a tour?"

"Yes, sir, we know it's odd, but—"

"This home is not for sale."

Bunny spoke before Hannibal could retort, "We desperately want to build a home of our own someday, sir. We love the old styles of homes such as yours. If you could humor us and just let us take a look around, oh, we'd be so grateful. We'd like to try to incorporate the elegance of these old homes in our own." Bunny began to giggle, "Oh, we've unsettled so many kind folks over the months, asking them to invite us into their homes. I promise you, we won't stay long. If you'd rather not, we understand. We didn't think it'd hurt to ask."

The antiquated face now revealed itself fully. Hannibal and Bunny both smiled at the kind-looking gentleman. He *was* a gentleman, too. That much was obvious judging by his appearance. He wore a vintage dress shirt layered with a wool vest, as well as vintage dress slacks. Of course, to him, they weren't vintage. They were simply his last attempt at high fashion.

"I don't usually trust strangers—"

Bunny and Hannibal had heard it a thousand times.

"—but, you two have a nice look to you. Please, come in."

"You're too kind," Bunny sang excitedly.

Hannibal and Bunny walked into the foyer, shaking hands with their benefactor.

"My name is Edmund Montress. Please, may I take your things?"

Hannibal handed over his ever-present umbrella; Bunny offered her rather flamboyant purse. Edmund opened a wardrobe off to the side and placed his guests' items within.

"Do you enjoy Beethoven, Mr. Montress?" Hannibal asked.

"Please, call me Edmund. Mr. Montress makes me feel old. Lord knows, I've got the mirror to do that anymore. Let's leave it to the mirror, shall we? Call me Edmund, I insist."

"Very well, Edmund," Bunny sweetly acquiesced.

"Of course, Edmund. My apologies."

"Think nothing of it, young man. Now, as for Beethoven, yes, he is divine. A direct link to God himself, if you don't mind me saying so. Are you religious folk?"

Bunny answered immediately, "Oh, yes, Edmund. We are. You?"

Edmund replied, "Been going to St. Patrick's my whole life. Every week without missing a beat for seventy-one years! You folks ever been to St. Patrick's?"

"No, but we have some friends who have visited there. They had nothing but nice things to say."

"Well, it's rare to find people who have nice things to say about the Catholic Church anymore!"

The portrait of manners, Hannibal and Bunny simply laughed.

"Well, let's start the tour then, shall we?"

Edmund walked them through the ornate dining room, the prestigious grand piano room, the rather formal family room, and then stopped in the game room. Edmund rested his withered hands on the lavish pool table.

"Now, most folks don't like to have a game room on their main floor. I love games, though. Can't get enough of them. This was a library, originally. Now, don't get me wrong, I still love the library. We just moved it upstairs, that's all."

Suddenly anxious, Bunny and Hannibal looked at each other before Hannibal offered, "I'm so sorry, Edmund. We didn't realize there was anyone else in the house! I hope we're not disturbing you!"

Edmund chuckled before he said, "Oh, there's no one here but me now. Lots of ghosts, maybe, but I'm the only one living anymore within these walls."

Edmund grinned slyly when he observed Hannibal and Bunny exchange nervous glances. "Relax, you two! Goodness, I'm old as dirt, twice as ugly, and you two are acting like I'm a serial killer! Ha! No, my wife, Elise, passed on decades ago. Nineteen seventy-seven, to be exact. She and I had the game room installed. We loved our games, you know." Edmund began to gaze off, obviously reliving some moment of his past.

Hannibal and Bunny waited a respectable amount of time before Hannibal cleared his throat, snapping Edmund back to the here-and-now.

Edmund flushed momentarily before asking, "Do you two enjoy games?"

It was all the couple could do to repress their laughter. Hannibal was a professional when it came to masking his emotions, however, and quickly answered quite seriously, "No, sir. Bunny and I don't care for games, I'm afraid."

Edmund's vibrant eyes grew wide in mock disbelief, "Why is that?"

"We just don't have that competitive drive in us. We hate for there to be winners and losers. No one should ever feel taken advantage."

"In our opinion," Bunny promptly amended.

"Ah, of course," Hannibal commented.

Edmund now seemed himself desperately suppressing the urge to laugh.

Hannibal remained the pillar of politeness to his tour guide, but he wanted to wipe that smirk off Edmund's face and find out what was so damn funny.

Proving victorious against his brief battle with laughter, Edmund said, "Please, forgive me. I'm getting a bit punchy in my old age. You two must be thirsty, and it's time for my medicine. Won't you please play a game of pool for me? I know you don't like to play games and all that, but I'll feel awful if I think you're bored while I'm attending my needs."

"Of course, how could we disappoint so gracious a host?" Bunny chirped.

"Do you know how to play?" Edmund asked.

"Yes," Hannibal replied. "I believe we picked it up somewhere along the way. Don't worry over us, Edmund. We'll be fine."

"We'd be happy to leave, if it would be more convenient," Bunny offered.

"Don't be silly!" Edmund nearly yelled. "The fun is just getting started! You haven't even seen the basement!"

"Nor the upstairs," Hannibal reminded.

"Of course," Edmund responded with a grin. "How does iced tea sound?"

"Wonderful!" Bunny cheered.

"I'll be right back, then." Edmund pointed to the pool cues along the wall, then shuffled off through a back door.

"Take your time, Edmund," Hannibal called after the old man.

✳   ✳   ✳

After leaving the game room, Edmund stopped upon entering the narrow hallway leading to the kitchen and listened. He pictured within his mind's eye the movements of his guests as he heard pool cues removed from their resting place, balls racked up, and chalk squeaking against cue heads. He then cracked the door just enough, just enough to see Hannibal expertly break. Edmund grinned cunningly after observing four balls ricochet into four pockets.

"Don't like games, huh? Hannibal, old boy, I think we're playing a game right now."

✳   ✳   ✳

"What do you think?" Bunny asked.

"I think this may be our easiest one yet."

Bunny sighed uncomfortably. "I don't know, Bull. This one is giving me the creeps. There's something not right here."

"Since when do you get the heebie-jeebies?"

"Call it women's intuition. I think we ought to call it a day."

Hannibal missed an easy shot to the corner pocket at Bunny's conclusion. "Are you kiddin' me? Look at this place, will ya? I bet he's got thousands stashed around here. Your shot."

"It's about time. What am I, stripes?"

Hannibal nodded.

"We've got enough this week. Let's hit the road." Bunny paused to point at a ball, then to the furthest pocket. She began to line up her cue. "I've got a bad feeling on this one. I'm tellin' ya, he ain't right."

Hannibal whistled after Bunny nailed her shot. "Look, Sin-a-Bun, let's just wait 'till we see the upstairs. If it looks good, we follow the plan. If it don't look good, we blow. Fair enough?"

"Yeah, fair enough," Bunny replied.

At that moment, Bunny and Hannibal heard the familiar shuffling of feet through the door.

"Get back in character," Hannibal commanded.

✳   ✳   ✳

"Here we are," Edmund declared, entering with his back to them because he'd used it to push the door open. He carried a silver tray with three tall glasses of iced tea, each with a quarter of a lemon wedged onto its lip. "How goes the game?"

"Quite awfully, I'm afraid," Hannibal moaned. "Unfortunately, we've resorted to rolling the balls into their pockets by hand."

"Oh, well, that's to be expected for those unfamiliar with billiards!" Edmund exclaimed while setting down the tray atop a nearby table. He raised his eyes to see the cues back in their places and a ball in each of Bunny's hands. He began to chuckle. "Well," he continued, "as long as you're having fun…Please, have a seat and enjoy your tea."

"Of course," Bunny concurred, setting the balls down upon the pool table.

"We do hate to take up so much of your time, Edmund," Hannibal apologized, taking a glass of tea and sitting upon a nearby stool. "Are you sure we're not an inconvenience?"

Edmund beamed, "You're quite a stroke of luck, young man. A veritable personification of convenience! Ha!"

Bunny made rapid-dread-filled-eye-contact with Hannibal. She took her glass of tea and sat at a stool. She thought it tasted rather unusual.

"So, are your friends thinking of joining St. Patrick's?" Edmund asked casually while gulping his iced tea down.

"Yes, I believe they said they were, didn't they, Bunny?"

"Yes, I remember them speaking candidly that St. Patrick's was the church for them," Bunny corroborated.

Edmund gently set his empty glass on the table. "You realize, of course, there is no St. Patrick's. Not in this city."

Hannibal and Bunny looked at each other briefly. Hannibal's eyes were composed. Bunny's were filled with terror.

"We've lived so many places, we must be getting confused. I do apologize, Edmund. However, I must say, I'm flabbergasted as to why you purposefully deceived us!"

"Hannibal, my friend, you are a pro," Edmund's feeble voice praised. "For a fella that doesn't like games, you sure are good at them."

"I don't understand," Bunny nearly cried.

"Ah, sweetheart. Don't play innocent with me. I watched your boyfriend break. He's been playing billiards for at least ten years, I can tell by his form."

Hannibal cursed himself.

"In fact," Edmund resumed, "you two have been fibbin' me since you walked up my path."

"Well," Hannibal shouted, standing up, "I'm afraid I've never been more insulted! Perhaps I *am* mistaken with St. Patrick's, forgive me for attempting to humor my elder. As for billiards, I have a rather sordid past that I didn't wish Bunny to know about—"

"The game's over, Hannibal," Edmund informed. "Give it up."

"We'll be going," Hannibal said. "Bunny, come."

Hannibal broke his stare at Edmund and turned to Bunny. He watched her fall to the floor as though she had boulders tied to her wrists.

"You can't leave now," Edmund laughed.

Hannibal's vision went fuzzy around the edges.

"You haven't seen the basement!"

✳   ✳   ✳

"Sin-a-Bun, wake up! Get up!"

Bunny opened her eyes, feeling as though she were on the bottom of the ocean. While her head swam, she began to sense an aching about her entire body, as though she'd been handled roughly.

"We got trouble, Sin-a-Bun! Wake up!"

"Bull, wha—?"

Bunny focused and faced the direction of Hannibal's voice. She saw him in a chair, directly beside her. He was bound with thick rope. She instantly looked down to find the same type of rope wrapped tightly around her.

"Oh, God," she moaned.

"Don't panic," Hannibal ordered. "We'll get out of this."

"What'd he do, drug us?"

"I think so," Hannibal muttered while taking in his surroundings haphazardly. All he could see before him was a wall with gardening tools attached to it. He couldn't turn his head enough to see behind him.

"Do you think he's callin' the cops?" Bunny asked.

"Do you?"

"No."

"Same here," Hannibal agreed.

"I knew this place was a mistake! We shoulda headed for the next state. I knew we shoulda—"

"Shut up!" Hannibal screamed. "We got enough problems without you bustin' my chops!"

Bunny grew silent.

"This ain't right," Hannibal groaned. "Something's off here. You were right, Sin-a-Bun. I can feel it, now. You were right. God help us."

Bunny huffed. "Why *would* He?"

✳   ✳   ✳

Edmund opened the door to his basement and slowly descended. He finally reached the bottom of the stairs. He looked to the far corner to see his guests, still bound. He noticed gleefully they had apparently worn themselves out struggling against the ropes.

"Hello, house guests!" he cried out in delight.

Both Bunny and Hannibal sat up rigidly at the sound of his voice.

"You crazy old man, what's this about?" Hannibal demanded. "I'll have you arrested for this—"

"Ha!" Edmund laughed. "The infamous 'House Hunters' dare to threaten me with the law! You must be joking. Such a sense of humor on you, young Hannibal. Quite amusing."

Bunny glared at Hannibal. He hung his head.

"Oh, yes," Edmund spoke as he approached his prisoners' backs, "you both have made quite a name for yourselves. How people kept falling prey to you is beyond me. Honestly, didn't any of the folks you picked to plunder ever bother reading the newspaper? Old people, I swear. Just because it doesn't happen in your hometown, nobody bothers to care. Well, unfortunately for you, I read the paper front to back. Imagine my surprise to read about a young blonde with a brunette lady friend who ask for tours of old homes, especially old homes owned by old folks, and then rob them blind. I have to admit, I'm just as guilty. I've got fourteen thousand sitting under my mattress right now. That's why you wanted to see the upstairs so badly, isn't it, Hannibal?"

Hannibal did not reply.

"It's a good job, if you're in it for the money. Pretty smart little gig you dreamed up, Hannibal."

"It was my idea, actually," Bunny asserted.

"Oops! Sorry about that, Bunny!" Edmund apologized.

"You knew the minute you saw us."

"Yes, sir, I did. Started in Sparta and worked your way clear up here to Moline. Probably figured you'd hit Iowa after me, didn't you? Why, I read you struck Litchfield, Taylorville, Jacksonville, Macomb, Galesburg—I can't believe you were so bold! So many towns in such an obvious pattern. Figured the country cops couldn't catch you, right?"

"They haven't yet," Bunny seethed.

"No, they haven't," Edmund agreed. "But I have."

"What do you plan to do with us?" Hannibal probed.

"Oh, I don't know. Maybe keep you here for awhile."

"They'll wonder why our Rendezvous is in front of your house."

"Your truck's been moved into my garage. Nobody will come looking for it. Correct?"

Hannibal and Bunny knew he was right. They both had no family with whom they cared to keep in touch. Her grandmother raised Bunny after her mother ran off with a trucker. After years of abuse, Bunny decided enough was enough. She stole every nickel her grandmother kept in the house, then started living on the streets. That's where she met Hannibal. She didn't know much about his past, he'd never cared to tell her, but they'd been together, on their own, for eleven years now. All they had were each other. That's all they'd ever need.

"Not much in that truck," Edmund resumed.

Hannibal winked at Bunny.

"Just some clothes in a few suitcases…Oh, and eighty-two thousand in cash stowed under the seats. Is that really the best hiding place you could come up with?"

The wink now seemed premature.

Enough was enough. "What do you want with us, old man? What's going on here?" Hannibal was in a rage.

"What's this about?" Edmund repeated. "This is about the game, that's all. The three of us, we've been playing a game all afternoon. I've greatly enjoyed it, personally. I hope you have as well. And, since I'm not tied up, I'd say I've won."

"So you turn us in now, is that it?" Bunny questioned.

Edmund began to laugh wildly, but his laughter soon became a fit of wheezing. Finally, he gained enough control to sputter out, "Oh, no, my dear. When you play the game with Edmund Montress, you play to the very last."

"Meaning?" Hannibal insisted.

Bunny felt a quick prick jab into her left buttock.

"What the hell!" she cried out.

"What's going on?" Hannibal screamed. He immediately felt a stick to his posterior as well.

"Meaning," Edmund answered, "that we still have quite a bit of fun left with each other. You see, I've won our little game. And now…now I get my reward."

Hannibal and Bunny both meant to usher threats against the old man, but only guttural gibberish escaped their mouths.

They were paralyzed.

"Tell me," Edmund requested, "have either of you ever heard of the 'Homeless Hijackers?' Have you?"

Edmund's manners dictated that he wait a few moments, even though he realized his hostages could not wiggle their pinky at this moment, much less answer his question.

"No, of course you haven't. That's because there is no proof the 'Homeless Hijackers' ever existed. Elise and I were very careful to leave no evidence. It was a little game she dreamed up, much as Bunny dreamed up robbing the elderly. What is it about some women? They can be so vindictive! Anyway, we tried it one night after a show in Rock Island. We picked up an old man—just some bum. Once we got him in the car, we promised him food and shelter. Oh, we did have our fun with him. That began a game we played for years and years. Unlike you two, however, we considered it just as much a game to see if we could avoid any publicity for our actions whatsoever, so that our fun could continue. Don't you see how the press can ruin everything? To think, if I hadn't read about your exploits, you probably would have whacked me over the head with your umbrella, Hannibal, and made off with fourteen grand in cash! Ah, well, it wasn't meant to be."

Bunny and Hannibal next heard a metallic object dragged off a flat surface. Bunny had no idea what she had just heard. Hannibal, on the other hand, would know that sound anywhere. The sound of a butcher knife lifted off a block.

They felt a hand grab the back of their chairs, heard a lock of some sort release, and then both were surprised to swivel in a half circle.

Horror seized their hearts.

"Elise loved saving their fingernails. That woman was quite odd at times, but I did love her so."

Edmund stood facing Bunny and Hannibal. Hannibal was correct in his deduction; Edmund weakly held a butcher knife in his right hand. He also wore goggles and an apron.

He turned his back to them and walked to a record player at the far side of the room. It was next to a ridiculously large oven.

Having moved, Edmund no longer blocked the view of the room, and the couple experienced more misery. Directly before them lay a mortician's table. Behind the table were shelves and shelves lined with skulls and jars full of what appeared to be fingernails.

"I always preferred to save their heads, myself. Of course, I cleaned them off. I mean, what a nut I'd be to let them rot and stink up the place, am I right?"

Edmund pulled a record out from a case and placed it upon the record player. He lined up the needle and then picked up his butcher knife again. He approached Bunny and Hannibal.

Tears streamed down Bunny's face.

Hannibal had liquid rushing down his thighs.

"Now, I'm not as strong as I used to be. I use to be able to lop off a whole arm with one swipe of this baby. I have to work it like a saw anymore. Takes forever, but that's okay. After all, this is the fun part."

Beethoven's *Für Elise* began to play throughout the basement.

Bunny screamed incoherently. Hannibal quickly joined in.

"I really have to thank you two for dropping by," Edmund offered sincerely. "It's been years since I've been able to go scrounge up any fun on my own. But with you two, it came right to me!"

He bent over Bunny.

"The game is over. Now comes the awful fun."

The Legend of Josiah Mibb

"Who is that?" Homer yelled from the storage room of Twilight Hills' Civil War Museum upon hearing a bell ring, alerting him of patrons.

"It's Wendell Krone, Mr. Benson," an even voice returned.

"Who?" Homer yelled back.

Wendell stood at the front counter of the diminutive museum with his wife of one year, Cassie. He glanced at her and rolled his eyes.

"Wendell Krone! I grew up here, remember? You were my high school history teacher!"

"Krone?" Homer repeated.

He finally emerged from the back and studied Wendell and Cassie as though he had discovered a hair in his cake. He had spectacles on as thick as bulletproof glass, yet he still squinted at them. He did so out of habit more than necessity.

Without removing his incredulous gaze from his visitors, Homer took his place behind the counter.

Eventually, he huffed, "I don't remember any Wendell Krone."

"Mr. Benson," Wendell began, completely mortified at being forced to regress to his seventeen-year-old self, "would you like me to bring you some beer and doughnuts?"

Slowly, Cassie saw Homer's eyes give way from cloudy confusion to sharp recollection.

"You little son of a—"

"We'd like to tour your museum," Cassie interjected while holding back her laughter.

Homer stared at Wendell, but his urge to whip profanities had passed. "Four dollars for the both of you," he mumbled.

Wendell handed him the fee. Homer took it and muttered, "I never did like you, you little smart mouth."

"I know, Mr. Benson. That's been well established."

Cassie and Wendell walked throughout the single room museum. As they strolled about looking at old dug up bullets, defunct rifles, authentic flags and uniforms, and antiquated photographs, the wooden floor beneath them protested with each step.

Despite his feelings for Mr. Benson, Wendell was quite impressed with the museum. While it paled in comparison to, say, Chicago's Field Museum, for a little town of two thousand, it was very well done. After Wendell's class graduated, Mr. Benson said he'd had enough and retired from teaching. He'd been left a considerable amount of his great-grandfather's paraphernalia from the Civil War, so, as a lover of history and that war in particular, he decided to educate the town in a less taxing manner. He opened his own museum. The museum had two employees—Mr. Benson and Reginald Benson, his grandson.

Of course, the museum was frequented mostly by people just passing through. All the citizens of Twilight Hills would sooner forget the Civil War had ever existed.

"You've done a great job with the place, Mr. Benson."

Homer paid no attention to Wendell's compliment as he stood behind the counter, tugging at his vest and scrutinizing the couple suspiciously.

"You have a wonderful collection. How long have you been at it?" Cassie asked.

Homer had always been a sucker for a pretty face, and Cassie's curls proved too much for him to resist, "Oh, I've been collecting my whole life. Good deal of this stuff was left to me by my grand-pappy, but I've picked up bits and pieces through the years. Now I've got my grandboy, Reggie, buying stuff for me on Bee-bay."

Cassie and Wendell giggled, but they knew better than to correct the old man.

"Well, I think it's wonderful," Cassie affirmed. "The town must really appreciate all you've done. Making history come alive like this is something every small town needs."

Homer left his perch behind the counter and approached the petite blonde. "You don't know how right you are, but I should have known better. This town don't give two tails about this museum."

"Why?" Cassie asked.

"Boy, are you telling me you've never told her the legend of Josiah Mibb?" Homer asked Wendell with utter disdain.

"It's all a load of sh—"

"No," Cassie interjected at the perfect moment. "Wendell's never told me about any legend."

"You're just like the rest of them," Homer chastised. "No sense of history."

"The town hates its own history," Wendell retorted. "Why would I even bring it up to people who didn't grow up here?"

"What are you two talking about?" Cassie asked.

"During the Civil War—"

"Mr. Benson, this is useless," Wendell interrupted. He knew that Homer would inevitably finish with the statue, and Wendell assumed, with his wife's sense of curiosity, he would wind up sitting in the cemetery tomorrow night.

"Let him finish," Cassie demanded with a grin to her husband.

"Thank you," Homer said. "I don't know how someone like Wendell Krone tricked a lovely lady like yourself into marrying him, but maybe you can clean up his act."

Wendell wanted to point out that he worked for a non-profit adoption agency now, that his act was quite clean, but he didn't get the chance.

"When the Civil War broke out, Twilight Hills was honored to have thirty-three of its finest young men sign up to fight the Rebels. The town treated them like heroes, and everyone took a great deal of pride in their sons, husbands, nephews, cousins, second cousins, third cousins, fourth cousins—"

"We get it," Wendell busted in. "Everyone was related to the thirty-three somehow."

"Wennie," Cassie whispered as she jabbed him in the ribs. She hated it when her husband was rude with people.

Homer grunted in victory, then continued, "Well, in 1862, our boys got their clocks cleaned at the Second Manassas. Even so, every one of them survived. Considering we'd lost 13,820 Union soldiers in that battle, that was quite a miracle. But, it didn't make no difference."

"Why?"

"They all got wiped out a month later," Wendell answered his wife.

"Not quite a month, young man."

Wendell bit his tongue.

"Although they had survived the Second Manassas, between September 17 and 18, at the Battle of Antietam, every last one of them died. And we thank God for that."

"What!" Cassie cried out. "How can you say such a thing?"

"Between Second Manassas and Antietam, our boys became war criminals!" Homer erupted. "They'd broken off from their march to Antietam and raided Dillowsburg. Their Second Lieutenant, Josiah Mibb, took a group of Union soldiers to stop them, but our thirty-three were too much for them. They killed all of their fellow soldiers, and in a final act of defiance, cut off Mibb's hands and tongue."

Cassie gasped.

"Yes, sick indeed. Mibb later reported, non-verbally, of course, that the boys had gone berserk; he didn't know why. To this day, none of us understand it. They murdered, pillaged, and even cut off the hands and tongue of some poor woman there along with Mibb. When they were through, they marched to Antietam like nothing had happened. There, they all died in battle."

"See why the town hates acknowledging it had a part in the Civil War?" Wendell asked his wife.

"I certainly do."

"Well, thanks, Mr. Benson. We'll be going now," Wendell spat out. He knew what was coming next, and he wanted to get Cassie out of there before he found himself forced to visit the cemetery.

"Wait just a minute, you know what's coming up, right?" Homer prodded.

"Wendell, stop!" Cassie ordered as she was dragged along behind her husband.

Wendell, of course, gave in just before he'd gotten her to the door of the museum.

Cassie patted down her clothes after Wendell had sent them into a flurry of disarray and questioned, "No, what's coming up?"

Homer plodded across the creaky floor, peering through his glasses with his glazed eyes, then said, "September 16!"

"Jo Lynn's birthday?" Cassie questioned before looking up to Wendell in confusion.

"Who?" Homer asked in puzzlement.

"My mom, Mr. Benson. She's lived here her whole life. She was the secretary at your school. You chewed her out about me on a regular basis. You remember," Wendell groaned.

"Jo Lynn? No, I don't remember anyone named Jo Lynn."

Wendell sighed and muttered something unintelligible to his wife. She giggled.

"What else is on September 16, Mr. Benson?" Cassie asked the feeble old man.

"Why, the statue comes alive, of course!"

"That's enough!" Wendell declared before he grabbed his wife by the arm and forced her out of Twilight Hills' Civil War Museum.

✳   ✳   ✳

"This meatloaf is excellent, Jo Lynn."

"Thank you, sweetie," Jo Lynn returned to Cassie.

Cassie and Wendell sat at the dinner table with Wendell's parents, Jo Lynn and Laymon Krone. They were enjoying a scrumptious meatloaf, baked potatoes, steamed vegetables, and sourdough muffins. And, of course, below the table pranced and trotted Peppy, the always-hungry mixed Collie.

"Thanks so much for coming home for my birthday," Jo Lynn said.

"I can't believe they gave you a half week off!" Laymon exclaimed.

"Well, I had it coming," Wendell replied.

"And you're not missing any classes?" Laymon questioned.

"I cleared my absences with my professors," Cassie replied, embarrassed at being forced to answer with a mouth full of sourdough.

Laymon huffed and then went back to his meatloaf. He had started his own garage at the age of eighteen, thirty years ago, and hadn't had a day off since. For obvious reasons, he became rather jealous and grumpy when anyone else got time away from work, or master's programs, for that matter.

Sensing Laymon's attitude made Cassie uncomfortable, Jo Lynn attempted to switch topics, "So, did you show Cassie around on your way into town?"

"I'm glad you brought that up," Cassie immediately returned.

Wendell threw down his silverware and complained, "I thought we agreed to drop it!"

"Drop what?" Laymon asked with his meatloaf suspended between the plate and his mouth.

"I don't want to talk about it," Wendell spouted in irritation.

"Don't want to talk about what?" Jo Lynn questioned.

Wendell huffed, "You know, if someone says they don't want to talk about something, and then you ask what it is they don't want to talk about, then we're *still* talking about it!"

"Well, excuse me!" Jo Lynn cried. "I just thought we could have a nice talk at the dinner table, but since your father is being grumpy, I guess you decided to join in on his parade. I made a nice dinner, and this is how you two—"

"Give me a break!" Wendell moaned.

"Aren't you being a little dramatic?" Laymon patronized his wife.

Peppy barked in accordance, although he actually only wanted some meat-loaf. Cassie was sure that the Krone men had been ganging up on Jo Lynn for years. Well, Jo Lynn had a partner now.

"We stopped by the Civil War Museum," Cassie told Jo Lynn.

"Why?" Laymon asked.

"Cassie's a history buff," Wendell replied to his father. He was aggravated that his wife had gone against his wishes, but he knew he'd never be able to control her. After all, that was one of the main things he loved about her. "We bumped into old Homer Benson."

"That old dumba—"

"Laymon!" Jo Lynn reprimanded.

Laymon went back to his meatloaf.

"What did you think of Mr. Benson?" Jo Lynn asked Cassie with a wry grin.

"He was…interesting," Cassie laughed.

"That's putting it mildly," Wendell mumbled.

"He started to say something really fascinating, but your son literally dragged me out of his museum before he could finish."

"The statue?" Laymon questioned without looking up from his plate.

"The statue," Wendell replied simply.

"What about the statue?" Cassie interrogated.

"Oh, I hate sharing a birthday with that darn statue!" Jo Lynn exclaimed.

"A statue has a birthday?" Cassie asked in utter confusion.

"Why would a statue have a birthday?" Laymon inquired sarcastically to his daughter-in-law.

"Well, I wouldn't think it would," Cassie retorted with her cheeks flushed, "but since no one will tell me what in the hell is going on!"

There was an awkward moment of silence.

Wendell chuckled. Along with the fact that his wife didn't take orders, he also loved the fire she could never keep contained when exasperated. He decided he'd break the silence and fulfill his wife's wishes: "Well, Benson told you about the thirty-three and Josiah Mibb and all that."

"Right," Cassie nodded expectantly.

"After the Civil War ended, the people of Twilight Hills were so embarrassed their boys had mutinied against a commanding officer, they erected a statue of Josiah Mibb in tribute. They hoped the gesture could somehow make up for the tragedy."

"Did the statue have its hands?" Cassie asked in total seriousness.

"Yes, and it still does," Laymon answered as he dug through his steamed vegetables looking for the cauliflower.

"It's still there?"

"Mm-hmm," Jo Lynn replied without looking up.

"Oh. Go on," Cassie encouraged.

"Well, the legend says that on September 16, at midnight exactly, the statue will come alive."

"You're kidding me!" Cassie blurted out, wide-eyed. She tried with all her might not to laugh.

"Not just that," Wendell continued, mortified, "but it will give you an order. If you don't follow its orders, it'll cut off your hands and tongue."

"That's ridiculous!" Cassie exploded, finally erupting in laughter.

Peppy barked at the sudden onslaught of noise.

"Maybe," Laymon affirmed, "but there were documented cases of men found dead in front of his statue with their hands and tongues missing. They bled to death."

Cassie stopped laughing.

"Dad, you know it was some sicko that did that, not the statue."

"When did it happen?" Cassie questioned. Now that there were documented cases of *something* happening at the statue, her thirst had been awakened.

"Let's see," Laymon began as he searched his memory. "September of 1911…1943…and…1968. After that, no one had the guts to take the chance."

"It was just some whack-job," Wendell asserted.

"Over fifty-seven years? No way. There's something more to it," Cassie lectured. She was a detective at heart, and had never been able to resist the temptation of a mystery, especially when the supernatural seemed at play.

"It's the statue," Jo Lynn responded. "It's not a copycat. The statue really does come alive. It makes Twilight Hills pay for what its soldiers did to him."

"Mom, you're an intelligent woman, I can't believe you'd say something like that," Wendell whined.

"It's not just me; the whole town believes it," Jo Lynn returned.

"Are you serious?" Cassie asked.

"As a heart attack," Laymon stated. "In fact, I dare you to find anyone outside their homes tomorrow night. No one is willing to take the chance. Been that way since 1911, the first time it happened. We knew we deserved it. The other two cases were out-of-towners, trying to prove us wrong."

"Honey," Wendell started, "you have to understand the psychological ramifications their mutiny had on this town. It's been over a hundred years, but Twilight Hills still suffers from what they did."

"Fancy college talk," Laymon muttered.

"Why in the world would an entire town nurture guilt over something from so long ago?"

"Small towns don't have much more than their pride," Laymon responded. "We've only got our reputation, and we're known as the town whose boys turned traitor. That's something we'll never live down, no matter how many statues we put up."

"Well, I think it's absurd," Cassie said.

"After tomorrow night, we won't have to worry about it for another year," Jo Lynn informed. "Let's just stay in, and I'll enjoy having my children home on my birthday."

Wendell could see in Cassie's eyes there wasn't a chance they'd be in bed at midnight the following night.

*   *   *

"No," Wendell said for what he knew would not be the last time.

"Why not?" Cassie questioned as her hand slid up his thigh.

"Don't try to seduce me into this, Cass," Wendell warned. "We are *not* going out there."

Cassie knew her husband, and she knew it was just a matter of time. She just had to keep chip, chip, chipping.

"For a guy who doesn't believe in ghosts, you sure sound scared."

Wendell rolled over so his back was to her. Some things he would not stand for. Questioning his rational mind was one of them.

"Oh, so you're gonna pout, now?" Cassie teased. "Since we're in your childhood room, you're going to act like a child?"

Wendell did not turn around, but yelled as loud as he could at her so long as it wasn't more than a whisper, "You're not getting your way this time, Cassie! I'm not scared, and I don't believe in ghosts, but something happened to those people out there. That's a fact. I'm not going to risk putting you in danger, and I don't care enough about that damn statue to stay up all night."

"I'm sorry, you're right," Cassie whispered into her husband's ear as she slid her hand up his thigh once more. "I know you're not scared. And I know you know there's nothing out there. Maybe once, when those people were attacked, but it's been over thirty years. I know you know there's no danger. I know you know I won't get off your back, even if it takes years, until I see this statue on September 16 for myself. Best of all, I know you know I'll make it worth your while if you take me out there, starting tonight!"

"Are you using your feminine wiles against me?"

"Is it working?"

Wendell smiled and informed, "It is now."

✳   ✳   ✳

The following night, Cassie and Wendell sat on the cool grass before the statue of Josiah Mibb. The statue was supposedly an exact replica of the man himself, but Cassie thought the jaw was a little too square, the shoulders a little too broad, and the mouth a little too righteous. Of course, if you're going to flatter someone in the hopes of making up for a grave wrong by erecting a statue in tribute, some exaggerations may not be uncalled for.

"You know, when I married you, I didn't sign up for sitting in cemeteries at eleven-thirty at night," Wendell complained.

"Really? Because I didn't sign up for scraping your poop out of the toilet, but it still happens," Cassie countered.

Wendell had been trumped.

✳   ✳   ✳

Finally, the hour of midnight arrived, September 15 gave birth to the 16, and nothing happened. The statue remained inert.

Wendell allowed thirty seconds to pass before he said, "You see, sweetie, it's just a legend. A ghost story. Nothing's going to happen, so, for God's sake, let's go back to Mom and Dad's and get some sleep."

"Sssh!"

Wendell looked up from his watch to see what had captured his wife's attention. His stomach felt as though it'd turned to lead as he saw the eyes of Josiah Mibb begin to glow with a hellish hue.

Ropes of red electricity snaked out from the base of Josiah Mibb and struck Cassie and Wendell simultaneously.

They suddenly heard gunshots exploding and people screaming.

Wendell and Cassie took each other in their arms when they saw actual, living Union soldier battling Union soldier. They saw women and children running down the streets of a tiny village with soldiers chasing them. Buildings were burning, sending huge black clouds into the sky.

Cassie screamed herself when she saw a soldier shoot a young boy in the back as he fled in terror.

"We've got to hide!" Wendell yelled.

He grabbed Cassie by the wrist and dragged her along once more, but this time he was not trying to escape a verbal assault like with Mr. Benson, he was instead attempting to evade death!

"What is this?" Cassie shrieked with panic in her voice.

"I don't know!" Wendell returned, equally horrified.

They weaved through the dead bodies in the streets, killed by Union soldiers, and tried to find cover. They were running straight toward a crossfire of Union soldiers shooting at their brothers in uniform when Wendell pulled Cassie into a mercantile.

There they saw not the statue, but the flesh and bone version of Josiah Mibb. Wendell expelled an audible cry of distress at the sight of the man who had been dead for well over a hundred years, and Cassie simply stared at him slack-jawed, dumbfounded beyond any hopes of capable logic.

"North or South?" a weak-chinned, slump-shouldered Josiah Mibb demanded.

Neither Wendell nor Cassie could answer.

"So help me," Josiah Mibb continued, "I'll kill you myself right now if you don't answer me. North or South?"

Wendell was the first to recover and asked, "What do you mean?"

"By God, I've a mind to kill you for your insolence!"

"North!" Cassie erupted. "We're from the North!"

This calmed the volatile Josiah Mibb considerably. "I didn't figure you were from Dillowsburg, not the way you're dressed. What are you, volunteers?"

"Yes, sir," Wendell stuttered, "we're volunteers." He looked down at Cassie and saw blonde hair sticking to her forehead from sweat. Much the same, he could feel the perspiration running down the crevice of his posterior.

"Well, for your sake, I hope you're better than the others. You odd-ducks have been popping up rather unexpectedly, I must say. Can you follow orders?"

A bit more collected but befuddled all the same, Cassie noticed the acne scars beneath Josiah Mibb's patchy beard before she replied, "Yes, sir, we can follow orders."

Josiah Mibb laughed heartily before he said, "Good. I guess I'll allow a woman to take part in the action seeing as how I'm a little short handed at the moment. Take these…" He paused, turned around, and lifted two of many, many blades of various shapes and sizes from the counter of the mercantile. Wendell saw a pair of feet sticking out from behind the counter, and grew horrified at the sight of blood running out from behind it as well. "Take these," Josiah Mibb continued, "and look for any townsfolk still alive. I don't care if they're lying in the street with half their head blown off, if they're still breathing, you cut their tongues out and their hands off. Understand?"

"What?" Wendell and Cassie cried out in unison.

Josiah Mibb glared at them through his penny-sized, serpent eyes. "By God, you follow my orders or you'll wind up like your fellow 'volunteers!'"

Josiah Mibb raised his .22 rimfire spur-trigger tip-up revolver. He kept the unofficial sidearm trained on them with his left hand while motioning for them to approach with his right. He maneuvered them around him so they could see behind the counter.

Cassie gagged and Wendell cried out involuntarily again when they saw two men and a teenager piled behind the counter. All had died from massive bleeding, all had their tongues strewn about the floor, and the hands had been hacked off of each of them. Cassie couldn't be sure, but she guessed the teen's clothing was from the early nineteen hundreds, and, as a result, she was sure the other two men were from the forties and sixties.

"Now, I don't know where you people are coming from, why you're dressed so strangely, or why you won't follow orders like them other boys, but you will do as I say or you will wind up like these folks on the floor."

"Lieutenant!"

Cassie and Wendell turned to see two Union soldiers explode into the mercantile. They shoved before them a tall woman with red, straight hair. Her eyes were blank, as though the terrors of what she'd seen had all but broken her. Cassie imagined that if and when those eyes were intelligent, she would have been a breathtaking sight.

"Ah! Good work, Privates," Josiah Mibb complimented. He apparently had all but forgotten Cassie and Wendell at the sight of the woman. He turned his back to the young husband and wife and sauntered to the redhead.

"Is this worth it, Murlene?" he asked her. "I told you if you spurned me I'd make you pay, and look at what's happened. Everyone you love—dead or dying. You tricked me, making me love you, making me soil my sense of pride by loving a Southerner, and then you reject me? No. No, Murlene, no one makes a fool of Second Lieutenant Josiah Mibb. These people of Dillowsburg have died because of you—remember that."

"Sir, the insurgents are getting the upper hand," one of Mibb's soldiers informed.

"How can thirty-three be winning against seventy-five?" Mibb asked in disbelief.

"I don't know, sir."

"I never thought I'd see the day when a Union soldier didn't follow orders."

Wendell, though terrified, had sniffed out the situation and said, "Ordering the deaths of innocent people because you got your feelings hurt is hardly an order worth following. Whoever's fighting against you is winning because they're doing the right thing."

Josiah Mibb spun on his heel and glowered at Wendell. "Sounds to me like I've got more traitors in my midst. Boy," he growled, addressing Wendell, "you'll cut off the hands and tongue of Miss Murlene Carpenter here, or you and your lady-friend will end up the same."

Josiah Mibb powered to the counter where the vicious blades rested and tossed one at Wendell.

Before he knew what he was doing, Wendell sidestepped the blade and it stuck point down in the wooden floor.

"Private Simeon, Private Edwin, remove the tongues and hands of these three war criminals."

"War criminals?" Cassie burst out. "You're ordering the murder of innocent people, cutting off hands and tongues, and you're calling *us* the war criminals?"

Moving like a rat, Josiah Mibb threw the butt of his Smith and Wesson against Wendell's head and shoved Cassie to the floor. She immediately threw herself over her half-conscious husband in order to protect him.

"I will never be spoken to in such a manner by a woman!" Josiah Mibb shouted. "Bring her here!" he ordered his men, referring to Murlene Carpenter.

Throwing her to the floor next to Wendell and Cassie, Josiah Mibb raged when Murlene made not a sound after crashing down. He suspected the object of both his hate and love no longer registered anything taking place in the real world.

"Start cutting, gentlemen," he ordered his soldiers.

Wendell and Cassie were astounded when Edwin and Simeon each took a knife from the counter and stalked them. They could see the confusion and regret in the soldiers' eyes, and Cassie, for a moment, felt sorry they'd been put in such a compromising position.

At that moment thunder reverberated throughout the mercantile.

Whatever pity Cassie had experienced for Simeon and Edwin doubled when she saw them drop to the floor with their backs blown out.

Wendell, shaking loose the cobwebs that resulted from the handle of Josiah Mibb's revolver, perceived three Union soldiers standing in the doorway of the store. Two of them had their rifles raised with smoke wafting from the barrels.

"What in the hell do you think you're doing?" Josiah Mibb bellowed at the soldiers.

One of them, a tall, lanky man of twenty-five years named Private Lucium Thornley sprinted to Josiah Mibb before he could fire his sidearm and crushed his nose with the butt of his rifle. Mibb fell to the floor with blood gushing like a geyser.

"We're not taking orders from you, Mr. Mibb," Private Thornley informed.

Seven more Union soldiers entered the mercantile after they heard the rifle shots.

"What happened?" Private Philo Lambert asked.

"They were about to maim these civilians," Private Lysander Conant replied. "We had to shoot them. We found Mr. Mibb, as well."

With blood streaming down his face, Josiah Mibb hissed, "I am your second lieutenant, Private! You will address me as such, and you will follow orders!"

"Not any more, Mr. Mibb," Private Conant answered. "The minute you used Union soldiers to kill innocent people between battles, you ceased to be an officer. You will be relieved of your duty and treated as a war criminal."

"I can't believe they were willing to execute his orders," Private Lambert mused as he wiped the sweat from his brow with the tattered sleeve of his uniform.

"There's a reason he picked all privates when he said he needed us for a special mission. He thought we'd be too green to question him. Well, you didn't count on having the boys from Twilight Hills with you, did you, monster?" Private Thornley asked rhetorically to Josiah Mibb before he kicked the Smith and Wesson away.

Wendell and Cassie stood up and then stared in wonder at ten of the thirty-three from Twilight Hills.

"Look at those two," Private Conant said, referring to Wendell and Cassie.

The soldiers had seen too much and killed too many to laugh outright at the strange appearance of the Krones, but some managed to smile in slight amusement.

"We need to resume our march to Antietam," Private Thornley reminded.

"In a minute, Lucium," Private Conant muttered. "I want to know what was going on in here." He looked down at Murlene Carpenter and he instantly read her condition. He'd seen the same look in former soldiers who didn't have the fortitude to witness the wretchedness of war.

Private Rufus had wandered behind the counter and found the three bodies of the men from the cemetery. "Good Lord!" he cried out.

"What?" Private Lambert asked.

"There's three men back here with their hands cut off! Looks to me like they done bled to death!"

"What in God's name was going on in here?" Private Conant turned to Josiah Mibb and aimed his rifle at the ashen man.

"You curs! How dare you defy me!"

"I'll explain," Wendell spoke up.

"Who are you?" Private Thornley interrogated.

"I'm Wendell Krone. This is my wife, Cassie," Wendell paused to gesture at his wife. Although the boys fought to hide it, Wendell could see them admiring her. "From what we gathered," Wendell continued, "Josiah Mibb loves this woman." He pointed at the pitiful Murlene still on the floor. She had yet to blink as far as he could tell. He continued, "He loves her, but I don't think she feels the same. He decided to take out his anger on the whole town. When we got here, he ordered us to find any surviving townspeople and cut off their hands and tongues. He said if we didn't, he'd do the same to us. Those men behind the counter," Wendell said, throwing his thumb behind his shoulder, "apparently didn't follow his orders either."

"You beast!" Private Thornley cried. Before anyone could react, he pulled an axe off the counter and chopped off the hands of Josiah Mibb. Twitching violently, Josiah Mibb howled in anguish on the floor. Private Thornley next took out his own knife, dropped his knee onto Josiah Mibb's neck, and sliced out his tongue.

Josiah Mibb's wordless shrieks of fury and anguish filled the room like a terminal plague.

"Lucium, what are you doing?" Private Conant wailed as he pulled his friend off their former officer who yowled uncontrollably.

"An eye for an eye, Lysander, an eye for an eye!" Private Thornley chanted.

"Philo, Oscar, try to staunch the bleeding," Private Conant told his friends. He next turned his attention back to Private Thornley, "Lucium, what have you done? We can't act as bad as him, or else we're no better. How are we going to explain this?"

Private Thornley watched Privates Lambert and Williams work to slow Josiah Mibb's hemorrhaging. He then growled with ice in his voice, "We've got to get to Antietam."

Private Conant turned to Cassie and Wendell and requested, "We've got to march. Can I trust you two to take care of Mr. Mibb until we find someone to come assist you?"

"I don't think so," Cassie answered sheepishly, fighting to ignore the insanity-inducing cries of Josiah Mibb. She had been studying the three men behind the counter and observed in amazement as they vanished one at a time. She figured they were returning to where they came from, and so she and Wendell probably would soon as well. "We're not going to be here much longer. I'm sorry, but you can't count on us."

"Well, then," Private Conant mumbled in agitation. "I guess Mr. Mibb will just have to make it on his own until we can send assistance. It's obvious she's not in any condition to help," he uttered, throwing his calloused hand in the direction of Murlene Carpenter.

"No!" Wendell shouted.

"What did you just say?" Private Thornley grilled.

"You can't just leave! You have to trust me; you have to have someone stay here to explain what happened or else Mibb will say you did all this. He'll make himself out to be the hero and all of you the villains!"

"We'll explain it to the officers at Antietam," Private Lambert reassured.

"Somebody shut Mibb the hell up!" Private Thornley bellowed. He couldn't face the man whom he had mutilated any longer.

"What if you don't get the chance?" Cassie whispered in response to Private Lambert.

The boys from Twilight Hills jolted at her words, but they knew what she said was a strong possibility. They'd been lucky so far, but how long could that luck hold out?

Private Conant thought for a moment, then said, "We'll draw sticks." He pulled a container of old style pick-up sticks from the mercantile shelves, broke three of them in half, threw the extra halves onto the floor, then put them, along with seven whole sticks, in his right hand. He made each of the ten Twilight Hills men draw.

When it was said and done, Privates Cornelius Gentry, Ansel Stucker, and Lysander Conant himself had to stay behind.

Cassie and Wendell watched as they said their goodbyes to the rest of the soldiers from Twilight Hills with constrained emotion. Everyone had a feeling it would be the last time they'd see each other.

After the thirty had left, Cassie comforted the remaining Union soldiers, "You'll be glad you stuck around to explain what happened. I know it."

Second Lieutenant Josiah Mibb howled in wrath and blinding pain as he saw his undoing fade away.

Privates Conant, Stucker, and Gentry spent the rest of their lives pondering the mystery of the two people who had once disappeared before their very eyes.

✳   ✳   ✳

"So, who are these guys again?" Cassie asked as she looked up at the statue of the three Civil War soldiers.

"They were the last three men to survive from Twilight Hills' thirty-three soldiers who fought in the Civil War. Plus, they caught a renegade officer who had a town murdered just because he was pissed about a girl blowing him off," Wendell explained.

"Wow. Somebody had issues," Cassie said.

"Sure did."

"Quiet everyone! It's almost midnight!" Mayor Sholtz called out.

Cassie looked around and saw the entire town of Twilight Hills surrounding the statue of Privates Stucker, Gentry, and Conant. As usual, Homer Benson had organized the event just as he'd been doing since his first year of teaching.

"This has been a town tradition ever since that boy discovered it in 1911," Jo Lynn whispered to Cassie. "We celebrate my birthday every year by coming out here!"

Midnight hit, and after thirty seconds of silence, the people of Twilight Hills heard Josiah Mibb's chilling cries of fury and pain.

"See, told you. The legend of Josiah Mibb is true," Wendell muttered in his wife's ear as he rubbed his head.

"I'll never doubt you again!" Cassie exclaimed as goose bumps rose on her skin from the eerie wails of a man who'd been dead for over a century. She noticed her husband's grimace of pain and asked, "What's wrong?"

"I don't know," Wendell groaned. "I've got a lump on my head the size of a golf ball all of a sudden. Hurts like crazy!"

Knight Writings

from the Chronicles of Purgatory Station

Entry 7579

Earlier today I witnessed something I thought I would never see, and that was the end of the Nether Man. More unbelievable was the fact that Pastor Irons played a major role in stopping the behemoth. Of course, without the man called Freedom and his heir apparent, Anthem, the rock man would likely have run his course and re-entered the sea, only to terrorize my city again.

Freedom seemed to be the sort of man I can respect. The pawn called Anthem was quite the opposite. I don't know what Freedom's situation is just yet, but it's obvious he's detached himself from his government control. I wish I could say that's a bad thing, but when you've been in the game for twenty-two years, you discover not all evil walks in the form of living rock or creates portals into nothingness. Some evils wear tights, some wear ties, and some wear stripes. Not just of the jail variety, either.

This Freedom has been at it publicly for a few years. He's proven himself time and time again. He is a good candidate. Technologically produced flight, low-caliber bulletproof skin, very high intellect, and more importantly, a moral heart in his chest. Could be perfect.

This brings me to Shadow Serpent. I found another of his victims tonight. I was first on the scene. Female. Caucasian. Brown eyes and a brunette. Appeared to be in the vicinity of five feet, three inches and around one hundred and fifty pounds. Late thirties. Body was found in an alley off O'Neil. Nothing stolen from her person. Other than four puncture wounds to the stomach, no trauma to the body. Death, as usual, caused by injection of a poison yet to be determined. Until I can get a sample of a victim's blood, or the perpetrator himself, the toxin will remain unknown.

This makes the Shadow Serpent's body count fifty-two in nineteen months of known activity. He has no method to his routes or choices in victims that I can determine.

I hate to admit this, but I may not be enough to stop him. He has eluded me since I began focusing my efforts on him thirteen months ago, when it became evident the PSPD could not stop him. I arrogantly thought the Nocturnal Knight, as the media long ago dubbed me, would succeed where they failed, as had been the case so often before.

The idea of a task force dedicated to stopping the serial murderer grows on me with every new victim.

Entry 7580

The Shadow Serpent claimed another victim tonight. Male. Hispanic. Looked to be in his late teens. Approximately five feet, eight inches. One hundred sixty-five pounds. Brown eyes, yellow and blue highlights to his hair. Two puncture wounds to his forehead. As usual, no witnesses. Body was found in a parking garage, top floor. Nothing stolen from person. No trauma to body other than punctures. Makes fifty-three in nineteen months.

I called it in and then departed the crime scene after determining there was no external evidence to be had. As I jumped the ledge, I noticed a silhouette on the building above. I knew it wasn't my prey for two reasons: anyone still living had never seen him, and the figure was that of a female. That being said, I don't like being seen, either. I would know my observer. What I found disturbed me greatly.

She called herself "Devil Woman." Strictly amateur. Don't get me wrong, I'm all for women bringing down Mega-Mals. Oime, if she didn't hate me, would be a candidate in a heartbeat, and she's as female as they come. This "Devil Woman," however, did not hear me approach from behind. She didn't even know I was near her until I tapped her on the shoulder. I'll give her this, she turned swinging, but it's obvious she had no combat skills beyond basic self-defense. The diamond-shaped mask; the red horns; the "DW" belt; it all screamed "wanna be." No function whatsoever. All form.

She will get herself killed if she keeps it up for long. I told her as such as rudely as possible. I've been intimidating the good, the bad, and the beautiful for decades. A smile didn't get you far when I started, and it gets you even less now. I'll follow her for a few nights; let her get roughed up just enough to call it quits. I don't need another corpse in my city.

Entry 7581

Even though I was shot, it was a good night.

A new Colossal appeared this afternoon. The boy told the press to call him "Excitor." He's young, but he's got power to spare. Seems to wield some form of bioelectricity in the super-Colossal range. Typical youth—brash, cocky, over-confident. He may be perfect. With him and Freedom, I'd have a tactician with muscle and flight and the enthusiasm of youth backed by raw power and fearlessness. Is the boy morally dependable? He'll need observing before any decisions are made. He brought down the criminal known as Barrage, however. No small feat.

Near First Redeemer, I found Devil Woman attempting to apprehend participants in a drug deal. She was quickly overtaken when they pulled out their nine millimeters. That's when I intervened. I disabled one of them immediately, but the other got a shot off. The Kevlar and leather armor held. He passed out when he saw me get back up. Ah, that little episode will drop non-Mega-Mal criminal activity by twenty-five percent over the next three weeks. I guarantee it.

The amateur put up a brave act, but I saw her hands trembling and the puddle at her feet. I pointed the puddle out. I haven't survived for two decades of taking on the city's worst by being nice. I don't want her dead. She seemed like a decent person. Can't say I approved of her garb, however.

Entry 7582

I found myself on the island's northwest side. The Serpent murdered yet another. This time it was an elderly African American. Male. Approximately seventy years old. Two sets of puncture wounds on each shoulder. Six feet, four inches tall. Two hundred and twenty, give or take. It's apparent the Serpent is using some form of needles to inject his victims. The media loves to propagate the notion that the Mega-Mal is literally "biting" his victims like a real snake, but all the evidence suggests nothing of the sort. There are always rectangles surrounding the sets of punctures. The rectangles are bruises. I've nearly come to the conclusion that the killer has two needles mounted to some contraption on each fist. As there are never any witnesses, I have no way to confirm this. Just a hunch.

As expected, it wasn't long before Turf arrived on the scene. As his name would suggest, he's very strict about maintaining order in his neck of the woods. He was not happy to find me sulking around, but he was even less happy to realize the Shadow Serpent had struck on his watch.

I don't know if Turf considers himself any more of a Colossal than I believe myself to be, but I've always thought highly of his efforts since he started protecting the innocent eight years ago. How a man who doesn't wear a mask maintains anonymity while fighting crime is a mystery even I can't solve. Of course, I discovered his real identity seven years ago in order to avoid a catastrophe.

In eight years, he's never killed. He doesn't use weapons. He depends on his enhanced strength, speed, and intellect to get him through the tough spots. I once heard a rumor that he also depends on a higher power. We may have something in common.

I told him that I was thinking of putting together a group to combine talents in order to terminate the Serpent's activity. He didn't seem interested. I'm thinking he's still miffed about not being allowed to join the old team, before most of us were killed trying to stop Quietus. I think Solar Flare knew what he was doing in refusing Turf's admission back then. I've always maintained that Solar Flare knew death was coming for some of us on that team. His powers gave him a strange talent for escaping time's parameters.

I should have been with them on that day.

Entry 7583

No Shadow Serpent victims tonight.

No Devil Woman sightings either.

I should consider myself lucky. I'm hoping both of them gave it up.

Trover brought in the young Colossal today to First Redeemer. Again, I don't know how these people who don't wear masks expect to fool anybody! He seemed very interested in finding a purpose beyond just being one of the nation's greatest heroes. Pastor Irons sat and spoke with him for a very long time. Trover simply faded into the background with a smile on his face.

The young man, Freedom, is a perfect candidate. In fact, if this new team works out and we stop Shadow Serpent, I'll gladly hand leadership over to him. Solar Flare was right; I'm not exactly the most diplomatic fella running around in armor and a cloak.

Speaking of armor, I'm thinking this "Silver Streak" could be a logical addition. His biomechanical suit gives him extremely enhanced speed. I'd love to know how it works. I didn't even know such a thing was in development, which leads me to believe it's not government related. The news has never been able to clock his speed. I find this rather odd. Like Excitor, however, Silver Streak has not been on the scene long enough to prove his morality. I'll not have any ethically ambiguous members on my team.

Entry 7584

The Serpent was mine!

It was on the Meltzer Building in Old Downtown, right on the edge of Grell Harbor. His back was to me, but as soon as I saw his figure I knew who it was. He had something hanging from his back, blowing in the wind. It almost looked like shed skin, but that's impossible. The killer is all too human, of that I'm certain. He was dressed in all black. I got about twenty-five meters away when I pulled out a tranq dart. I wish I could tell you that I find it dishonorable to take down an adversary from behind, but when their body count is closer to a hundred than zero, honor goes out the window.

It's a moot point anyway. His latest victim was still alive.

Shadow Serpent turned to face me even though I hadn't made a sound. I couldn't make out his build due to the skin-like cape billowing behind him. I could see two piercing crimson eyes, two fangs, and a red, forked tongue.

I was right about the needles. On the end of the knuckle-guard on each of his gauntlets were two needles. Big needles.

After the half second it took to take in the features of Purgatory Station's most talented serial killer, I next observed his victim.

This took considerably less time than I spent on the Serpent.

It was the Devil Woman.

I could see nothing in those red eyes, and the Mega-Mal remained silent. He merely stuck one of the two needles from his left hand into her left arm, then shoved her off the building into the harbor.

He ran and jumped to the next roof; I sprinted the twenty-five meters to the ledge, lost as much armor as I could en route, then dove in after the amateur.

Entry 7585

Twenty years ago a man named Trover nursed me back to health after Odium cut me to shreds. This, of course, was before I began wearing much more durable armor.

Back then, I wore a mask instead of a helmet. He did not remove it in the nine days he, his brother, and his brother's girlfriend took care of me.

Out of respect to him, I won't remove the Devil Woman's mask.

It is obvious the Serpent did not want her dead. He simply used her to distract me from pursuing him. I'm certain he was ready to be seen. I walked right into his plans. He had choreographed all of it perfectly.

I quickly pulled Devil Woman from the water and rushed her to my quarters. It took a few days, but she's finally coming around.

Unfortunately, the Serpent did not pump enough of his venom into her for me to get an accurate read of its composition.

Was this also part of his plan?

Could the Serpent be more intelligent than any of us?

Entry 7586

I have my work cut out for me.

Devil Woman is up and moving, and she is thirsty for vengeance. She demanded I train her to take on the Serpent. I tried to explain to her that even I don't know if I can take the Serpent, and I've been trained by the best and have over two decades of experience.

She wouldn't take no for an answer. If I don't train her, she'll be killed within the week.

To make matters worse, she's a heathen. I suppose that is not without its irony.

Entry 7587

It has been days since my last entry. I have been very busy. Devil Woman is coming along sufficiently in her training. She does not remove her mask, and I do not unfasten my helmet. There is no personal connection whatsoever.

I keep telling myself that.

Although she is an amateur, she is not entirely clumsy or unintelligent. I've begun training her in the art of the staff. It will allow her to keep her distance from criminals while engaging them. I did not respond when she mentioned a gun would be easier.

On another note, the Shadow Serpent killed once again over the last few days. Again, no witnesses. Two set of puncture wounds along the collarbone. Female. Asian. Forty to forty-five years old. Five feet, one inch. Approximately one hundred and seventy pounds. No irregularities in appearance other than the wounds. Killed while cutting through Morrison Park. Supposedly on her way to the graveyard shift at work.

Where is the connection between the Serpent's victims! I cannot believe that anyone, Mega-Mal or not, can kill so many so indiscriminately! Even history's worst murderers had a method to their viciousness. What is his method?

It is time to put a force together. Loathe as I am to admit it, I can't protect the innocent *and* track down and stop the Shadow Serpent at the same time. I will need assistance. Devil Woman asked me who I would like to have working with us. I told her the names of my candidates, then I reminded her that she is not one of them, therefore negating the term "us."

She did not respond to my latter statement positively.

Entry 7588

Even though I had explained to her that I needed a few days to observe some of my candidates, Devil Woman summoned them.

She and I were to meet tonight on top of First Redeemer for a training run on rooftop combat. When I arrived, she was standing with an impressive cadre of Colossals.

Freedom stood in his red, white, and blue with his cape flowing behind him, looking exactly like the Colossal everyone believes him to be. He was the only one I was sure would join.

To my surprise, Turf was there as well. He didn't appear happy, but he did look resolved to put an end to the killings. That's all I ask.

Silver Streak stood with his suit gleaming in the moonlight. I wish Devil Woman had given me more time to watch over this fella, just to be sure. His membership is probationary in my book.

Also there, on a trial basis, were Excitor and some other kid I've never seen before. Excitor had blue electricity jumping from hand to hand looking as though he was ready to save the world.

The other one was covered from his boots to the top of his forehead. Only his hair was exposed; it was black and hanging down to his eyes. His suit had an orange flame riding up his legs and chest, set against black. He called himself El Fuego. Unlike Excitor, he gave no clues to his abilities beyond the suit and the name, but I think it's fairly clear.

I don't know how in the world Devil Woman convinced these men to join my little club, but I saw in her eyes that she expected to be admitted for her deed. I guess that makes four probationary members.

The Shadow Serpent will be stopped.

Entry 7589

It's been weeks since I began training my recruits to battle as a team. While we've been training, the Serpent struck time and again. I've now had fifty-seven murders in my city over the last twenty-one months, all accredited to the Shadow Serpent.

He will pay dearly.

In the meantime, the recruits have progressed tolerably enough. I've come to rely on Freedom and Turf for their veteran experience. They seem to get along well. As well as anyone can get along with Turf, that is.

Silver Streak is a different story. He's not a particularly gifted combatant. He doesn't have any passion for our drills, either. I don't know why he joined up with us. He said he wants to take down the Serpent, he owed a friend, but his heart isn't into what we're doing. I've seen that suit of his in action. Actually, I haven't seen anything more than a blur. He refused to explain to me how it works, but I'm beginning to think it's got nothing to do with enhanced speed. If he's going to stay a part of this outfit, he'll detail the specs or else.

Then we have Excitor and El Fuego. That's Spanish for "The Fire," by the way. We have a "no real names" policy amongst ourselves, although I've already figured out by happenstance three of my six recruits. I'm not going to commit their names to record, but Turf and Freedom were figured out a while ago, and I just happened to come across El Fuego's as well. The rest would be easy if I wanted to put some real effort into it, but I don't. My only concern is the Serpent.

At any rate, those two kids—Excitor and El Fuego—do not get along. Every drill we ran that had them coordinating as a team wound up a pissing contest. If they both didn't have such raw power, I'd kick them out on general principal. But, I need them.

Devil Woman is doing fine. Even though she's driving me crazy with all the personal questions she asks, she's got more passion in her little finger for taking down the bad guys than Silver Streak has in his entire body. But, like Excitor, Silver Streak, and El Fuego, she's an amateur. These kids will probably get Freedom, Turf, and me killed if I don't take every precaution. The only problem is, the rookie boys have enough power to keep their hides safe in a crunch, while Devil Woman's only got her heart and her brain. Not many of us survive doing what we do with just those. Until I met her, I thought I was the last.

If we could just catch a break; if the Serpent would slip up just once…

Entry 7590

Devil Woman is off the team.

After a training session, I caught her taking notes. She thought we had all left. In fact, we had. I came back because I had a hunch. My hunches are always right. There she was, huddled in a shadow, jotting down everything.

I can't believe I let her get the best of me.

I should have known when I first encountered her that she wasn't the real deal. I mistook her greenness with just being a novice. I never dreamt someone would risk her life over something so trivial. I'll never understand her sort.

I threatened to break every finger she had if she breathed a word of what she learned to the public. When I first met her, she probably would have started crying. I'd made her tough, though. She handed the notebook over to me without saying a word. I turned to leave, and then she asked me to wait. It killed her pride, but she begged me not to tell the rest of the recruits about her. I agreed, though I'm not sure why.

I'd like to think it was because I didn't want to hurt team morale.

It's not that.

It's a good thing what happened; I'm too old to get mixed up with women like her. Besides, Pastor Irons would never approve.

Entry 7591

More weeks have passed since my last entry, more people died.

Sixty-one people in twenty-two months.

Finally, we caught a break. Last night, Turf was on patrol on his own when he came across a dead body. It was a female African American. Turf doesn't bother to analyze details as I do, but I got him to remember that he thought she was around twenty years old, about five six, and probably one hundred and sixty pounds. He said she had one set of puncture wounds to her right cheek. No other signs of damage.

Also, she had a note attached to her.

It said that I was to meet the Serpent tonight, alone, at Waid's Wharf. It's on the northwest side of the city, the rough part. An old shipyard. Barely used anymore, not for anything legal, at least. That's Turf's part of town; he'll know where I can stash away the team.

I'd love to take you down myself, Serpent, but I won't risk another innocent life for my own pleasure. Tonight, you will be no more.

Entry 7592

It has been four weeks since my last entry.

Just like with my other team, all those years ago, things went wrong.

Terribly wrong.

I got to the wharf. Turf, Freedom, El Fuego, Excitor, and Silver Streak were a quarter mile behind me hiding in a warehouse. They had a clear view of me, and with Silver Streak in the crew, I could have help instantly if I needed it.

I saw him.

Again, his back was to me with some sort of skin hanging from it, whipping in the wind.

He turned to face me.

Once more, I saw those bloodlike eyes, those white fangs, and that red, forked tongue. He stood perfectly still, utterly relaxed. I've seen such a stance before. It is a stance that only the most deadly and capable of warriors employ. I knew if he wanted a fight, I'd have my hands full.

Keep in mind, I've never gone against someone I wasn't sure I could beat one way or the other.

He held up his arms for me to take a look at the needles protruding from his gauntlets. I think he was reminding me, just to make it a fair fight.

I reached behind me and detached my escrima sticks. I kept them at my sides, beneath my cloak. I did not feel the urge to let him know what I had waiting for him.

He motioned for my approach.

I rolled my shoulders as though warming up for combat. It was the signal to attack.

I saw a blur pass me, and then, next thing I knew, Silver Streak lay on the ground. He had not been punctured, but it was obvious from the boot mark on his face that the Serpent had somehow reacted to his attack. I had it in my head that his suit was actually a temporal displacement unit rather than a speed machine. I guess I was wrong.

Phase one of "Operation: Head Crush" had failed.

I dove on the ground as phase two initiated. Blasts of flames and electricity soared over my head, aimed at the Serpent. All that remained where he had been were sparks and flares.

I got up and positioned my escrima so that I was ready for both offense and defense.

Excitor, El Fuego, and Turf formed a perimeter around me. We kept Freedom hidden as our ace in the hole if things got worse.

Freedom is wanted as a traitor to the government, after all. He tries not to go out in the open unless it's absolutely necessary. The last thing I needed was Meta-Agents like Hell Hound and Anthem crawling all over us.

We looked everywhere, and finally, atop a crate as big as a truck, we saw him.

The Serpent stood, glaring at me. I had betrayed whatever sense of honor he thought existed between us.

I recognize no honor in murderers.

He picked up a remote control device of some sort and pressed a button.

The crate fell to pieces, extending outwards, and within, the nightmare initiated.

He had four people strapped to a table.

As the crate disassembled around the hostages, the Serpent leapt into the air, executed three somersaults, and then landed on the table in the middle of his victims. He immediately sank a pair of his needles into the poor soul on the far left. He twitched violently before dying. Excitor vomited. I think it was the first time the boy had seen someone die violently.

We all made a move to rush the Serpent, but he threatened to drop his "fangs" into yet another victim.

He kept the needles just above a woman's forehead, then stared us all down. We froze.

With his left hand, he pointed at me and motioned for me to approach him. I did.

He allowed me within ten feet of him, then gestured that I stop.

Though it pained me, I followed his instruction.

He pointed at the three men twenty feet behind me and gesticulated that they remain in place.

He then exploded from the table and commenced attacking me.

I got the escrima up just in time to block a set of his needles. When he pulled his hand back, he took one of my wooden attack sticks with it. I couldn't allow him the time to pull the escrima free from the needles; I had better odds against one set than two.

Then, El Fuego and Excitor did something stupid.

I heard Turf scream, "No!" before streaks of unrefined energy blazed past me. Again, the Serpent easily dodged them, landed next to the hostage on the far right, then punctured her trachea with his venomous spikes. Another innocent dead.

Shadow Serpent waved his finger sternly back and forth at the boys. I didn't have time to yell at them myself because the battle commenced anew.

It became obvious to all that he was only toying with me.

Freedom didn't dare come out of hiding for the sake of the victims; Excitor and El Fuego had been rendered useless, and Turf wouldn't risk movement either. Silver Streak remained unconscious. And I was just an old man getting the tar beat out of him.

It'd been a long time since I had taken that kind of punishment. I knew he could have stuck me anytime he wanted. The only part of my body that wasn't armored was my chin. He made a point to strike it with an open palm and kick it with the heel of his boot as often as he could. And trust me, that was quite often. He was showcasing my vulnerability to his needles.

I didn't land one blow against him.

Finally, he stabbed me under the chin with only one of his needles. He didn't have enough surface area to get them both in. My face immediately went numb and I dropped.

I watched him bend down to unfasten my helmet. He knew one poke from one needle wouldn't be enough to do me in. He meant to finish the job.

That's when Freedom made his move.

The boy's got guts, I'll give him that. He broke through the wall of the warehouse, hoping to get the edge on the Serpent, but the killer was too quick.

He back flipped from me to the table with the victims, tore loose the escrima, then placed both sets over the two remaining hostages.

Freedom had no choice. He'd almost made it, but he had to land next to my body, just mere feet from the Serpent.

He almost made it.

With the top half of my body now ice-cold, I looked up to see Freedom staring at me. He knew he'd failed. I could see he was a man who didn't fail often, and hated it when he did.

In the time it took Freedom to make the quarter mile, the rest of the team had gotten halfway to the hostages. They stopped, thankfully, when Freedom did.

We had a good old stalemate. None of the Colossals dared move. The Serpent knew if he killed his last two victims he would have no collateral for escape. He had nowhere to go. My men blocked his only route. He only had the harbor behind him.

He meant to take it.

He fluidly scooped up the smaller of the still living hostages, threw her over his shoulder, then motioned for Freedom to back away from me.

With one set of his poisonous darts pressed against the butt of his victim, he knelt down and lifted my helmet half off. My entire jaw and mouth were completely exposed.

I felt the needles push against my skin when thunder erupted.

Before I blacked out, I saw Devil Woman standing over me with the PSG-1 sniper rifle.

God forgive me.

Entry 7592

It has been five days since my last entry.

My healing goes well.

Bodily, at least.

My soul is a different matter.

As an absolute last precaution, I implemented "Phase: Omega" in the stratagem against the Shadow Serpent.

He could not be allowed to continue.

I was ninety percent sure we'd be able to take him, but the hostage situation changed matters drastically. When Devil Woman saw that all other phases were a bust, she made the move I had instructed. Long range termination.

I abhor guns, and I detest killing.

I don't know which is worse, that I ordered the death of a human being, or that I used someone else to execute the action.

When all was said and done, I couldn't condemn just myself, I had to bring Devil Woman down with me.

I was told that the Serpent had been hit squarely between the eyes, yet he still managed to bolt for the water. No one was willing to dive in after him, and I can't say I blame them. There were innocents to tend after. There were the dead to see to.

His body never surfaced.

The team disbanded.

Freedom, while no stranger to death, couldn't condone my actions. Turf is a natural loner. Silver Streak doesn't have it in him to continue, said he'd missed first place yet again. Excitor and El Fuego are simply too green. They have to deal with the death of those hostages for the time being. They'll get over it, eventually. I hope they've learned a lesson from what took place.

And Devil Woman, well, I owe her a great deal. She was the only one I knew would be willing to kill. She was the only one who saw the big picture. She was the only one prepared to do anything to get back in my good graces.

The question is whether *my* good graces have cost her someone else's?

Entry 7593

I was able to get out of bed today.

Thankfully, there is no permanent damage. Pastor Irons and Devil Woman did a fine job of nursing me back to health.

My soul still aches for the death I caused.

Is it right to kill in order to keep others from dying? Was it right for me to assume the mantle of judge and jury? Was it right to appoint a naïve young woman as an executioner?

I don't know.

After doing this for twenty-two years, I'd always found a way other than killing. Now that I've done it, will I resort to it again?

More so, even if I don't, will Devil Woman? She was nearly massacred by the Shadow Serpent when she took him on hand-to-hand, yet she defeated him soundly from a half mile away with the aid of a rifle! That sort of success is difficult for people to ignore.

I will call on her today to see if she'll meet with me. I must see her again. I wish I could say it is only to discuss the actions I ordered.

Entry 7594

When Devil Woman came to my quarters, it was not the Nocturnal Knight she found, but rather, it was Pastor Irons.

He handles these sorts of situations better.

Pastor Irons first asked her to remove her mask.

Although she hesitated, the Devil Woman disappeared, and Pastor Irons found Sydney Attwater standing before him.

She asked Irons what this was about. He told her it was about several things. He told her the story she'd been working on for WPUG News was now out of the question since she had committed murder. He informed her that her days as the Devil Woman must end, for Devil Woman had killed. He alerted her to the fact that the redemption of her soul was all that mattered after what she'd done.

Of course, Sydney is an atheist, so Irons' last proclamation did little to stir her.

Sydney argued that if she hadn't done what she'd done, the body count would be in the seventies by now. She was right. She also reminded Irons that it was me who'd ordered her to exterminate the Serpent to begin with, it was me who taught her how to fire the sniper rifle, and it was even me who assigned her vantage point for the shot. She may have pulled the trigger, but the Nocturnal Knight killed the Serpent for all intents and purposes.

Irons told her I was misguided in my sense of righteousness and needed help.

The pastor will never forget the look on Sydney's face after he said that. She looked at him as though he were psychotic.

She replaced her diamond-shaped mask and left Irons, that old, unassuming fool, standing alone in my attic headquarters within First Redeemer.

He contemplated deeply as I rubbed his bandaged chin.

The Coat

Ten minutes into his walk across campus, Terry realized he had made a terrible mistake. The temperature outside was beyond the freezing point, and our genius had yet another ten minutes in the elements to somehow endure until he reached The Pint's Cranny, his favorite bar. The dilemma he faced prior to his trek was what to do with his coat once he reached his destination. He, of course, didn't want to stand around holding it while trying to make nice with the ladies. Only a chode would be that moronic. So, he did what so many college-aged kids of his mental capacity did—he went without.

It wasn't long before he noticed there was absolutely no one else out and about. Typically, at that time on a Thursday night, there were throngs of students walking to parties or bars en masse. Not this night, however. On this night, there stirred not even a spirit. There was only silly Terry and his warped devotion to appearing "cool."

He found his snot hardening within his nostrils, and each breath he sucked in burnt his lungs with an icy fire. His thin sweater provided no protection at all, and although he wore a stocking cap, it was for pure fashion only and offered little in retaining warmth.

Only ten more minutes 'til I get to The Cranny, he thought to himself. While not the smartest junior out there, he was with it enough to realize he was half way to his destination, and to turn back home at this point would not save him from any extra exposure to the cold. *Better make sure I save some dough for a cab after the bar closes.*

Terry came to the end of the sidewalk and powered up a steep embankment to the railroad tracks. The tracks were a very busy shortcut during the school day that many students utilized. By walking along them, students could save themselves several minutes of winding around traffic, buildings, and parking lots.

He muddled along with his hands stuffed in his pockets for a few more minutes when, down the hill, he saw a car full of girls drive by. Of course, he couldn't resist looking at them and took his eyes off the ties just for an instant. That instant was all that was needed, and Terry found himself toppling down the embankment with arms and legs flailing like an out-of-control, human landslide. After rolling on cold ground laden with rubble for what seemed like an eternity, he came to a rest at the bottom of the little hill. He took stock of himself and realized he was unhurt. To his terror he turned his head and perceived, just inches away, a great jagged rock jutting out of the ground and grinning at him with malice.

I could've been killed if I'd hit my head on that rock!

"Hey!" a voice called down to Terry from above.

He pried his eyes away from the nefarious rock and saw a young woman looking down at him from the top of the embankment.

"Are you okay?" she cried down with great concern.

Terry sat up with a grunt and rolled his eyes. "Yeah, I'm fine."

"Do you need help getting out of there?"

"No, I got it," he returned. Although relatively unscathed, he immediately felt the effects of the hard ground's pummeling as he stood. He was growing sore all over. In the dark and with the distance between them, he could hardly see the girl looking down at him. He decided he wanted a closer look, so he did what he would have had to do anyway, he climbed back up the embankment from his pit. He hoped he would have a hottie waiting for him when he got up top, but when he came face to face with the young lady, he found himself more than a bit unsettled.

He noticed immediately she had dried blood caked to the side of her temple. He was absolutely disgusted by the sight before him. He'd never really been one for blood. "Are *you* okay?" he asked as he pointed to her head.

She gasped as though he had just reminded her of it and returned, "Yes! Yes, I'm fine. I just bumped my head earlier, that's all."

"You should get it looked at," Terry replied without any real interest. He was one of those people who would say what he knew he was supposed to say, but rarely had any sentimentality behind such statements.

"You shouldn't be out here without a coat," she rejoined. Unlike our coatless prodigy, she sounded as though his well-being was the only concern she had in the whole world at the moment.

Terry just shrugged his shoulders and winced as they screamed in stiffness.

"What's so important that you have to be out in this cold without a coat?" the young woman questioned.

"I'm going to The Pint's Cranny," Terry responded rather curtly. Had the girl been less bloody and less of a "plain Jane," he may have been interested in their conversation. Since she was neither, he just wanted to get to some warmth, some beer, and some sorority chicas.

"You're risking your life just to go to a bar?" she asked incredulously, placing her hands on her hips.

"Whatever," he responded in typical Terry Imbissile fashion. He was bored beyond words already. Plus, he was freezing more and more by the instant.

She next folded her arms across her chest at his rudeness before saying, "You've still got at least ten minutes to go; you'll freeze to death out here without a coat!"

Terry made a noise somewhere between a spit and huff, watched in brief amazement as condensation left his body and nearly froze in mid-air, then quickly followed in a whine, "If you're so worried about me freezing to death, why are you making me stand here and listen to your lecturing when I could be gone by now?"

She narrowed her eyes and stared right through him. He could feel her assessing him. Then, as though she had made her conclusion and decided within her mind that Terry wasn't as bad as his personality indicated, she said, "I'll be home soon. Take mine." She began to remove her thick, wool coat.

He laughed and sarcastically responded, "Thanks, but you look about fifty pounds lighter than me. I can handle the cold a lot better than you. Keep it."

She continued to stare at him until her coat was completely off and then attempted physically forcing it onto Terry.

"Hey, dang it!" Terry yelled at her while trying to twist away. "I said you keep it! I'm not walking into The Cranny wearing a girl's coat!"

This time she laughed. His misplaced sense of importance seemed to strike her as quite amusing. Once she finished her little giggle, she changed gears and scoffed, "Wearing a girl's coat won't kill you!" She grabbed him by the elbow and slid his arm through one sleeve of the coat. "But guess what? Walking across campus in this weather actually could kill you, and I'm not going to have your death on my conscience."

He found himself overpowered by the young woman who was every inch his height. Terry tried to squirm away from her, but she was eerily robust. Part of him, however, didn't mind her apparent physical superiority, for he instantly felt quite warm and cozy as he settled within his newly acquired coat.

He decided it would be polite if he said, "What about you? You could die in this cold too, you know?"

She simply smiled at him and said, "I don't have to fear the cold; it won't kill me. But I do appreciate your concern. You're not as big a jerk as you seem; that's nice to know. Anyway, I'll be home in a little while. You go on!"

Finding himself unable to resist her command, Terry turned and sped down the tracks away from her. He pulled the coat's collar up around his neck and felt, in a rather non-Terry moment, quite appreciative for his benefactor. In an even more unusual moment, he suffered a flash of genuine courtesy. He suddenly turned and yelled, "How will I return it to you?" He did not see her, though. Where she stood, only moments ago, was nothing but cold, empty air.

Terry shrugged and turned back around, stuffing his hands into her pockets. He felt something plastic and rectangular in one of them and pulled out her student ID.

"Olivia Miller, huh?" he said to himself. He then went on his way to drink the night away in Olivia's warm, dependable protection.

*   *   *

The next day Terry awoke to the mother of all hangovers. He forced himself out of bed and into the shower. After having finished with the shower, he got dressed and made himself breakfast, or lunch actually, as he noticed he'd slept through all three of his Friday classes. Of course, this was nothing new. Attending class, in Terry's world, tended to interfere with his social life.

Speaking of his social life, he had a quick thought about how that girl had almost pulled one over on him last night. (He still couldn't believe the idiot she'd made of him, muttering an expletive illustrating his interpretation of her personality.) He then decided he wasn't quite ready to take on the new day after all, so he stumbled back into his bedroom to catch a few more z's. Upon reentering his bedroom, he noticed Olivia's coat slung over his desk chair. In yet another rare moment of courteousness, he thought he should return the coat as soon as possible. He had no idea why he was stricken with such thoughtfulness lately, but he went ahead and staggered back to the kitchen and picked up the apartment's only phone. He dialed the number for student information.

"Name, please," the operator said.

"Terry Imbissile," he answered.

The operator spoke a number to Terry, and he quickly realized that it was his own. "You meant the name of the person I wanted to call, didn't you?" he stupidly asked the operator.

"Name, please," the operator repeated, this time with frost in her voice.

"Olivia Miller," Terry informed with confidence.

Fully expecting the operator's ensuing words to be numbers, Terry was shocked to hear, "What is your business with Olivia Miller, sir?"

"What do you care?" Terry snapped in typical fashion. "Just give me her number! Do what you're paid to do."

"Sir, I'm not allowed to give out any information about Ms. Miller without determining the inquisitor's business with her."

Terry thought this was one of the strangest things he had ever heard of, but he answered the operator nonetheless, "I just want to return her coat, lady. What's with all the cloak and dagger crap?"

"Sir, it's standard procedure for us to have you call the following number in regards to Olivia Miller. Would you like me to connect you directly?"

"What the—? What is this crap? Yes, give me her number! That's all I wanted to begin with! Why are you giving me the run around with this?"

"Thank you and have a nice day," the operator said, devoid of any emotion.

Terry instantly heard the phone ring on the other end before someone finally picked up. He heard not Olivia's voice, but instead, "This is Detective Amadeus Jordan; you've got information about Olivia Miller?"

"Wh—what?" Terry fumbled.

"Don't waste my time, pal. You got information on Ms. Miller or not?" Jordan barked.

A detective? Terry became befuddled beyond belief and instantly wondered if the girl from the night before meant to make good on her threat against him. He grew even more exasperated by the fact that the detective's voice was the highest voice for a man he had ever heard!

"What's…Why did the operator connect me to a cop?"

"What's your name?" Detective Jordan demanded.

"Terry Imbissile."

"You're kidding me, right?"

"What's that supposed to mean?"

Detective Jordan realized the caliber of genius he was working with and decided to move on, "You a student at the college, Terry?"

"Yeah, why?"

"What year?"

"I'm a junior, but—"

"Good. You're capable of answering questions; you just proved that to me. Now, why did you want to get in touch with Olivia Miller?" the detective interrogated.

Terry saw her face, that minx from the bar, and began to sweat. This has to be a trick. He was sure the cop was using Olivia as bait to ensnare him. This couldn't be about anything but the girl from The Cranny. "I just wanted to return her coat, dude. Would somebody tell me what is going on?"

"I want you to describe Olivia Miller's appearance to me, Terry."

"Why?" The sweat beaded on his forehead. This cop was smooth; he'd give the high-pitched son-of-a-gun that much. Terry thought he was pretty smooth too, though. He'd been questioned by the police before. He knew everything was about leading you into saying something on accident. He didn't know how this Jordan knew about Olivia Miller, but Terry wasn't going to let himself be lulled into admitting jack as far as the girl from the bar was concerned.

"Why?" Jordan choked out, repeating Terry's question. "Because I'm with the police, and I'm telling you to! Got it, you smart-mouthed punk?" he shouted through the phone in a voice so high it was barely audible.

"Okay! Jeesh! You need to chill, man." Terry forced himself to concentrate and only stick to facts about Olivia Miller. He wasn't going to be fooled by a cop like back when he was a sophomore. Stick to describing Olivia Miller, that's all he needed to do. "Um, she was about five-ten. I don't know, maybe a hundred and forty pounds."

"Anything else?"

Terry focused hard. "Um, let's see, she had brown hair. She was okay looking, I guess. I'd never date her. Looked a little too much like a goody-goody to me, you know? I like girls with a little edge to them. You know, like rocker chicks and those types." Crap! He needed to stick to the facts and there he was having diarrhea of the mouth! Poor Terry. He just wasn't blessed in the brains department.

"Right, got it. Rocker chicks. Back to Ms. Miller. Did she have any distinguishing characteristics or marks?"

Terry pushed his limited intellect into overdrive and suddenly remembered, "Oh, yeah! Weirdest thing, she had dried blood on the side of her head—on her temple. Said she had bumped it earlier. Pretty gross, if you ask me."

There was a long pause of silence on Jordan's end, and then he said with deadly seriousness, "You want to return her coat, right?"

"Right, you're a real genius. I told you that to begin with. What's this have to do with the police?" Although he tried to put on the punk kid who wasn't scared of authority act, he'd noticed the detective's very serious tone of voice and immediately worried this definitely had something to do with his drinking excessively the night before and that devil of a girl from the bar. As already made apparent, he was not very astute, but he did have an uncanny knack for sensing trouble whenever he was potentially involved. His radar kicked into overdrive at the moment.

"Terry," the falsetto-voiced detective began, "you're going to give me your address, then you're going to get her coat ready for me, then you're going to sit tight until I get there. Understand?"

Baffled and more than terrified, although he would never admit as much to anyone with a pulse, Terry responded, "Okay…"

Twenty-sweaty-armpit-minutes later Terry opened the door to see a ridiculously tall, long-haired man wearing a tweed jacket and corduroy pants with a face like a horse lurching before him.

"You Terry?" the man asked in a voice that did not match his body whatsoever.

"Yeah," Terry replied while unsuccessfully trying to hide his dismay. "Listen, is this about last night? Because I swear, she told me she was a freshmen in *college*. I didn't know, seriously. I don't even do drugs. I mean, yeah, okay, I've dabbled in them, but—"

"Kid," Detective Jordan interrupted while he plodded into the apartment, "I don't know what you're talking about and I suggest you clam it with that stuff right now. I've got one concern and that's with the coat only. Now, where is it?"

Terry took one look at the expression of the detective and was no longer worried about his excessive drinking the night before. He also decided this was not about his apparent transgression with a much younger lady looking to score some stuff. Unfortunately, however, now he had a whole new problem. He realized this was not a trick at all and really did have something to do with Olivia Miller and her coat. This was *only* about Olivia Miller and her coat. That freakin' coat he was supposed to have ready for the cop.

"Kid, you got the coat?" Jordan probed impatiently as he pulled some licorice out of his pocket.

Jordan brushed past Terry and entered even further into the student's grimy apartment while searching it with his eyes. When there issued no response to his question, the detective turned on his heel and growled, "Quit messing with me, kid! Get me the coat, now! I've got other cases to worry about besides this one."

He saw Terry's lips tremble and had all the answer he needed. The boy thought this was about something else. Now that he knew what Jordan really wanted, he realized he might still be in grave trouble after all.

"It's gone, right?" the detective asked with no surprise in his voice whatsoever.

"I seriously thought this was about the bar. I mean, I thought it was weird, but I was thinkin' about last night, you know?"

"No. In fact, I have no idea what you're talking about. But answer me, kid, is the coat gone?"

"I looked everywhere!" Terry blurted out. "I swear, not more than an hour ago it was hung over the chair in my bedroom! I didn't really think this was about the coat! I thought it was about that girl from the bar. When I wouldn't get her drugs after we, uh, well, you know, she said she was going to have her father report me. I figured she was lying; after all, it didn't make sense. But then, the operator patched me through to you, and I started getting paranoid."

Ah, Terry swore he wouldn't be tricked in order to make a confession. And indeed, he hadn't been tricked. He revealed all of his dirty secrets completely on his own accord.

Luckily for him, Jordan was overworked and dead tired. Beyond his captain hating him and giving him more work than the rest of the guys, he'd just been served a lawsuit for urinating on his neighbor's dog. That's something else he didn't want to think about, so he kept both Terry and himself fixated on his reason for coming over to Terry's apartment in the first place. "The coat, did a roommate take it?"

Terry instantly replied, "I only have one roommate, and he left for a wedding yesterday morning! No one's been here but me all day! I don't know how that girl got into the bar, but I didn't bring her home! We just messed around a little in the bathroom, that's all. I've been alone here—all day! I swear I don't know what happened to it. Did this Miller chick tell you I stole her coat? She gave it to me; seriously, she all but forced it on me—"

"Let me guess," Jordan cut in. "You were walking on the railroad tracks along Bradbury Avenue in the cold, and she approached you and insisted you take her coat."

Terry narrowed his eyes in bewildered confusion, "How'd you know that?"

The detective sat down on one of the stools lining the breakfast counter and sighed, "Ah, it's always the same."

"What?"

"Yeah, we thought it was a prank at first. After a while though, all the witnesses, all the folks who'd been approached by her, they all had the same key identifier."

The blood on her temple, Terry thought to himself instinctually.

"She's given her coat to other people?" Terry questioned.

The detective just chuckled and informed, "Oh, yes. You're the third person so far this winter. You'd think more people would wear their coats out in the cold. Mostly college kids on their way somewhere by foot. You all think you're going to live forever and all that. Can't say I blame you. I was an idiot at your age. Heck, I'm still an idiot."

This was far too much for Terry to handle. He babbled, "I don't know how I lost it! It was in my room not more than an hour ago. I promise, I'll pay for it! Did she report me or something? She gave it to me to wear! Why do girls hate me so much? They're always trying to get me in trouble! Why is she setting me up like this?"

Again, Detective Jordan could only chuckle. "Don't worry about the coat. Olivia Miller didn't set you up, and you don't have to pay for it. People have been losing her coat for years."

"What are you talking about?"

"It's always the same, kid. She gives people her coat; they try to return it, only to find it's disappeared. People with your exact experience, down to the missing coat, have been telling me the same story ever since the winter she fell down into a little ravine along the railroad tracks. She fell down that hill, hit her head on a big rock."

Terry had a sudden enlightenment, "But, that must've just happened last night. The blood was still on her temple."

"No, it wasn't last night. It was three years ago."

Terry's mouth dropped in disbelief. "I don't get it!" Terry cried out. "Why doesn't she wash the blood off? Is she some kind of messed up freak? Why does she give her coat away to people with blood on her face?"

"I don't know, kid," Detective Jordan replied with something approaching boredom. It was rather obvious he had been through all of this before. "All I know is that this woman plays the coat fairy when she's supposed to be at Shepard's Field."

This was far too much for the college student. "That's a cemetery!" he screamed at the top of his lungs.

"I know. That's where they put dead people. That rock she hit her head on—it killed her."

Son of Eloehiem

The Mianthon plowed through the stars, just as it had done for centuries. Its mission was one of peace, of healing the systems of the galaxy. When it had left dock so long ago, only thirty-two men and thirty-two women, all over twenty-one, none under forty-five, inhabited it. In the years that have passed, those one hundred spawned a mini-civilization. The Mianthon now carries eight hundred and fifty-nine people, still nowhere near its maximum capacity of twenty-seven hundred.

The denizens of the Mianthon cultivated and distributed the herb called Nolion. It was the only herb in the known galaxy that had proven, thus far, to have superb medicinal effects for the hundreds of sentient life forms discovered as yet. When they began, they gave it away freely, for theirs was a mission decreed by Eloehiem, the creator of life for whom they paid homage. Eloehiem had blessed this civilization by giving them Nolion, easing the burden of their mortal frames, and they heard His calling to share it with the galaxy both known and unknown.

However, in the three hundred and sixteen years since heeding His edict, they have drifted off course. They now demanded trade for their Nolion, instead of giving it away as told. Only a handful still offered true, heartfelt reverence to Eloehiem; most only recognized Him when it proved advantageous.

Those not responsible for the commanding, repairing, and maintaining of the ship's many aspects were required to help farm the Nolion in the Gestation Chamber, a vast portion of the ship where abundant quantities of Nolion were produced yearly.

When the mission originated, the ship was to always have a Commander, a Commission of Virtue, and a Voice of Eloehiem. After the second generation of the ship's initial crew, the Commission of Virtue became the Commission of

Reason, and the Voice of Eloehiem became a token figurehead, utterly power-less in the eyes of the people.

In the year 2999, the story of Jaesua began under mysterious circumstances. They found him as a baby, floating through the vacuum of space. Cold and lifeless, the crew of the Mianthon towed his form in so they could incinerate it properly, the only tradition of Eloehiem still practiced by all. Just as the baby was to be reduced to ashes, it sprang to life. After much study by the scientists on board the vessel, they determined he was nothing more than an anomaly of nature. Many theorized he had been jettisoned from some other craft, and then preserved by the iciness of the void. The scientists found no more use for him once they agreed unanimously he was perfectly normal, just like the rest of them, and they offered him for adoption.

No one wanted the child, until two people, a man and his wife, members of the anemic Body of Eloehiem, volunteered to take in the baby.

✵   ✵   ✵

Thirty years had since passed. Dul now served as the soundless Voice of Eloehiem. Isian, Cudco, Yanmon, and Oarink were the Commission of Reason, and Commander Pylite, who was bred for his position through unalterable lin-eage, appointed all after he came into power at the age of thirty-three only four years ago.

Choosef, one of the many mechanics of the Mianthon, worked on an oxy-gen converter with his fellow mechanic and adopted son, Jaesua.

"What's the output read?" Choosef asked after he replaced the interface plate.

"Eighty-nine percent," Jaesua replied.

"Okay, that's within acceptable range. Job done."

Choosef and Jaesua crawled out of the mammoth oxygen duct and loaded into their transport. It was just large enough to hold the two men and their tools, taking up no more room than a person lying down.

"Home," Choosef spoke into the navigation console.

The transport beeped alive and rolled them through the many large corri-dors of the ship.

"I've been thinking," Jaesua initiated while they passed fellow crewmembers on foot. Some were on their way to the Gestation Chamber, some were on their way to a maintenance shift, and some were simply out for a walk.

"What about, Son?" Choosef asked as he filled out a report form to transmit to the Belly, the unofficial name of the Mianthon's Control Center.

"You and Mother, you see what's happened to the people of this world, don't you?"

"First of all, Son, remember, this isn't a world. This is a microcosm of the world we come from. This is just a ship."

"The world *you* come from," Jaesua reminded.

Choosef flushed and apologized, "Sorry, Son. I forget."

"I know it's hard, Father, but you have to accept…"

Choosef set down the report grid, unfinished. Regulation stated that reports must be transmitted within five minutes of all repairs, but he didn't care. This was far more important.

"I do accept, Son," Choosef assured. "Your mother and I knew where you came from the minute we heard about you. You were foreseen, remember? Even if you hadn't told us as much when you were eight, we know who you are."

"But the others don't think so."

Choosef sighed. He felt ashamed of his people. How far they had fallen. "Son, it's not just the passengers on this ship who don't believe, it's most of the members of the Body as well! I'm afraid we are beyond redemption."

"You're not," Jaesua informed. "This is all His Will. Once my time here is over, they will remember Him."

Choosef and Jaesua passed over the Gestation Chamber. Both of them peered over the bridge their transporter drove along to look at the thousands of Nolion plants blooming. They appeared as red sunbursts, spreading the light of wellness to all, or at least they did in the beginning. Now they only healed those who had something of value to exchange.

"What's that supposed to mean?" Choosef questioned. He had never heard his son speak in finite terms before. "'When your time is over?'"

"I spoke last night with Eloehiem. Tomorrow, my journey begins."

Choosef only nodded in understanding. He and his wife suspected this day would come.

✳   ✳   ✳

Five months had passed since Jaesua left his quarters to live off the compassion of the people of the Mianthon. Already, seven had joined his cause, listening to his stories, and following his example. Included in that seven were his childhood friends, Maree and Peedor.

They had set up residence within the Gestation Chamber, and it was there that Jaesua taught any willing to learn.

Slowly but surely, some whose families had long ago turned their backs on Eloehiem faced Him once more through the words of Jaesua. But, ironically, it was the Body of Eloehiem that proved his greatest opposition. They argued there existed already a voice of Eloehiem, as appointed by Commander Pylite, and that appointee was Dul. After only five months, the Body had grown uneasy.

$$*\qquad*\qquad*$$

In the seventh month, Dul meant to confront Jaesua directly.

Amongst the lush red Nolions, Jaesua stood in nothing but a tunic and pants among his followers. His inner circle had grown to nine, made up of Maree, Peedor, Movsern, Carschad, Wilf, Ary, Frantone, and Zalk. Most of them had been Nolion Attendees—farmers.

With the dissipation of the Commission of Virtue and the birth of the Commission of Reason, so too was born a militaristic faction under direct control of the Commander, the Commission of Reason, and, to a lesser degree, the Voice of Eloehiem. Dul made sure he had several security officers with him as he approached Jaesua and his most trusted friends.

"Dul, it is good to see you here," Jaesua greeted. "I focused we could work together on bringing the people back to Eloehiem. He has answered my focus."

Dul studied the benign faces before him. He hated them, but he sensed not an iota of maliciousness amongst their numbers. "We will not be working together, insurgent. There can be only one Voice of Eloehiem, and that is me."

Jaesua grinned and said, "The Voice of Eloehiem is an important position when held responsibly. It is not my wish to *take* it from you. My position is greater."

"Are you saying I am not acting responsibly as the Voice of Eloehiem?"

Jaesua glanced at his friends lightheartedly and answered, "That is for the people to decide. It is the people I'm concerned with, not you."

"And who are you to be concerned with the people? I am the Voice of Eloehiem! I will care for the people!"

"Then tell me," Jaesua demanded as he walked toward Dul, "what is Eloehiem saying right now?"

Dul stared stupidly at his questioner. A crowd of workers and pedestrians had gathered in curiosity. Nearly spitting he was in such a rage, Dul interrogated, "Who do you think you are?"

"He is the Son of Eloehiem!" Maree yelled from behind Jaesua.

Dul, the security officers, and the citizens of the Mianthon laughed at this outburst uncontrollably.

"We are back to this again, are we? This was amusing when you were a child, Jaesua, but such statements as an adult will yield far more dangerous results. Eloehiem would not beget someone of flesh! That is why I am here!" Dul chortled, his confidence regained.

"You are no longer the Voice of Eloehiem, you are the corrupted pawn of the Commander and the Commission of Reason," Peedor seethed.

Jaesua glanced over his shoulder at his boyhood friend. He spoke, "Calm yourself, Peedor. Anger leads to the very corruption you speak of. All is happening just as it is meant to. You can experience Eloehiem's Will with honor, as He would like, or your actions can make you a disappointment; however, what He has planned *will* pass."

"You dare, even now, to say you are the Son of Eloehiem?" Dul hissed.

"Eloehiem gave us the Nolion to heal those in need. He did not decree that anything should be given in return for the healing powers of the Nolion. When people are sick, Eloehiem helps them however He can. Sometimes, the Nolion is not enough."

Many of the crowd squinted their eyes as they fought to deduce the meaning of Jaesua's words. Dul himself appeared bewildered. The friends of Jaesua, however, only smiled. Although they looked a bit confused themselves, they had gotten use to spending hours working on the meaning of Jaesua's words.

"You break the First Rule of Eloehiem," Dul growled.

"No, I am not putting *myself* before Eloehiem...like others onboard this vessel are prone," Jaesua returned.

Dul huffed, turned his back to Jaesua and his friends, and left. He took his security officers with him.

The eight friends cheered for their teacher. They were genuinely happy he had won his first battle with those in power, those blocking Eloehiem's Will, but Jaesua did not give the impression of being pleased.

Maree took him by the hand and asked, "Jaesua, what's wrong? You just defeated a blasphemer of your Father! You act as though you're unhappy!"

Jaesua motioned for his friends to form around him, then said, "Dul is powerless. He is merely a token figure. When the Commission of Reason replaced the Commission of Virtue, the true Voice of Eloehiem became a thing of the past. No, if we want the people to regain the Grandeur of Eloehiem, we must shake their devotion to Pylite and the Commission."

"You want to overthrow the Commander of the Mianthon?" Ary asked.

Jaesua chuckled, "No. I've got all the power I need, and I'm given it through Eloehiem. Commanding a ship will not bring the people back to Him. We will lead by example. We will teach His ways to the people who have forgotten. This ship used to be a beacon of hope throughout the galaxy with Eloehiem's gift of the Nolion. All Eloehiem asks is that we honor Him as we live out His Will. That is our goal."

✳   ✳   ✳

Thirteen months had passed since Jaesua began his mission. In that time, Trice, Patrace, Jaspeh, and Andrid joined his cause. They continued to live in the Gestation Chamber, accepting charity from those who supported them, turning the other cheek to those who hated them for their beliefs.

One day, Choosef and his wife, Maerae, were shocked to open their quarters to the Commander of the Mianthon, Pylite himself!

He walked in without being asked—tall, broad, and handsome—with corruption lingering about him. He had not changed the practices of the people concerning the free distribution of the Nolion personally, but he had supported such change. In his mind, obtaining goods for their healing herb to trade for other items with alien societies made perfect sense. It seemed, after all, the logical thing to do.

"Commander Pylite, to what do we owe this honor?" Maerae asked.

"I am not here to socialize," he responded curtly.

Such a statement did not surprise Choosef and his wife. Hundreds of years ago, when the mission of the Mianthon first began, the Commander, the Commission, and the Voice always intermingled with the people. There was no sense of class, no display of power over another. The Commander just happened to run the ship, the Commission decided what was best for the people as a whole, and the Voice told them Eloehiem's Will. They were of the commoners. Now these leaders acted as though they were above the people. In their minds, they were better than the ordinary citizens. Eloehiem served *them*, from their perspective, not vice versa.

"May I ask what brings you to us, then?" Choosef prodded.

"Your son," Commander Pylite began. "He is dangerously nearing treason against Eloehiem."

"*Against* Eloehiem?" Maerae inquired incredulously.

"Yes."

"How?" Choosef requested.

Pylite's jaw set as he nearly growled, "He already has twelve members of this ship following him blindly, and he has turned many to thinking of him as the true Voice of Eloehiem. Usurping loyalty from Eloehiem—"

"Why don't you just say what you mean?" Maerae interrupted. Pylite stared at her, astonished, as she boldly informed, "He is bringing the people to Eloehiem. He is the first to truly act on Eloehiem's behalf on this ship for a hundred years! What you mean to say is that he is turning power away from you and your lackeys!"

Pylite slapped her harshly across the face.

Choosef moved to protect her, but security officers rushed into their quarters and hit him with a discharge from their weapons. He fell in a heap next to his wife.

"May I remind you the punishment for treason is death upon the scroo? If you are not careful, you will find yourselves accompanying your son there!"

"You cannot kill the Son of Eloehiem!" Maerae screamed from the floor.

"We shall see," Pylite seethed before he turned and powered out.

After Pylite left, Maerae tended her husband. He still twitched involuntarily from the jolt he received.

Finally, he regained control of his fine motor functions. He looked up at his wife kneeling over him, and then mumbled, "My father once told me he could remember when there wasn't a weapon on the entire Mianthon other than the gas Nolion gave people."

Maerae could only laugh, despite herself.

✳   ✳   ✳

Between the twenty-fourth and the thirty-fifth months after his teachings began, Jaesua performed the miracles.

He healed several of the sick who had not yet ingested Nolion. For instance, with just a touch of his hands, he ceased the hemorrhaging in two separate women, restored the sight of three different men, corrected the withered hand of a child, and revitalized the hearing of five people who had been rendered deaf by a gravity-inducer's explosion. He made nutrients appear from thin air, he turned water into zodru, and, in a feat none could believe, he levitated to the top of the Gestation Chamber.

❋   ❋   ❋

It was in the thirty-sixth month, days before his thirty-third birthday, when he was finally taken in for treason against Eloehiem. He had accumulated too large of a following for the powers in control, and when the wife of Lascuroos brought her dead husband's body to Jaesua, and he restored the departed to life anew, they were taking no more chances.

In a few weeks they would finally enter a solar system that had taken years to reach. The Commission and the Commander expected a great deal of profitable trading, but Jaesua had the people of the ship clamoring for Nolion to be distributed freely once more.

The people were slowly coming back to Eloehiem, and it was through the work of Jaesua that it was happening.

One night, Jaesua gathered his twelve closest friends and had dinner with them.

Once dinner had nearly finished, Jaesua spoke into Maree's ear, "In a moment, I must say goodbye to all. But before I do, promise me you will be strong."

"What do you mean?" Maree asked.

"Just promise me. No matter what happens to me, I will never be gone. I exist perpetually, and I will always be with you. This is my purpose in life; this is why Eloehiem sends me. I have done this many times. I will do it many more. I am Eloehiem's Will. Be strong for me?"

"I will," Maree swore. Her eyes were glistening in the corners, and although she didn't know why she was overtaken with sadness, she knew her time with Jaesua was coming to an end.

"You will see me again before your days are over, Maree. But now, I must speak to the others."

Jaesua stood up among his students and said, "In a few minutes, security officers of the Commission of Reason will enter the Gestation Chamber and imprison me. Tomorrow, I will stand trial for treason against Eloehiem. I tell you now that I am the Son of Eloehiem. I will never die, yet, in forty days, I will be executed upon the scroo. I will then be incinerated, and my ashes will be spread into the void. If you recall, I was given to you in the form of a lifeless infant from the very place to which I will be returned. I tell you this not to frighten you, but to prepare you. We have brought the people back to Eloehiem. That was why I was sent.

"However, all we have done will be undone during the trial. The people will turn against me. After I am gone, they will regret their treachery and look to my teachings anew. Though I will return to life, I will not be on this ship any longer. It will be up to eleven of you to continue my teachings."

All twelve of the friends were shocked! Trice found his voice first and asked, "Why only *eleven* of us, Jaesua?"

"Because one of you will testify against me during the trials. In fact, one of you has already promised Pylite that you will aid him in my fall."

The students glared at one another, their hearts full of suspicion. None knew who the traitor was in their midst.

"Wipe such tainted thoughts from your minds, friends," Jaesua commanded. "The traitor will be revealed soon, and the traitor will repent. This person was promised five percent of the profits taken from the trading done with the new system we are entering, but those trades will never come to pass, and there will be nothing for the traitor but the guilt of the heart. Take my student back when he repents, and hold no grudges."

"We will do no such thing!" Peedor cried.

"You will," Jaesua returned softly to his oldest friend. "Eloehiem commands it. The follower of Eloehiem who turns his back on Him is worse than those who do not follow Eloehiem whatsoever. You will accept all those who are sorry for what they have done. Especially you, Peedor. For you will be the cornerstone of a new way on this ship. You will be the foundation from which my teachings will be built."

The twelve students lowered their eyes in utter bafflement. The teachings had been going so well, they had never suspected tragedy such as this would strike.

"We do not have much time," Jaesua continued. "I want you to uphold a tradition. He pulled a Nolion leaf off from the gargantuan plants for each of his students. "The leaf you have in your hand represents my body, and I represent Eloehiem. Ingest it, and do so in memoriam of me, and in honor of Eloehiem."

The followers all ate the leaf Jaesua had given them.

Jaesua then said, "Pour zodru into your cups."

He waited for all to follow his orders, even the traitor, and then, with a quick wave of his hand, he said, "The zodru represents the blood flowing through my body. Drink it, and do so regularly, in memoriam of me, and in honor of Eloehiem."

Once all had completed his command, security officers burst into the Gestation Chamber and quickly whisked him away.

Peedor rushed after them to protect his old friend.

The security officers turned to confront their pursuer, and Peedor stopped. He looked to Jaesua for guidance, for he knew he would not last a minute against trained officers of the Commission of Reason.

"What did I tell you, Peedor?" Jaesua whispered.

Peedor lowered his head in shame.

They took Jaesua away without incident.

The following day, the trial began. Jaesua was charged with treason for breaking the First Rule of Eloehiem. Dul and the Commission of Reason presented a terribly solid case against Jaesua. Of course, Jaesua, Choosef, Maerae, Peedor, Maree, Dul, the Commission of Reason, and Pylite himself knew it was nothing more than a pack of lies. But, it was a convincing pack of lies, and when Jaesua's own student, Frantone, substantiated all that Dul and the Commission claimed, it was not difficult to sway the people.

During the trials, Jaesua said nothing. Finally, Dul asked him if he was the son of Eloehiem.

Jaesua responded, "Yes, I am the Son of Eloehiem."

Dul replied, "But, to say you are the son of Eloehiem would make you, in part, Eloehiem himself! Do you claim to be Eloehiem himself?"

"I am the Son of Eloehiem."

"So you admit you are putting yourself before Eloehiem; you are claiming to be Eloehiem!"

Jaesua said nothing.

"People of the Mianthon," Dul shouted as he addressed the crowd who had come to witness the trial of Jaesua, "our worst crime is to break the First Rule of Eloehiem. For this crime, death on the scroo is not enough; this man of treason must suffer before death! Do you agree?"

Jaesua closed his eyes and offered a focus to his Father as he heard the very people he had healed cry for his suffering and impending death.

Over the next forty days, Jaesua was punished publicly for the people of the Mianthon to witness. They were shocked that he never cried out, he never begged for mercy. Even as skin tore from his body, even as sodium chloride was doused into his open wounds, even as he was humiliated time and time again, his will never broke. Many could see that he focused without fail during the punishment.

On the thirty-ninth day, Maree visited Choosef and Maerae.

"Maree, come in," Maerae said to one of her son's oldest friends.

Maree entered the quarters of her love's parents and fell into the arms of Maerae, sobbing uncontrollably. Choosef entered the main quarters and saw the women holding each other. He approached them and took them into his arms. And he shed tears as well.

The next day, Jaesua was made to carry the very scroo he would be fastened to until his death. He hauled it from the prison on one end of the Mianthon all the way to the Execution Platform found at the top of the immense Gestation Chamber.

As he made his way, the people of the Mianthon scoffed at him. He heard the people say that anyone could heal the suffering in a room full of Nolion, that Eloehiem would never take the flesh, that he was just a crazed con artist, or, even worse, a zealot.

What Jaesua did not hear were words of sympathy, words for Eloehiem, or words of repentance.

Jaesua was finally led before Pylite, Dul, and the Commission of Reason. They would address him before he was anchored to the scroo and raised to the Execution Platform.

"This is your last chance to repent for the horrible claims you have made, Jaesua," Dul spoke not to Jaesua himself, but to the bloodthirsty crowd who had come to observe the death of a man many had once followed.

Jaesua only focused as he conversed with Eloehiem.

"You wretch!" Dul exclaimed. "Look at me when I speak to you!"

Noticing that Jaesua would offer no response to the Voice of Eloehiem, a Voice he had himself appointed for Dul's weak will, Pylite decided to take matters into his own hands. "Jaesua, look at me."

Jaesua slowly lifted his eyes to the Commander of the Mianthon. Pylite took notice of the cuts and swollen features of the supposed Son's face.

"People of the Mianthon!" Pylite called out. As he scanned the crowd, he saw many of Jaesua's most devoted followers, including Maree and Peedor. "We have not had an execution on this ship for over a decade, and I am open to staying this man's death to avoid such barbarity. Although he is the worst enemy of Eloehiem, I'm sure he would repent if given time. I know the Commission of Reason usually makes the difficult decisions, but this decision we will instead put into *your* hands. Tell us, should we stay his execution?"

New tears fell from Maree's eyes as the crowd roared for Jaesua's death.

"Then know this," Pylite bellowed, "his death is on your hands, for you have made the decision on your own. Remember that."

The crowd continued to plea for Jaesua's death.

"Jaesua," Pylite began. "Do you have anything to say before you are fixed to the scroo?"

Jaesua lifted his hunched shoulders and spoke with a voice impossibly strong, "You, Dul, and the Commission of Reason have manipulated these people into your bidding. They know not what they do, and I forgive them. You have put yourselves before my Father, you are guilty of the very thing for which you accuse me, but I forgive you. I die so that Eloehiem will offer you another chance at redemption. That is my purpose. Know this, however, the moment I die, your opportunity of trade with the next system will fail, and you will spend the next forty years repairing the Mianthon until you reach the next system. At that time, this ship will have returned to its original mission, you and those you appointed will no longer be in positions of power, and this will be a vessel of Eloehiem once more."

Pylite chuckled and then muttered, "Fasten him."

The next half hour was spent painfully attaching Jaesua to the scroo. Once this was torturously accomplished, the scroo was raised to the Execution Platform for all to witness.

Just over seventy-two hours later, Jaesua died.

At the moment of his death, the engines of the Mianthon cut out, and it would be ten years before they could be restored to full power. Until that time, the Mianthon drifted in perpetual motion, avoiding the dangers of space as best it could.

Jaesua was taken down from the Execution Platform. His lifeless body was displayed openly as it was transported to the Incineration Wing. The people of the Mianthon instantly regretted their decision. After laying eyes upon Jaesua's body, many sought out Peedor that night. Within only a few years, Peedor led the Body of Eloehiem into a golden age. He did so with the original ten followers of Jaesua, and with Darroo, who served as Frantone's replacement. After his treachery, Frantone could not live with his guilt and ended his own existence.

After his incineration, Jaesua's ashes were given to Maerae and Choosef, and they, with Maree and the rest of the followers of Jaesua, spread those ashes into the void.

They returned him to Eloehiem.

✳   ✳   ✳

A few weeks later, the Mianthon passed the only inhabited planet of the system they currently drifted through. This was the planet they had hoped to trade with, but without engine power, they could not stop. They helplessly floated past, and Pylite remembered the words of Jaesua before he was fastened to the scroo.

"You're sure about this?" Choosef asked Maree.

"I'm sure," Maree returned.

"You'll be alone," Maerae said.

"No, I won't," Maree answered. "Your son is with me. I can hear him speaking to me at all times."

Choosef opened the portal to one of the hundreds of escape pods on the Mianthon.

"Will you get in very much trouble for this?" Maree questioned as she entered the pod.

"Probably, but nothing compared to what Jaesua went through for us."

Maerae said, "Are you sure this is what you want?"

"I'm sure. I've thought about this since the moment he was put to death, and I know this is the right thing for me to do. Even though I know Peedor and the rest will reconnect the people with Eloehiem, I cannot suffer the people that cried for his execution. I know it goes against all he taught, but I'm going to try to teach his words elsewhere. If we cannot give them the gift of Nolion, at least I can spread the teachings of Jaesua."

"Your shuttle will be useless once you land," Choosef informed. "And the Mianthon will never return to this system. You'll be stranded."

"I know."

Maree hugged them both and then closed the pod's hatch.

Pylite was informed the minute an unscheduled shuttle launched, but he let it go. He knew it was useless to raise questions, they couldn't turn around in their out-of-control ship anyway. Besides, he had a hunch he knew who it was. He would find out later he was correct.

✳   ✳   ✳

Thirty-three years later, Maree had grown quite elderly. She adapted to her new surroundings rather quickly all that time ago, after her ship had crashed unnoticed into a series of caverns. Although it was damaged beyond repair, she emerged unscathed.

Soon after a few days of journey, she settled into the outskirts of a local civilization. Within months, she was considered a wise woman that many sought for council. Always, she told the people she helped that her wisdom derived from Jaesua, and that he promised he would return for them.

Now she was sixty-seven years old. She had heard rumblings in the town of a man who claimed he was the Son of Adonai, as the locals called him. Some felt he was a prophet, some thought he was a teacher, and some even thought he was nothing more than a crazed fool.

She heard he had performed miracles, however, and she remembered Jaesua's promise that she would see him again in her lifetime.

Maree set out to find this man they called Yeshua.

She questioned all she came across, no matter what their race, religion, or nation of origin. She finally determined this Yeshua was being held prisoner, and was to soon be crucified.

✳   ✳   ✳

She had arrived too late.

On a cross overlooking all, she saw the man they called Yeshua nailed to it, dead.

She looked at his face and realized Jaesua had kept his promise.

Ghost of the Bed and Breakfast

I roll over, unable to sleep. Trist is next to me, sleeping like a child without a care in the world. He's never had trouble sleeping.

I always have.

Right now we're in an old bed and breakfast visiting the hometown of an author that's been dead for just over a century. I'm something of a book nerd, and I make a point to travel to all of my favorite authors' childhood homes.

Tristopher is not nearly the book lover I am, but he does love me, and so he puts up with these silly little trips I plan.

He hasn't ever had much use for the dead.

Me, I can't get enough of them. One day I look forward to meeting all of my heroes. All those authors who have delighted me over the years.

Hopefully, though, that won't be anytime soon. I've still got a lot of homes to visit!

I crawl out of bed, careful not to rouse Trist, and go for a walk through the house. According to its owners, it was built in the early eighteen hundreds. Of course, it's located in the historic district of town, not more than three blocks away from our point of interest, Mark Clemmons' boyhood home.

The house we're staying in is rather simple in design. It has two floors, each with four main rooms. The ceilings are quite high throughout. The first floor has a kitchen, a dining room, a living room, and what is now a music room. There are also two bathrooms. The second floor has four bedrooms, divided by a staircase that splits into a "Y." Each section of the upper floor is bisected by the stairs and has two bedrooms and a bathroom.

I love old houses. They carry so much history and soul with them. Sometimes I feel as though I can hear the ghosts in the walls calling out to me. I've never told Tristopher such things. He doesn't believe in that sort.

The one thing that bothers me, however, about this particular old house is that there are no doors separating the bedrooms. They only have a small hallway between them leading to the stairs and the bathroom. Needless to say, if you plan on doing anything more than sleeping while staying at the Historic Petersburg Bed and Breakfast, you may want to think again. Either that, or be willing to endure several pointed glances the following morning.

I move smoothly down the steps, momentarily interrupted by a slight stumble, then walk through the dining room to the kitchen.

The Jades—the owners of the house—make sure to leave plenty of nightlights all over the house for their guests. They are also courteous enough to keep several glasses out for anyone needing a drink during the night. I'm not particularly thirsty at the moment, although I am known to frequently get up during the night for such a thing. Trist tells me I should make a habit of sleeping with a bottle of water next to the bed, but I prefer my little midnight jaunts.

I pass through the kitchen and enter the living room, strolling through the first floor of the house, admiring the antiques. There is nothing—and I mean nothing—in this house that comes from modern times unless they are the barest of essentials. Meaning there is a refrigerator, the plumbing is up to date, I assume there is a washer and dryer, and although there is no television or computer on the main floor, I suspect the Jades have them in their master bedroom. After all, we decided to stay at their home due to their thorough website.

I'll be honest with you. I picked this place not only because it's so old, but also because they advertised it may be haunted. I've never told Trist this either, but I have a deep fascination with the supernatural. I was hoping during our two-day stay we might run into a spirit of some sort. Oh sure, as I said before, I can hear the old house talking to me as old houses tend to do, but I'm hoping to see a real-deal, walking, talking ghost. Well, maybe not talking. That could be rather uncomfortable.

I stop in the music room. Mrs. Jade has an old grand piano set up in the dead center of the room with padded benches lining the perimeter of the walls. It's a lovely room, decorated quite elegantly. As I walk past the piano, enjoying its appearance in the moonlight that overpowers the room's little nightlight, a cat leaps out from under the bench, hisses at me hellishly, then darts out of the room.

That damn cat scared the life out of me!

I finally tire of my spree and the lack of the supernatural, so I climb the stairs back to our bedroom. I walk as softly as I can so I don't cause the temperamental steps to groan in complaint.

As I enter our bedroom, I get my wish.

There one stands—a ghost.

It appears to be a little girl, no more than ten years old. She has beautiful long, dark hair. She's wearing a nightgown like those that must have existed in the early twentieth century. Her appearance is pure white, except for that lovely hair of hers. She's not glowing, but it's as close to glowing as something can be without giving off any actual light.

Needless to say, I'm delighted.

She's standing right next to Tristopher's side of the bed, staring down at him in keen interest. Her head shoots up, and she then regards me sadly. Her eyes are flickering like those old silent movies, but they burn with a sort of hazel I've never seen before.

She shakes her head at me sorrowfully and then disappears like a fog burning from the new day's rays. There is nothing left of her but a quickly dissipating mist.

But, I got my wish.

Finally content, I crawl back into bed with Trist.

Of course, he sleeps on as though nothing has happened whatsoever.

✳   ✳   ✳

The next morning, I roll over and Trist is gone.

Trist is a good man, the best man I've ever met next to my own father. He is not one to simply run away from a fight.

Let me explain.

Before we returned to the bed and breakfast for the night, Trist and I had a terrible argument over dinner. He did not want to stay at the Jades; he thought the house was too old and not up to code. I assured him there are laws for that sort of thing and the house was perfectly safe. For goodness sake, if it had been standing since the eighteen hundreds, why would it pick two thousand and three to have a catastrophe? He didn't agree. We fought far longer than we should have, but he eventually brought us back to the house. We went to bed without a word to each other, but I assumed all would be right with the new day and our miraculous survival.

Apparently, I thought wrong.

Glancing at the clock, I see that it is seven-thirty. I peek over the edge of the bed and notice his running shoes are gone.

That answers it.

I knew my Trist wouldn't stay mad at me.

He started running about three weeks ago. Out of nowhere he told me he felt like he was getting old (he's only twenty-six) and needed to get back into shape. So, he took up running. He started with a half mile and has been trying to add a half-mile each week. That'd make his run this morning only a mile and a half, so he should be back any time now.

I bounce out of bed, feeling light as air, and glide down to the dining room. I'm not feeling hungry, which is the norm with me; I'm not really one for breakfast. But, I do sit down at the dining room table where Mrs. Jade has set out an armada of breakfast dishes.

Once again, out of nowhere, that infernal cat explodes from under my chair, screams at me, sending chills through my bones, and then sprints out of the room.

Mrs. Jade then walks in, carrying a cup of coffee.

"What in the hell is the matter with your damn cat?" I seethe at her pointedly. I'm not really a cat person, and sometimes my temper gets the better of me. Sadly, this is one of those times.

I apparently offended her gravely because she does not even acknowledge my existence. The old, blue-haired woman simply sits, sipping from her coffee and reading today's paper.

"I'm sorry, Mrs. Jade," I apologize. "I didn't mean to curse at you. I hope you'll forgive me." She does not even lift her head! How dare she! "Could I have a cup of coffee, please?" I ask, testing the boundaries of her grudge.

Apparently it has none, because she doesn't even fulfill the request of a paying customer.

Just as I'm about to berate her, some other guests, a middle-aged husband and wife, come pouncing down the stairs gleefully.

"Mrs. Jade!" they cry as they leave the stairs and rush to the dining room table. They're dressed remarkably well and I suddenly realize I haven't changed out of my pajamas. Perhaps that is why they disregard me so utterly; perhaps they are embarrassed for me. Snobs.

"Mrs. Jade," they continue, "we saw one!"

"What's that, dears?" the old woman asks quite pleasantly. I'm amazed at how she can switch moods so easily. She gives me the cold shoulder one minute, then treats them like royalty the next.

"We saw a ghost!"

"Hey, I did too!" I inform in elation. They're too excited, though, to notice a twenty-something too lazy to change out of her pajamas.

"What did she look like, dears?" Mrs. Jade asks them.

"She was a little girl," the woman responds. "Very dark, long hair."

"I saw her, too!" I blurt out. They ignore me still. How rude!

"Beautiful child!" the man cries.

"Did she say anything to you?" the old woman asks.

"She did," the woman answers. "She told us to beware the stairs!"

I spin in my seat and leer at the stairs. I guess they're kind of steep, but that's what a ghost chooses to say from beyond the grave? *Beware the stairs?* I think it's kind of lame, to be honest.

"Why would she say such a thing?" the man questions.

It's like he read my mind!

"Her name was Peggy Huston. Her parents, Willard and Martha, lived in this house from 1900 until 1915. Their only daughter was born in this home, and their only daughter died here at the age of ten in 1913."

"How did she die?" I ask.

Mrs. Jade, still not looking at me, at least decides I'm worth answering. She says, "Poor little Peggy fell down those very steps and broke her neck. She now visits the guests of this house and warns them to mind the stairs. She doesn't want anyone else suffering her fate."

"They are a little difficult to negotiate," the woman agrees.

"Yes, we've had many accidents, despite the railings."

"That's why we had to sign the waiver?" the man asks.

"Yes. We had a terrible mishap a few years ago. Luckily, there wasn't a lawsuit involved, but my husband and I decided better safe than sorry. This house has been in our family ever since the Hustons moved out. We'd hate to lose it."

Wow. I want to ask what happened two years ago, but I suspect she's still mad at me for cursing at her over her hell-spawn kitty.

Just then, the side door of the house flies open and Trist barrels in. He's covered in sweat and looks as though he could keel over. He tramps past the middle-aged couple and Mrs. Jade, regarding them politely, but ignores *me* completely! Don't tell me he's still upset after all!

I stare after him in shock as he powers up the stairs, stumbles slightly, regains his footing, then completes the ascension, disappearing from my sight.

"He a runner?" the woman asks Mrs. Jade as she seats herself at the table next to me.

"Yes," I answer. "But he just star—"

"He's a marathoner," Mrs. Jade interrupts me.

My jaw hits the table. Figuratively, of course. What in the world has given them the impression that Trist runs marathons? Couldn't they see what a mile and a half just did to him? He looked like he'd run ten!

"Is that the ruckus I heard this morning?" the man inquires with a grin. It was obvious to me he didn't truly mind the noise Trist must have made leaving for his run.

"Yes, I'm afraid so. I'm sorry for that," Mrs. Jade apologizes.

"Not at all," the man assures. "But, he must have gone quite a ways, leaving at five in the morning and all!"

"You must be mistaken," I say to the man. "Trist couldn't have left much before seven if he were only running a mile and a half."

They all ignore me. Again.

I've had enough. "You bastards!" I scream at them. "My husband and I are leaving this minute, and I want a full refund! I've never been treated so callously in all my life!"

I then erupt from my chair and run up the stairs, tripping embarrassingly as I do so.

✳   ✳   ✳

Trist is already in the shower by the time I enter our bedroom. No matter. I'll be dressed and packed to leave by the time he's done. I can't remember the last time I've been so upset.

Where the hell's my suitcase?

I see Trist's bags, but where are my things?

"I told you," a childlike voice from behind lectures.

I spin around and there she is—Peggy.

She's as amazing now as she was last night when I saw her. But, unlike the night previous, she's not disappearing and she is apparently intent upon having a few words with me.

I'm so exited by the prospect of talking with a real ghost that I'm able to put the rudeness of the human inhabitants under this roof behind me.

"What's that, sweetie?" I ask her, trying to overcome my exhilaration.

"Don't talk to me like I'm a child," Peggy replies. "I've been aware for over a hundred years now, compared to your twenty-five."

Twenty-five? She's not as smart as she makes herself out to be. I'm only twenty-three. Close, though. I have to give her that.

"Okay," I say encouragingly. "Are you Peggy?"

"You're so annoying, Dena. I wish you'd come to grips already."

"What are you talking about? How do you know my name?" I ask her. In all my imaginings of what it would be like to converse with a spirit, this is about as much the opposite as can be fathomed.

Whoops! The bathroom door just opened. I peer out the bedroom and see steam floating out from Trist's shower. When I turn back to Peggy the Ghost, she's gone.

I jog over to Trist as he stands in the bathroom, combing his hair. He's already dressed. That doesn't surprise me. He was mortified at the prospect of someone peeking in on him in the bedroom while he dressed and undressed.

"Hey, buddy, what'd you do with my bags?" I ask him with a smile.

He ignores me.

That's not the Trist I know. He's not like this. Why is he being so mean to me? He's never treated me like this in our entire four years of marriage!

"Trist, please, stop this! Everyone in this house is ignoring me, and it's driving me crazy!"

Tristopher then walks right past me without saying a word.

He enters our bedroom, puts on his shoes, grabs his bags, then leaves the bedroom just as quickly as he entered.

"Do you expect me to simply ride home in my pajamas?" I yell at him. "This isn't funny anymore, Trist! Enough is enough! Where'd you put my stuff?"

I have to chase him down the steps as he continues to pretend as though I don't exist. The legs of my pajama bottoms are too long, and I trip over them as I hurry down the stairs.

I roll end over end and next find myself on the floor, lying face up, staring at the ceiling. I sit up to see Trist still descending the steps.

He's acting like nothing happened!

But...how did I get past him?

This isn't making sense. I should be in some sort of pain after a tumble like that, but I pop up without a sore spot on my body!

"Care for some breakfast before you're on your way, Tristopher?" Mrs. Jade asks him.

Strange. I don't remember Mrs. Jade and Trist bonding remotely enough in the last twenty-four hours to warrant such a casual tone.

"Please," Trist answers as he takes his seat next to the middle-aged man who has now finished his breakfast and is reading the paper. The middle-aged woman must be using the restroom, because she's nowhere to be seen.

"How was your run?" Mrs. Jade asks Trist.

I stand at the foot of the stairs, utterly perplexed.

Peggy resides at the head of the stairs observing me sympathetically.

"It was good," Trist answers without much emotion.

"How far did you go?" the man questions in genuine interest.

"Just a bit over ten miles," Trist informs.

"Training for a marathon, huh?" the man replies.

"Always," Trist answers simply enough.

Marathon! Trist hasn't even run a 5K yet! What is he talking about?

"Dear," Mrs. Jade begins, "don't take this the wrong way, but I truly hope this is the last time I see you here."

So, the rudeness continues. Glad to see it's not only me she treats like dirt.

"No, I'm afraid it won't be the last time," Trist mumbles as he chomps down on some bacon.

"Honey, you have to let go," Mrs. Jade pleads.

What is going on here?

"I should gather up my wife and get our day started," the man says as he excuses himself. It's obvious he's detected a conversation which he has no business being a part of.

"I'll let go when she tells me to let go," Trist groans without making eye contact with Mrs. Jade. He chews his food relentlessly in lieu of gnashing his teeth. "I'll keep coming back every anniversary until she tells me not to."

"Trist, sweetie, what's wrong? What's happened?" I beg of him from behind. I'm too freaked out to move, but I want to run to him and wrap his arms around me tightly.

"It's been two years," Mrs. Jade reminds softly. "You come on each anniversary. Don't you think she would have contacted you by now if she were going to? I think she's moved on, dear."

She thinks *who's* moved on? What is she prattling on about? I look up when I notice Peggy moving, coming down the steps. She takes her place by my side. I'm too confused to enjoy the novelty of a ghost standing directly next to me. I can't handle seeing Trist so upset.

"She's still in this house, Mrs. Jade. I can feel her. Her spirit is still here. I know it is."

Trist doesn't believe in ghosts. I don't understand anything he's talking about. He's never even been here before...has he?

"You have to let go, son," Mrs. Jade reiterates quietly. "We all have to release our loved ones so they may move on to their next place." She reaches over and takes Trist by the hand. He immediately begins to cry. In the six years I've known him, I have never seen my husband cry.

Ever.

Oh, Trist, oh, baby! What is this? What's wrong?

"You don't understand!" Trist sobs as he breaks down and climbs into the approaching embrace of old Mrs. Jade, "I never got to tell her I was sorry! I never got to tell her I was sorry! We went to bed mad, and that's the last chance I had to apologize. That's the last chance I had to tell her I loved her, and I didn't take it! All because I was mad at her and too stubborn to settle it before morning! Why didn't she sleep with water next to her bed? Why?"

A sensation unlike any other suddenly comes over me.

I look down to see my hand within Peggy's.

She whispers, "Two years ago I told you to beware the stairs. You did not heed my warning."

Freedom's Acquiescence[1]

from the Chronicles of Purgatory Station

Allen walked into the living room to find Sophie and Franklin, his elderly roommates, working on dinner together. Of course, Sophie, being the tremendous cook that she was, needed absolutely no assistance from Franklin, but her boyfriend loved to observe the minute delicacies of her sometimes-supernatural prowess at the culinary arts.

Allen smiled when he noticed they were making the same meal he had first consumed in the apartment above Franklin's bookstore, which was called Trover's Fine Literature. He had been nothing more than a starving stranger to them that night. So much had happened since then, all those months ago.

He had fallen in love within days of being given refuge by Franklin and Sophie, and he had alienated that love almost immediately. It'd now been seven months, and Julie Carmah still had yet to talk with Allen. He didn't even dare step foot in her shop, Carmah's Cup, located directly next door. In a reversal of their original understanding, Franklin must now get all of Allen's coffee for him.

The tall, muscular man sat at the breakfast bar and watched the old lovers adoringly bicker with each other as one of them cooked and one of them impeded the process of cooking. Although he loved the only role models he'd ever known, or remembered, at least, and was psychologically inclined to behave in the most moral of manners, Allen still felt a pang of jealousy at their happiness.

---

1. This story takes place seven months after "Freedom's Resurrection" found in the short story collection, *The Imagination's Provocation: Volume I* (iUniverse, 2005).

For the briefest of moments, he thought he and Julie would have that joyfulness, even though he was indirectly responsible for her husband's death.

"You look upset, Allen," Sophie commented as she shooed Franklin away.

Allen snapped to and faced the lovely woman. Was he upset? He supposed so, for a variety of reasons. At the moment, one of those reasons loomed at the forefront of his mind.

"I just got an encrypted e-mail from one of my former, um, associates—"

"A member from MAP?" Franklin interjected incredulously.

"Yes."

Sophie and Franklin both stopped what they were doing. Allen had deserted his post in the government's highly classified Meta-Agent Program months ago. He had once served as a public Colossal for the government, acting as a patron of goodwill for several years. However, the program had many, many more agents than just Allen, code-named Freedom, but none of them acted as Colossals—none were heroes of the people. Nor were they expected to be. Instead, they executed covert operations for the security of the United States of America, and most of those maneuvers involved sabotage and assassination.

When Freedom had become too comfortable in his position as a Colossal, MAP officially decided to put him in his place. They assigned him a mission to purge the leader of Ulrakistan, a country his own currently warred with, but he refused. They could have gotten any other MAP operative to fulfill that order, but they selected him as a lesson. Although a difficult choice, he wouldn't become a killer. As a result, the war still rages on, men and women continue to die over there, and Allen can't help but blame himself for each of those deaths. Julie's husband, soldier Trent Carmah, perished only weeks after Freedom had gone AWOL.

"Are you in danger?" Sophie asked, looking quite nervous.

"No," Allen answered promptly. "It came from an ally; maybe the only ally I have left in the whole program. He wanted me to know that the botched mission I ran with the Nocturnal Knight and the others brought me all the wrong kind of attention from MAP.[2] I'm apparently back on their list, although I don't think I ever really went off of it."

"This is my fault, Allen. I never should have suggested you work with the Knight," Franklin apologized, placing his withered hand on Allen's powerful shoulder.

---

2. To learn of this mission, read "Knight Writings" found in *The Imagination's Provocation: Volume II* (iUniverse, 2006).

"Don't be so hard on yourself, sir—Franklin!" he corrected after an immediate glare from the old man who hated such formality from a friend. "The Shadow Serpent had killed nearly a hundred people; I had to take action. The Knight had been working on the case; it only seemed reasonable when Devil Woman approached me to join their cause."

"I never dreamt it would end so badly. The Knight isn't the same man he was twenty years ago, not the man I remember," Franklin muttered pensively. His eyes were laden with shame.

"We all make mistakes," Allen reassured, this time placing his strong hand on Franklin's tiny shoulder. "I'll deal with both the Knight and the Shadow Serpent when the time is right."

"So did your friend have anything else to say?" Sophie questioned. Of course, she asked this while busying herself with the nuances of preparing a meal.

Allen noticed she kept brushing aside her gray hair as it fell into her eyes. "I don't know I'd go so far as to call him a friend. We weren't really produced to think in those terms at MAP. But, no, he just wanted to offer a warning."

The three of them sat in silence for some moments, contemplating the implications of such dire news. The man who had replaced Allen was known only as Agent 0104, or, to the public, as the newest government sanctioned Colossal called Anthem. Unfortunately, Anthem was anything but a Colossal. He represented everything Freedom did not, and that included assassination. But, he *did* follow his superiors' orders, so in their eyes, that made him perfect.

Franklin's brother, Walter Trover, had worked for MAP in his younger years as a scientist. When he discovered that Allen tested off the charts in morality and conscience, he fudged the books a bit to keep the young boy in the program. Such attributes were generally not held in high regard for a program creating super soldiers. Walter Trover considered Agent 0099, the man now called Allen, his penitence for all the killers he'd helped create. He'd died long ago, apparently, but left a post-hypnotic suggestion for Allen to come to Purgatory Station if he ever found himself in trouble, to a bookstore called Trover's Fine Literature. And so Allen did just that when he first defied orders.

"You need to tell him," Franklin mumbled to Sophie.

Sophie glared at her boyfriend and replied harshly, "I think he's had enough for today, don't you?"

Allen could hear most conversations taking place at a normal volume from well over a hundred feet way. A few mumbles directly before him proved infantile as a challenge.

"I can take it. If I need to know, I need to know," he said.

"Put the meat in the oven, won't you?" she requested of Franklin with ice in her voice. She wrung her hands on a dishtowel, obviously distraught at delivering bad news to her young roommate. "Allen, sweetie, I saw Julie last night, after she closed, over at Malko's Café. You know they stay open quite late."

"I know," Allen returned patiently. He knew what came next. It seemed only natural.

"She was on a date, honey."

His face did not change expressions one iota, but Allen felt quite sure his heart split directly in half at the conclusion of Sophie's statement. He had cried only once before, and as the tears welled up again, he fought them back. He had, after all, already cried for Julie. He told himself months ago he must let her live her life, even if that meant she wanted nothing to do with him. He understood such logic at his most rationale level. However, he had always been the atypical member of MAP due to the fact he retained much of his humanity rather than changing into a heartless machine. His face flushed.

"Anyone we know?" Allen asked with his voice a steady tone despite the tempest wreaking havoc within his heart.

"No," Sophie answered, raising her nearly non-existent eyebrows in sympathy.

"I should talk to her," Allen muttered after dropping his chin to his chest. His mussed hair fell into his eyes.

"You can't," Sophie immediately imposed, far more directly than she had intended. "Oh, sweetie, I'm sorry to be so abrupt, but she deserves a chance at happiness. You understand I love you, Allen—"

"We both do," Franklin called out as he put some green beans on the stove, nearly catching his long-sleeved plaid shirt on fire in the process.

"—but we love Julie also. We know why you had to do what you did in Ulrakistan, and she does too, in her head; in her heart, though, she can't help thinking what might have been."

"I can't kill," Allen growled in irritation. His ears felt as though they'd been doused in gasoline and lit.

"Honey, I realize that. That's what makes you the hero you are. But, she doesn't see it that way. You realize that. She only knows Trent would still be here if you'd been the soldier she thinks you were supposed to be."

"You know I respect the soldiers," Allen volleyed. "And you know if I could trade places with Trent, I'd do so in a heartbeat. But the entire world views me as a symbol of justice. I can't commit cold-blooded murder, even if it is my government that orders it. I may have been just another soldier to my superiors, but the children of my country see me as their champion! I can't cross that line, no matter what."

"Allen, we don't think ill of you for your decision, of course," Franklin pronounced, walking towards him from the stove. "We all have to make our decisions in life, and my brother recognized even when you were a baby there were just some things you *wouldn't* do. He realized it almost immediately when he worked as a scientist for MAP and you were in your early developmental stages for their little super-solider factory. You can't blame yourself for who you are."

"But Julie can, and she probably should," Allen proclaimed barely above a whisper with his head still lowered. He spread his palms out wide on the breakfast bar, stretching his fingers as far as he could in an effort to relax.

"We're sorry, dear," Sophie offered.

"What should I expect?" Allen asked them. Then he spat, "What kind of a life could I offer her when Allen Hemmingway doesn't even officially exist?"

❋   ❋   ❋

Five days later…

"Nick, I'm home!" Julie notified as she entered the apartment she shared with her brother-in-law. She was the only family he had left, and it'd be a cold day down below before she would abandon him.

She entered the television room and saw the red-haired teen watching a late night movie.

"Shouldn't you be in bed?" she asked him as she removed her coat and tossed it over the old, patched-up recliner.

"It's Friday night, Julie," Nick grinned at her.

"Yeah, I bet you had an awesome Friday night closing down the shop for me," Julie half-joked, half-apologized as she plopped down and extended the footrest.

"It wasn't bad," Nick reassured. "Franklin and Sophie helped me. Then we played euchre for a while."

"They're good people," Julie acclaimed.

"The best," Nick agreed with the light from the television reflecting off his face.

"So, what are we watching?" she asked as she pulled her brown, curly hair back in a ponytail and took off her jewelry.

Nick cleared his throat and informed awkwardly, "It's a film based on the end of the Absolutes. You know, that old team of Colossals."

"Yeah, I know," Julie muttered disapprovingly. She'd never been a fan of the overabundance of Colossals that Purgatory Station seemed to have, but since her encounter with Allen Hemmingway, she'd become even less favorable of their existence.

Nick, contrastingly, couldn't get enough of them. His experience with Freedom at the defeat of the Nether Man was something he'd cherish for the rest of his life.

Wishing to switch topics, Nick inquired, "So, how was your date with Hunter?"

Now it was Julie's turn to feel rather awkward.

"Oh, it was fine. We had some coffee and took in a quick one-man show."

"How was it?"

"Pretty funny, actually. I didn't think it would be, what with being titled after a cave man and all that."

Nick glanced at the television and saw the destruction of the Absolutes at hand by their greatest adversary, Quietus. Of course, no one actually witnessed the end of the Absolutes' lives, so this scene, and the movie as a whole, was largely taken from poetic license. That being said, Nick knew it upset Julie to watch it, so he turned it off.

"Thanks," she said breathlessly.

"No problem, I've seen it before."

"It came out when I was your age," she informed.

They then sat in silence for quite a while, both quietly reflecting on their evenings.

"He's a nice guy," Nick finally blurted out.

"Who?"

"Hunter."

Julie studied her brother-in-law closely to search for sarcasm. She knew Nick though, and it wasn't part of his personality to purposely be a smart mouth. So many of them were such jerks at that age, but not Nick. Not now, probably not ever.

"Yeah," she agreed. "He is a nice guy. You know, if it's weird for you, I'll stop seeing him."

Nick smiled gently and affirmed, "I know my brother's your first love, Julie. Nothing will change that. No one expects you to die an old maid, least of all me. Hunter's good for you. He's a lot like Trent, really."

"You're wise beyond your years, boy," Julie grinned. "Good thing I met Trent before you, who knows what could have happened?"

"Yeah, I'm sure you'd love to date a sixteen-year-old. Just what you want, a boyfriend ten years your junior with acne and a cracking voice!"

They both laughed, then Julie grew quite serious and said, "I mean it, though, Nick. You say the word, and I'll break it off with Hunter. It hasn't even been a year yet, after all."

Nick rolled his eyes, then informed, "The only way I'd ask you to dump Hunter is if you'd give Allen a chance—"

Julie huffed in irritation.

"—but I know you've got some grudge against him, and I know you refuse to tell me what it is, and I'm going to respect that. So, unless you'll give Allen a shot, I'm good with Hunter if you are."

"Allen's not right for me, kiddo. Just take my word for it," she seethed.

"Franklin and Sophie think he's okay."

"They're old, Nick. They don't know any better."

Julie saw the look of disgust come over Nick's face, even with only the light from the kitchen behind them offering illumination, and instantly realized what she'd said. She couldn't believe she'd uttered such filth. Franklin and Sophie had been nothing but pure gold to her and Nick, and she had the audacity to speak against them because she had a chip on her shoulder.

"Oh, Nick. Oh, Nick, please forgive me for saying that! I'm such a heel; I didn't mean that. You know I didn't mean that," she pled.

"I know Julie. This kind of thing can't be healthy, though. Your beef with Allen is turning you against your loved ones. That can't be good."

"You've been watching Dr. Gill again, haven't you?"

"No comment," Nick laughed.

"Oh, I don't know how long it's going to last with Hunter anyway. He's a great guy, but he doesn't make me feel the way Trent did," Julie admitted as she began to play with her own ponytail, staring off into space.

"Has anyone?" Nick asked, swinging his feet off the coffee table and onto the rest of the couch so he could face her better. He pulled the old quilt off the back of the decrepit couch and covered up.

Julie's face turned red, but she refused to answer.

"Hey, speaking of Allen, I've got some hard news for you."

With thousands of thoughts flashing through her mind instantaneously, Julie immediately asked, "What?"

"I saw him last night at The Machine in the Ghost."

"What the heck's that?" Julie inquired in utter confusion.

"It's an all night internet café. He was having coffee."

"He's drinking someone else's coffee!" she exploded.

"You know, we've been studying this play where someone says something like, 'I think you protest too much.'"

"Hardy har-har," Julie mocked. "We need every customer we can scrounge up! Whether I like him or not, we need his business! How dare he go somewhere else!"

"Yeah," Nick chuckled. "How dare he enter another coffee shop when you won't let him step foot in yours..."

"First of all, it's *our* coffee shop, not just mine. You know that. Secondly, that's not the point, and you know that, too."

Nick leaned his head back on the pillows and stared at the ceiling. He loved his sister-in-law, but he sometimes wished she could ease back the throttle a little. Trent loved the fire she had in her belly, and Nick knew he'd never settle for someone who didn't have it as well. It still annoyed him, however, when it made her beyond unreasonable.

"What time did you see him there?"

Nick felt very tired now that he had leaned his head back on the pillows and gotten cozy with the blanket, and answered rather nonchalantly, "Oh, I guess it was around one-thirty."

Julie sprang up from her recliner like she'd been shot out of a canon and screamed, "What the hell were you doing out at one-thirty in the morning?"

Startled by her explosion, Nick sat up, stunned, and realized he had just gotten himself in a heap of trouble. Crap. He knew he should have just gone to bed earlier, but he thought Trent would have wanted him to wait up for Julie and make sure she got home okay. Now he'd just thrown himself into the proverbial fire.

"Um, I was, uh...well, you see, I was, um—"

Just as Julie prepared to issue forth a stern ultimatum, their phone rang. She glanced at the clock and it read eleven-thirty at night.

"Who in the world?" she whispered to herself. She hadn't asked Hunter to call her when he got home. She walked into the kitchen to grab the cordless, but pointed at Nick with her eyes wide, feeling it unnecessary to say anything before she did so.

She answered the phone.

Nick watched her, relieved at the reprieve from the hot water, until he saw a look of shock come over her face.

"Nick, honey," she said between sudden and choked sobs, "would you mind going to bed now?"

"Is everything okay?" Nick asked in genuine concern. His heart suddenly raced, for he immediately thought something had happened to Franklin or Sophie. After all, his parents, grandparents, and only brother were all deceased. There wasn't much more bad news left for him to take.

"Please, sweetie, just go to bed; we'll talk tomorrow morning, okay? We'll talk tomorrow morning, I promise."

Before he left for Ulrakistan, Trent had made his little brother promise to mind Julie in every way, shape, and form, and so Nick had done everything Julie had ever told him to do. Although it pained him to leave her obviously distraught, now would be no different.

He squeezed her shoulder as he walked past her and shut himself in his room for the night.

"Okay, I'm back," Julie sniveled into the phone.

Twenty painful minutes later, Julie stood at the window facing out over Geoff Avenue. The tears flowed more slowly now, but there was no sign they would end. She already had a headache from the tears, and her sinuses felt as though they'd been packed with mud. A million unorganized thoughts raced through her head uncontrollably.

She then saw a familiar, tall figure walk by on the other side of the poorly lit street. She would know him anywhere.

"Someone else's coffee, huh?" she sniffed, suddenly wiping at her eyes with the sleeve of her shirt. "We'll just see what's so great about this Spirit in the Computer or whatever the heck it's called."

She grabbed some tissue, rubbed the little mascara off that had ran a bit with her tears, threw on her coat, then pursued the man who had not only betrayed his country, but had now betrayed her business as well.

✶   ✶   ✶

Allen Hemmingway glanced through the immense windows of The Ghost in the Machine internet café as he walked by. If all went according to plan, he wouldn't have to offer his patronage any longer after tonight.

He powered three blocks past the café until he came to an alley leading nowhere. There was entirely no reason for this dead end to be in this particular spot, but it remained standard MAP protocol to have a "clean street" in every city. They were streets incapable of falling victim to any sort of electronic surveillance. Although Purgatory Station paled in comparison to its larger neighbor, Boston, across the bridge, it still found itself the host of many, many unproven meetings. Smaller cities were more inconspicuous, after all.

Allen, now a renegade of MAP, had avoided this alley as though his life had depended on it. At present, ironically, his new life depended *entirely* upon this familiar place.

The muscular bookseller stood in the center of it, perfectly still. He knew he was being watched, studied. He expected nothing less.

"Serve the country first," a hallow voice said from nowhere.

"And the people second," Allen returned without an ounce of conviction in his voice.

Out of the shadows stepped a large, powerfully built man. From the chest up, a sculpted metal shell fit his body perfectly. It seemed to react to his every movement flawlessly. It covered every aspect of his head, and all Allen saw were two glowing eyes staring at him. In another alley, one that wasn't masked with electronic buffers, those eyes could figure out an awfully lot just by scrutinizing something. His arms were bare from the biceps down, except for gloves that fit tightly up to the wrist.

"You know I don't actually believe that, right?" Allen reminded.

"I think the entire MAP facility knows that by now, Agent 0099," the man said as his sidearms slightly rapped against his legs while walking toward Allen. In a voice that sounded filtered through an electronic microphone, he said, "I suppose I should be calling you 'Mr. Hemmingway' now though, correct?"

"I prefer it, Agent 0091," Allen returned. "Or do you prefer 'Cyber Spy?'"

"I do prefer Cyber Spy, if you're serious," the large man returned.

"How are you?" Allen asked, extending his hand.

"Fine, Allen. You look well," Cyber Spy affirmed, taking Allen's hand and shaking it briefly. Allen could see the man felt more than compromised by this action.

The two men walked side by side to the end of the alley, sticking to the shadows. Even though they were in pitch darkness, Allen could see the yellowish slits glowing at him where Cyber Spy's eyes should be located.

"Been on any missions lately?" Allen asked in an effort at levity.

"Classified, Allen. You know that," Cyber Spy replied curtly.

They both realized Cyber Spy had been successful on at least one mission seven months ago. After all, he had located Agent 0099 for MAP, and Allen had suffered a high caliber bullet to the temple as a result. Even though Cyber Spy had not fired the actual shot, both men thought it best not to specifically bring that mission up. Allen had gotten his dig in; that was quite enough.

Orders were orders. Allen didn't follow his last order. They considered him a bad solider. Cyber Spy maintained his standing as a good soldier. He had yet to mutiny. He probably never would. Walter Trover had allowed Agent 0099—Allen—to retain an aspect of humanity as a child that was seldom evident in MAP prospects. While Agent 0091, Cyber Spy, was the only other member of MAP that Allen had warmed up to, he was still far from an ordinary human with typical emotions. Cyber Spy, like the other agents, had been bred to follow orders. Period. No matter what. If he were ordered to kill Allen, he would do it. No questions asked, no hesitation.

However, hadn't Cyber Spy broken protocol already by warning Allen? And if this meeting went as planned, wasn't Cyber Spy defying his superiors even more so? Perhaps Cyber Spy had held on to more humanity than Allen had given him credit.

"You're risking execution," Cyber Spy reminded.

"I know," Allen confirmed. "It's worth it."

"What's worth it?" Cyber Spy interrogated.

"You're the master spy, figure it out," Allen jibed.

"We're not produced to be normal citizens of the nation, Allen," Cyber Spy lectured. "You can't offer anyone the 'American Dream.' MAP members are not made for what you're thinking."

"I haven't even told you what I'm thinking," Allen chuckled.

"I *am* a master spy," he responded flatly.

"Then you'd know I'm not a member of MAP any longer."

Allen's eyes shot up to the rooftops when he heard a sudden howl erupt, filling the night with maliciousness and wrath.

Before he knew it, he found himself roughly thrown to the hard pavement beneath.

He made an effort to explode to his feet, but a heavy boot planted itself firmly onto his chest and forced him back down again.

"Stay put!" a gnarled voice roared.

Allen looked up and saw Agent 0050 standing over him, nearly foaming at the mouth. The most feared agent in the entire Meta-Agent Program had located him. A hybrid of all the most dangerous aspects of both wolf and man glared at him.

He had been hunted and caught by Hell Hound.

Cyber Spy started to make a move, not entirely sure what he would do, but Hell Hound immediately yowled, "Stand fast, Agent Cyber Spy. I am your superior officer, and you're in it deep enough as is."

MAP agents were manufactured to follow orders.

Cyber Spy remained motionless.

Hell Hound gave his attention back to Allen.

The long, forked beard, the crescent, reddish eyes, the elongated incisors, the lanky fingers tipped with razor sharp claws, and the brown down covering his entire body unnerved even Allen, who had dealt with things during his time as Freedom that most humans couldn't begin to imagine.

Hell Hound removed his boot and mocked, "Now, get up, traitor. Make your move. Give me a reason to call in Shootdown and Anthem. Give us an excuse to party tonight; we finally get to eliminate a deserter of MAP."

"I serve the people, Hell Hound," Allen announced. "And I don't serve the people by blindly assassinating world leaders."

"Well, don't worry your pretty face about *that*, Agent 0099. We knocked off your target a few months ago anyway. We cleaned up your mess. Don't bother thanking us."

"I didn't miss, and it wasn't botched. I chose not to kill him. By the way, the assassination did a lot of good, didn't it? The president announced we've got at least another four years in Ulrakistan. So, great job with that."

Hell Hound narrowed his animalistic eyes, then grumbled, "I've got orders against terminating you unless you're in Freedom uniform or attacking a member of MAP. So do me a favor, fight back!" Hell Hound barked fiercely and then let loose a vicious onslaught of kicking and punching Allen bestially.

Cyber Spy backed away and leaned against the wall of the alley as he watched the closest thing he had to a friend cover up and endure Hell Hound's thrashing. He had been ordered to stand down, and he would follow his orders. It simply wasn't a matter of choice for him.

"If we'd caught you during that Shadow Serpent fiasco you'd be dead by now, you know that, traitor? You'd be buried in an unmarked grave in the middle of Siberia right now!"

"The Serpent's killed countless citizens of this city!" Allen choked out between Hell Hound's kicks. "Why doesn't Anthem stop him?"

"Because the Serpent's doing exactly what MAP—"

Cyber Spy cleared his throat loudly, effectively ceasing the finale of Hell Hound's near slip.

Hell Hound ended his attack against Allen, turned to face Cyber Spy, then nodded in near appreciation.

"The lust of the kill," Hell Hound shrugged, taking deep breaths in an attempt to calm himself. His narrow but freakishly muscular chest expanded with every intake of air beneath the tight black shirt he wore.

"Understood," Cyber Spy responded.

Hell Hound glowered fiercely at Allen once more and spat, "This is your last warning, 'hero.' You show your face in the red, white, and blue one more time and you won't have a face left, got it? Stay off the grid and MAP won't bother with you."

"Got it," Allen gargled.

Hell Hound huffed roughly, then leapt straight up to the edge of the rooftop above.

Cyber Spy strolled over to Allen, offering his hand to help up the beaten man.

The spy dared say nothing; Hell Hound's hearing was amplified beyond imagination.

He heaved Allen up when a roar thundered down from above, "Desist aiding that traitor!"

Cyber Spy immediately released Allen's hand, and the trampled man fell in a heap to the cement once more.

If Allen could have seen the eyes behind that expressionless faceplate, he was certain he would have detected a wink from Cyber Spy.

That would be the last friendly meeting they would ever have.

✳   ✳   ✳

"You okay?" Julie asked with such little sympathy that she surprised even herself.

Allen looked up and saw the woman he loved, but hadn't actually spoken with in seven months, approaching him.

He got up, rubbing his ribs a bit, then inquired, "How much did you see?"

"It was dark; I didn't see anything," she replied simply.

"Stick to that story, would you? I think it'd be better for both of us."

"Sure thing," she agreed. She walked with Allen as he started to leave the alley. "So," she began, "what's so important that you'd let yourself get beat up like that?"

Allen drew to a stop right as they nearly crossed the threshold of the alley onto the sidewalk. He faced her, taking in her lightly freckled, statuesque countenance, and found it difficult to keep eye contact. He held his hand out to her.

She looked down to see a small electronic card blinking in the palm of his massive hand.

"This is what was so important," he declared.

"What is it?" she asked while staring at it in fascination.

"It's a key. And it's got a time limit. Once we leave this alley, we're going to have to make small talk. We can't discuss what just happened, and we can't mention this key. If you want to tag along and get some answers only by watching, that's fine. We're not in any danger as long as we don't talk on the street about what we're doing. If you want to go home, that's fine, too. You're going to find out what all this was about one way or the other. It just depends how quickly you want it to happen. So, what's it going to be?"

"You know me, Allen Hemmingway. Lead the way."

✳   ✳   ✳

As they walked through the chilly night, Allen and Julie spent more time together than they had in over a half a year. Although nowhere near ready to forgive him for, as she believed, the death of her husband, Julie felt far too upset to simply go back home. She needed to be out, doing something, to take her mind off the terrible news she had just gotten, and if this was it, so be it.

"You've been crying," Allen noticed as they strode along.

"So?"

"Would you like to talk about it?" Allen offered.

"About what?" she snapped.

"Well, I don't know. You'd have to tell me first, wouldn't you?" Allen returned with more sarcasm in his voice than he would have liked. He had never behaved so immaturely in his life, even as a toddler. His time away from MAP had made him more and more human, for better or for worse.

"No, Allen, or whatever you want to be called, I don't want to talk about it."

"I want to be called Allen," he confirmed.

"Whatever."

Several moments of silence passed until both of them felt a cold rain divebomb their heads. They looked up only to meet much more of the same.

"Great," Julie muttered under her breath.

"We're too far out for you to walk back by yourself," Allen lectured. "You're going to have to deal with it."

"Easy for you to say, I've seen you shrug cars aside," Julie mumbled as she pulled her coat up over her head.

Allen trusted Julie never to tell anyone of his other identity, but she knew it irritated him when she spoke of it out in public. He wasn't going to let her get under his skin, however. He would instead simply change subjects.

"So who's this new guy you're seeing?" he asked over the plops of cold rain.

"How'd you know about him?" Julie called out from the innards of her coat. "Sophie."

"I should've known."

"So? What's he like?"

Allen thought she either hadn't heard him or, more likely, ignored him until she finally replied, "He's not Trent."

Millions of thoughts flashed through Allen's head, and most of them dealt with the guilt over a man's death he had never met. In Julie's mind, if Allen had followed orders, the war would have ended weeks before a child suicide bomber had killed her husband.

Allen not only refused to kill, but he always suspected removing the leader of Ulrakistan would do nothing to curb the activity of the insurgents, and he had been right. It seemed his nation was going to be there for the long haul, and his countrymen and women were dying daily for a war no one seemed to believe in.

He thought it best to change subjects again. "How's Nick?"

"Still a devoted fan of Freedom and any other Colossal who puts on a pair of long underwear."

"Good to hear," Allen returned.

Despite her chagrin at such a comment, Julie disregarded it. She did have a concern, however, that perhaps Allen could help with. "Actually, he told me, on accident, of course, that he saw you at some café the other night."

Allen did not even break stride. "That's true; I was communicating with the gentlemen you just saw. Not the furry one, obviously."

"I didn't think so."

"I didn't want to risk a trace on Sophie's computer."

"That's happy news. I thought I'd lost your business."

"No. You may not allow me in your shop anymore, but I'm still a loyal customer. As long as Franklin's willing to go get it for me, at least."

Julie threw her head back in frustration beneath her coat, then continued, "Anyway, he saw you there at one-thirty in the morning."

Allen stopped in his tracks, water streaming down his chiseled face, and asked, "What in the world was he doing out at one-thirty in the morning?"

"That's what I want to know. I plan on talking to him about it, but I think, now that it's confirmed, this has been going on for a while. Little signs, here and there. I thought it was just my imagination, but now…"

"You need to know what he's been up to."

"I worry about him. Trent left his upbringing to me."

"I'll check into it."

Nearly inaudible, Julie whispered, "Thanks," without meeting Allen's blue eyes.

They walked anew, their shoes making flatulent sounds as the chilly water seeped into their soles.

Several more blocks passed, and then, abruptly, Allen muttered, "We're here."

"We're where?" Julie asked.

Allen guided her through a doorway, though it was devoid of any doors, into an old, abandoned building. Julie had feared upon entering they would meet with some unsavory characters seeking shelter from the rain, but then she remembered she was walking with the nation's former greatest hero, so her fright readily subsided. She actually grew rather ecstatic at escaping the dampness.

They descended some decrepit stairs that groaned under Allen's heavily muscled frame and entered a cellar of sorts.

Julie watched as Allen approached a brick wall, pulled out the electronic key, then swipe it through what appeared to be absolutely nothing.

She heard an efficient purr, and before Julie knew it, a small portion of the wall slid aside, revealing a hollow no larger than a shoebox. Allen reached in, pulled out a black leather pouch, dropped the key inside the cubbyhole, then watched as the wall moved back into place once more.

"You wanted to know what was so important?" he reminded.

Julie watched as he unzipped the pouch and spread it open for her inspection. She had dropped her coat back into its orthodox position upon entering the old building, and when she leaned in to look, with water dripping down her forehead from her wet hair, she saw dozens of documents—cards, identifications, forms—all detailing the existence of Purgatory Station's newest official resident, Allen Hemmingway.

"Yale, huh?" she said, looking at one certificate in particular.

"His idea of a joke," Allen dismissed. It seemed that would be all he had to say on the matter.

Julie pulled her head out of the pouch, after which Allen promptly zipped it closed again and stuffed it somewhere inside his coat.

"What would make you put yourself completely out in the open like this, Allen? I thought you and the government had agreed to be cool as long as you don't put on the long johns?"

Allen answered before he could think about it too hard, for he knew to think about it too much would result in saying nothing at all. "I realized if I'm ever going to share my life with someone, I need to have a real life *to* share."

Julie stared at him blankly. She then turned and left suddenly, back into the downpour.

✳   ✳   ✳

The next morning, Allen sat with Sophie and Franklin at the breakfast bar. They ate toast, fried eggs, as well as sausage, for their morning meal. While Franklin craved coffee, he'd have to wait a half-hour until Julie had Nick bring it over, as was habitual. In the meantime, he settled for hot tea.

"And so she just walked away?" Sophie asked after crunching into her toast.

"That she did," Allen answered. "Without a word. I followed her, of course, to be sure she got home safely. I knew better than to push my luck, though."

"Good point," Franklin agreed. "That's the most she's spoken to you in quite some time."

"Yes," Allen confirmed simply.

"Well, there's nothing more you can do now other than wait her out and see what happens," Sophie figured.

The three of them all nodded together, without anyone voicing anything otherwise. They finished their breakfast as such, in silence, contemplating this new turn of events. After all, Franklin and Sophie had, previous to last night, been boarding a man who didn't exist for any and all official purposes. Now they had a real, certified citizen of the United States living with them.

"Crap."

"What is it, Franklin?" Allen questioned, alarmed by the elderly man's outburst.

"Now I'm going to have to keep you on the books," he groaned.

*   *   *

"Are you still in business?" one man asked another in the shadows of a tavern few knew about.

"Always," the second man answered.

"Good. I've got a job for you," the first said.

"Where?" the second asked.

"Purgatory Station."

"What is it?"

"Your specialty," the first man said.

"Same rates as last time."

"Worth every penny," the first man praised.

"I'd ask what you get out of it," the second man mused, "but you don't pay for that."

"Just like a good soldier, you don't question my orders," the first man grinned.

*   *   *

The clock struck two in the morning, and Allen lurked in the darkness across the street from Carmah's Cup. He'd been waiting since midnight, waiting for some sign, and now, finally, his stoic patience had paid off.

"I love reconnaissance…" he muttered to himself with a slight smile as he looked down at his garb. He wore black, from head to toe. Not so thoroughly as to draw attention to himself, however. No, he'd been trained better than that. He simply attired himself in a black long-sleeved shirt with black pants and black boots. To wear black gloves or a black hat would have been overdoing it, and more likely to pique the interest of the local law enforcement. He simply looked like some sophisticate on his way to or from a swanky shindig.

"What are you up to?" Allen asked under his breath as he followed his target, careful to stay a half-block behind at all times. Thousands of disparaging scenarios fluttered though his head. Drugs? Gangs? Weapons? Worse? Could it get worse than those? Allen didn't know. What he did know, however, was that on this night, he would keep his promise to Julie and find out what Nick had been up to.

Allen knew in his heart that Nick was a good boy, a boy who strove always to make his brother's spirit proud, but Nick was also at an age when it was most easy to be swayed by fools. Allen hadn't experienced such things personally, but he had a basic knowledge of child psychology, just as he had a basic knowledge of virtually any topic one could dream up.

Members of MAP may have been brutish, but that didn't make them brutes.

He watched Nick enter an alley and disappear. Allen readily followed. He soon witnessed Nick standing before the back door of the business called Malko's Café.

"What's all this about?" Allen questioned in a whisper, remembering this was recently the site of one of Julie's dates.

Suddenly, the back door slid open just a sliver and Nick slithered though like a greased snake. The door immediately closed ever so softly.

Racing to the back door, Allen gently took its handle and turned.

Nothing happened; it'd already been locked.

Allen took a step back and looked up at the building Nick had just penetrated. He could see that, like so many other businesses in Old Downtown, the owner lived above in an apartment.

He hated to do it, seeing as it was two in the morning and all, but to pick the lock and possibly set off an alarm would do no good for his newfound status as an official citizen of the world. Although a travesty to possibly wake up a hard working neighborhood, Allen had to make sure Nick was not exposing himself to any sort of danger within the walls of Malko's Café.

He pounded on the door, careful to hold back so that he didn't knock it off its hinges.

Sooner than expected, a middle-aged man yelled down from the window above the door, "What the hell do you want, you moron! It's two in the morning, here! I'm gonna call the cops, you freakin' idiot!"

"Sir, please, there's no need to shout," Allen called up as quietly as he could while still projecting loudly enough to be heard.

"You wake *me* up and you tell me not to shout?" the man shouted more resolutely than before. "I'll shout all I want, you miserable—"

"Sir, please," Allen interrupted. He held up his identification for the man, who, in turn, squinted in an impossible effort through the darkness and distance. "My name's Allen Hemmingway. I'm a friend of a woman whose brother-in-law just entered your café."

"I got a burglar in my shop!" the man yelled hysterically. "Maria, call the cops! Some punk broke into my store!"

"Why isn't the alarms going off?" a nasally, somewhat feminine, voice returned from behind the irate shopkeeper.

The middle-aged man looked back at Allen with his thin eyebrows raised skeptically.

"Someone let him into your shop," Allen informed. "Sir, really, can you come down and open your door for me so we can discuss this inside? We're waking up the whole neighborhood."

The man hesitated.

"Sir, my friend is very concerned about him. She was left in charge of him after her husband—his brother—died."

Once more, no response issued.

"Sir, do you have any children?"

Again, no answer.

"Look, sir, I live with Franklin Trover of Trover's Fine Literature. If you want to call him right now and check my credentials…"

The rotund café owner's eyes lit up and he blurted, "My Poppi was friends with those Trover boys! I'm glad to hear Franklin's still up and running that store of his. Why, just the other day I thought about—"

Allen abruptly caught movement within his peripheral vision. As trained, he resisted the urge to turn his head and notify the quandary that they'd been spotted. Instead, he shifted his eyes sideways to see the happenings on the man's left.

Oh, Nick.

The boy eased out of a window just three rooms away from whom Allen could only assume was Mr. Malko. He appeared resigned to scale the lifted stonework of the building downward.

Allen knew an accident just waited to happen.

"Sir," Allen interjected rapidly. "Could you just search your home and café for me? You're not being robbed, of that I'm certain, but I need to know what my friend's brother-in-law is doing in there."

Suddenly, the window to the man's right opened up and a young girl appeared.

"Poppi, what's going on?" she asked.

Allen's heart breathed a sigh of relief. Now he knew what this was all about. Nick had good taste. The dark-haired girl not only was cute, she also seemed quite smart. After all, she currently strove to misdirect her father's attention, and Allen's, from the boy crawling down the wall to her father's left.

"Irene, this guy says there's a boy in our store, but there ain't no alarm going off. Did you let anyone in?" the man asked with absolutely no hint of actually believing such a thing possible.

"Poppi!" Irene cried out, obviously offended. "Of course not!"

Irene next gazed downward at Allen with eyes so pleading they nearly broke his heart.

"There you have it, fella," Mr. Malko said in irritation.

"My mistake, sir. Please accept my apologies."

"Yeah, well, if you wasn't friends with Trover, you can bet your ass I'd be callin' the cops right now."

Mr. Malko then slammed his window shut.

Allen shot Irene a look somewhere between amusement and scorn before she blew him a sincere kiss and gently closed her window. Although he didn't have time to wait for it, Allen would have bet anything the cracked window Nick had climbed out would be closed as soon as Mr. and Mrs. Malko were back to sleep.

Allen left the alley and there stood Nick, waiting for him like a good boy.

"You were smart enough not to run, huh?" Allen asked gently while putting his solid hand on the boy's shoulder.

"You're in pretty good shape, Al. I knew better."

They strolled along the lighted sidewalks of the city, heading back to their respective homes.

"So that's what this has all been about?" Allen questioned with a chuckle.

"What what's all been about?" Nick asked genuinely.

"Julie knows you've been sneaking out a lot. I told her I'd get to the bottom of it. Now we know."

"Yeah. Are you going to tell her?"

"No, I'm going to leave that up to you. It's not to punish you, Nick, although I imagine Julie will do that as well. Purgatory Station is a dangerous city. It won't do for you and Irene to be out so late on the streets. You could literally be killed if caught alone by the wrong people."

"I know, Al. It's just, we go to different schools, we both work all night at our families' shops; if we ever want to see each other, we *have* to sneak out!"

"I understand, Nick," Allen sympathized. "We'll have to work something out. That is, assuming this is something you want worked out."

"What's that supposed to mean?" Nick asked incredulously.

"Well, if you really care about this girl, I'll try to help you somehow, but if this is just about…well, if you're just after, um, well…"

"Sex! You think I'm just with Irene for sex?" Nick erupted.

"Well?" Allen countered.

"No!" Nick volleyed. "We're too young for sex, Al! Cripes, what do you think I am?"

"I mean, I'd hoped you knew you were too young, but, I guess, I mean, I've heard the temptation—"

"What's that supposed to mean? You've 'heard?' Are you saying you're a virgin?" Nick interrogated.

Allen's cheeks flushed. Truthfully, he was a virgin. Members of MAP were not allowed to have any meaningful relations with anyone, nor did they ever have an opportunity to bond with anyone on a personal level. They were regularly given access to the opposite sex in order to satisfy certain needs, but Allen had never taken part in such things. His instinct told him it was worthless if done with someone you didn't care about. He couldn't blame his fellow MAP members. After all, they were incapable of feeling any emotions that dealt with love—other than love of country, of course.

"Oops, here we are," Allen said as he let loose a sigh of relief. They had finally arrived at Carmah's Cup. "Listen, I'll talk to Julie in the morning; don't wake her up now. She's going to have to talk with Mr. Malko so you and Irene don't put yourselves at risk any longer by being out so late. But, after certain consequences, I'm sure they'll come up with something so you two can date at reasonable hours."

"Thanks, Al. I know I can always count on you to be fair," Nick offered.

"All right, I'll see you tomorrow," Allen said as he patted the boy on the back.

"Good night," Nick returned before leaving Allen to sneak back into Carmah's Cup and his apartment.

"Good night," Allen returned once he saw the boy enter safely.

✳   ✳   ✳

He pulled the ridiculous suit on.

When the zeroes got long enough, he threw on the tights. After all, he was one of the most feared Mega-Mals in the nation, and for legitimate reason. He had yet to be defeated, though the official scorecard said otherwise. But, that wasn't important to him. When it was said and done, if the numbers got bigger in his account, his pride could take any blow. He was a business, in the end. He was a franchise unto himself. Those other guys who were just plain nuts or seeking vengeance, well, that wasn't him. He didn't have any personal vendettas. He didn't consider himself to be a truly evil individual.

He was all about the green.

It'd been a long time since his last hurrah. Come to think of it, Freedom "took him down" last time as well. Not today, though. Today, Freedom would be embarrassed, and Anthem would be the hero.

His paycheck made sure of it.

The black mask slid over his face with a hard tug.

✳   ✳   ✳

Julie heard the ring signifying a new customer had entered her shop. She looked up, brushing a curl out of her vision as she did so, and saw Allen approaching her. It was the first time he'd attempted to enter Carmah's Cup in months, and it marked the first time she wouldn't stop him from doing so in the same amount of time.

"We need to talk about Nick," Allen said plainly after he came to a halt before her counter.

"He told me a little bit before he left for school this morning," Julie informed. "Thanks for checking up on him for me."

"Not a problem," Allen returned. "So, you know it's nothing bad then."

"Well, other than all the problems that can spring from late night rendez-vous with the opposite sex, no, nothing too bad."

"I think he's serious about her."

"He's just a kid, Allen. You know how fleeting high school is."

"Actually, I don't."

Julie blushed, then said, "Right, I'd almost forgotten. Well, anyway…"

At that moment, the door rang again and a tall, powerful, strawberry-haired man entered her store. He walked briskly up to the counter, leaned over it, and pecked Julie on the lips.

Allen unwillingly clenched his fist into a solid bone-crushing mass.

Julie, rather mortified for reasons she wouldn't consciously acknowledge, pushed Hunter back a little and stumbled, "Hunter, I have a customer."

"I'm not a customer," Allen seethed. This was so below him. He knew it was, but he couldn't deny the infantile hatred he felt for this man who kissed Julie right before his eyes. "I work next door."

"Ah, well," Hunter began, sensing Allen's tension. "Whatever the case may be, I'm sure you've seen two grown-ups kiss, right?"

"Of course he has," Julie interjected. She hoped a giant cockroach would devour her on the spot, and she hated cockroaches more than anything imaginable.

Just then, several more customers entered the coffeehouse. They appeared to be businessmen and women hoping to hone their morning's presentation over some coffee. Forced aside next to Allen, Hunter noticed Allen stood just as tall as did he. He glanced over and saw Allen's blue eyes still penetrating his.

"Got a problem, Mr.—?"

"Hemmingway, with two m's," Allen retorted. "And I do have a problem."

"Would that problem happen to be me?" Hunter interrogated, turning squarely to face his doppelganger in size and stature.

"Yes, it is you. But, it's no fault of your own," Allen answered, backing down from Hunter ashamedly. He was acting like an imbecilic cretin, not a Colossal! Provoking a civilian out of pure spite because of his own jealousy! What was happening to him?

"Then whose fault is it, Hemmingway?" Hunter demanded.

"My own," Allen responded.

"Got a crush on Julie or something?" Hunter asked directly.

"Isn't it obvious?" Allen fired back.

"Yeah, in fact, it kinda is. Well, that's tough, isn't it? She's with me now, so deal with it. You should have made a play earlier."

"Yeah."

Although he never backed down from a fight, Hunter also didn't see the point in egging one on. He thought he'd change the subject.

"So, Hemmingway, what do you do?"

Allen watched as Julie took orders from the table full of suits and skirts. "I work next door, Trover's Fine Literature."

"Book nerd, huh?" Hunter grinned.

"Yeah, I guess I am. How about you?"

"Soldier. Just got back from Ulrakistan."

"Don't say?"

"Yep."

"How's it going over there?" Allen asked, more than slightly uncomfortable. He still felt a slight pang of guilt about that war, although it'd been well established his actions would not have changed the outcome, or lack thereof. At least, not at a national level.

"How the hell do you think it's going?" Hunter countered. "We're still there, aren't we?"

"So you're against it?" Allen inquired.

"No, I'm not against it," Hunter declared, aghast. "I just wish they'd let us take off the kid gloves and kick some ass. You?"

"I think we should pull out. Immediately."

A rock-hard set of knuckles shocked Allen as they smashed into his chin. He instantaneously rolled with the strike to spare the man a broken hand, but the savagery of the attack confounded him! He fell to the floor, not hurt in the least. After all, most small arms fire couldn't rupture his epidermis. It quite surprised him, nonetheless.

"You're nothing but a damn coward!" Hunter bellowed at Allen while shaking his fist in pain. "Weak-kneed wimps like you are the reason we won't take our panties off and get down to business!"

The entire patronage of Carmah's Cup stopped what they were doing and took in the ruckus playing out before them.

Julie came running across the shop and sternly demanded under her breath, "Hunter, what are you doing?"

"This chicken thinks we ought to pull out overseas! Tell him to get lost, will ya, Julie?"

Allen stood up, rubbing his chin in order to sell an injury, though he felt no pain at all from the considerable blow, then said, "My opinions are my own, Hunter—"

"That's Sergeant Ares to you, turncoat."

Huffing, Allen continued anew, "My opinions are my own, and the fact that I think we're not doing anything but getting ourselves and a lot of innocent civilians killed and should leave immediately does not make me a coward or a turncoat. I can't believe you would assault someone without warning just for disagreeing with you."

"Yeah, well, you didn't just watch twelve of your buddies die three weeks ago, did you?"

Dropping his head in genuine sorrow, Allen pleaded, "Don't you see? Those soldiers didn't have to die needlessly!"

Hunter made a fist and took a step toward Allen again, but Julie held him back rather insufficiently. He bellowed, "You call dying for your country a needless death? They died performing the duty they swore to fulfill! You pansy people in this country just don't get that, do you?"

"Hunter, you're upset. Please, go back in the kitchen, have some water, calm down," Julie requested, rubbing his thick, lightly-haired arm.

"No, damn it!" Hunter cried out. "Are you going to get this guy out of here, or do I have to throw him out?"

Julie met Allen's eyes and answered, "No, I'm not going to throw him out. He's welcome to his opinions, as misguided as they may be. But…no…I'm not going to kick him out."

Hunter tore his arm free. He glared down at her, and though quite menacing, no one in the shop believed for an instant he would harm her. Hunter had an air of honor and courage about him, and, after learning he had lost so many so close to him so recently, all were willing to overlook his brash aggression.

"What would Trent think of you?" Hunter hissed before he powered past her, flung the door open, and then left Julie's life forever. She would never see him in person again.

The shop quietly resumed its functions. The presenters went back to their notes, the readers went back to their papers, and the daydreamers went back to their daydreaming.

Allen took a step toward Julie and whispered, "I'm no coward."

"Prove it," she growled at him before storming back into the kitchen.

✳   ✳   ✳

"So you know Freedom's gonna show up?" Agent 0104, also known as Anthem, asked his superior.

"I've taken care of it."

"What's that supposed to mean?" Agent 0050, Hell Hound, barked.

"Are you questioning me?" the superior interrogated.

"No, sir," Hell Hound snarled.

The superior looked about the hold of the stealth ship in which they flew. He saw Agents Anthem, Hell Hound, Cyber Spy, and Shootdown all suiting up. Anthem, of course, was the only one that looked the part of a Colossal. He dressed in a garish uniform of black, red, and blue. His cape hung loosely about his body, all the way to his ankles, fixed in place by a silver star at the end of each collarbone. That was his job, after all—to be the government's officially sanctioned Colossal. The rest of them were covert agents who dealt mostly with overseas issues or concerns the people of the nation were never to know about. They were each dressed to most efficiently deal with their area of expertise. All wore masks or helmets but for Hell Hound.

The time had arrived to bring Freedom and his stolen G-Repulser, the belt that gave him the ability to fly, back into the fold. He was too expensive to be left out in the field to do as he liked. They'd made a promise, however, that Allen Hemmingway could live his life freely. Freedom, on the other hand, would be taken in on sight. For that to happen, he needed the current elite members of MAP. And he needed an exposed Freedom.

Good thing he hired someone to make sure Freedom crawled out of the woodwork.

✳   ✳   ✳

"She saw me take on the Nether Man! How can she call me a coward?" Allen complained.

"She didn't call you a coward, Allen; she told you to prove you *weren't* a coward," Sophie reminded.

"Semantics," Allen mumbled.

"Not really," Sophie replied. "There's a big difference."

Allen threw his head back in utter despair. "What was I doing? For an instant, I was ready to annihilate that guy in the middle of Julie's shop simply because he kissed her! I've gone from being a disciplined super-soldier to a soap opera reject!"

Franklin laughed heartily at Allen's comment before he said, "Oh, now, sure, you're developing a penchant for the dramatic, what with all those Fitzgerald and Shakespeare works you've been reading, but don't go overboard. After all, some of your changes have been for the better."

Allen glanced over at the Bible Walter Trover had left behind for his unusual prospect. It still retained the bloodstain on its cover from when Agent Shoot-down had attempted to assassinate Allen. He'd read it twice now, and currently found himself in the middle of his third run. Much of it confused him, but much of it also made perfect sense.

"I know you're right. I'm just becoming so darn…"

"Human?" Franklin finished with a smirk.

Allen said nothing in return.

"We know you're no coward, Allen, but face it, some fears you're not facing head on," Sophie reprimanded.

"Like what?" Allen asked in sincere curiosity.

"Well," Sophie began, "why don't you tell us?"

"What? What my biggest fear is?" Allen questioned.

"Mm-hmm."

The powerfully built hero sat inertly upon the couch, unable to verbalize that which immediately sprang to mind.

"Well, if you're anything like Walter, I know what your biggest fear may be," Franklin hinted.

"What's that?" Allen inquired.

The silver-mustached old man rose creakily from the couch and disappeared for a few minutes. When Allen studied Sophie for an answer, she looked even more perplexed than did he.

Finally, Franklin returned, holding a very small box.

He cracked it open, and Allen saw before him an engagement ring.

"What in the blue skies above is that?" Sophie called out in alarm from the loveseat she sat upon with her favorite magazine on her lap.

"Relax, old gal," Franklin eased with a wave of his liver-spotted hand. "I'm not going to break our promise to each other. This isn't for you."

"Who's it for then?" Allen questioned, looking at the ring in keen interest.

"This was for my brother's lady, way back when."

"I never knew Walter had thought about marriage!" Sophie interjected with her mouth hanging ajar.

"Thought about it!" Franklin exclaimed. "He dated that woman for six years, and he bought this blasted thing after only their sixth month together! He darn near thought about marrying her since the moment they laid eyes on each other!"

"I don't believe it!" Sophie blurted out while moving across the room to admire the diamond she had no interest in having for herself.

"I didn't either. He showed it to me after a year and a half with her. Said he was going to pop the question any day now. Well, after four and a half years had passed beyond that, she got tired of waiting on him to work up the nerve, so she moved on. Within months she met some school teacher and they married later that same year."

"I don't believe it!" Sophie repeated, stunned the brother of her boyfriend she thought she had known so well could surprise her so thoroughly from beyond the grave.

"Said it was the biggest regret of his life, God rest his soul," Franklin enlightened. "I'd sure hate to see someone else make that mistake."

Allen couldn't remove his eyes from the object before him.

✳   ✳   ✳

A man wearing a black trench coat and a black fedora stepped into the middle of the busy street. Motorists immediately barraged him with insults and complaints. Rush hour threatened any minute.

He threw off the coat and hat, revealing a skin-tight costume beneath of black and white.

"Time for a little ordered-up death and destruction," he whispered to himself in perverted glee.

✳   ✳   ✳

"Okay, soldiers," the superior called to his MAP operatives. "We've got reports of Mega-Mal activity in Old Downtown Purgatory Station."

"Where there's a Mega-Mal in Purgatory Station..." Hell Hound began.

"There's Freedom," the superior finished.

He then continued, "Despite your personal feelings, your orders are to bring him in...Got that, Agent 0091?"

"Yes, sir!" Cyber Spy replied robustly.

"And," the superior continued, "I want him brought in *alive*. Do you copy that, Agent 0104?"

"Piss on that," Anthem muttered under his breath. Then he shouted, "Yes, sir!"

"Superb. Remember, Anthem plays to the cameras, the rest of you are not to be seen. I don't want this country knowing about you all just yet," the superior commanded, feeling quite satisfied. "Get ready, gentlemen, we're bringing in the last of MAP's defectors."

✳   ✳   ✳

Allen entered Carmah's Cup with a sense of fear he had never experienced in all his years of battling the worst the world of Mega-Mals had to offer. His feet were melted to the tile floor as he trudged through the doorway.

His thoughts were momentarily distracted by the stunning sight of Nick working tables side by side with his girlfriend, Irene!

"Oh, I'm so glad you're here!" Irene called out to Allen. "I never got a chance to thank you!"

"Thank me?" Allen questioned as he shook the slender hand the young lady offered. "I thought you two might be upset with me for, well, you know…"

"No way, Allen!" Nick chimed in. "Julie and Mr. Malko talked it over, and they decided Irene and I could work together at each other's shops during the week. Sure, we're working extra hours, but—"

"—at least we get to be together!" Irene finished.

"Well, that's good news," Allen affirmed. "I'm glad this has worked out for you two."

"Who would've thought my dad could be so reasonable?" Irene laughed.

"What do you need?" Julie suddenly interjected from the counter. She had a scowl on her face that did nothing to hide the disdain she felt for Allen.

"I wondered if we could talk, um, in private?" Allen asked, moving past Irene and Nick, toward Julie.

"No, we can't talk in private, Allen. I mean, you ruined the only relationship I've had with a man since…well, in a long time, and you didn't seem to mind doing *that* in public."

"You could've told me to leave like Hunter wanted you to," Allen reminded.

"Why don't you just tell me what you want and get out?"

"Fine," Allen mumbled.

He dropped to one knee and pulled out Walter's engagement ring.

Julie, Nick, Irene, and everyone else in Carmah's Cup gasped at the sight of the diamond and all it entailed.

Their gasps coincided with hundreds of panicked screams from the street outside.

Allen turned his head to gaze out the windows of Carmah's Cup. His eyes bulged at the sight of street tables and chairs, papers, and all manner of debris hurtling through the air. People clung to light posts and mailboxes to fight against the unseen force compelling them to its source; others smartly rushed through the nearest doorway. The wind howled with the fury of a hundred tornadoes, yet the sun shone brightly, and stormy weather had not been called for on this day.

Allen dropped the ring box and sprinted out the door.

Just as he laid eyes on the villain not more than a quarter mile away, the city's alarms sounded. Unfortunately, Purgatory Station had become quite accustomed to the noise. The city had more than its fair share of Colossals, after all, and with that came a disproportionate number of Mega-Mals.

"What is that?" Julie shouted over the thunderous winds as she followed Allen out of her shop. Her hair immediately whipped and flailed about, and she yelped as she lost her footing and slid.

Allen grabbed her quickly and flung her back into her coffee shop, then slammed the door shut in Nick and Irene's faces as they intended to exit the business as well.

"Get to cover!" he shouted through the glass.

Nick looked down at Allen's feet and saw they had burrowed an inch into the concrete. His eyes bugged at the sight before they locked with Allen's.

"Get them to cover, Nick," Allen commanded in a familiar voice.

Nick followed Freedom's orders.

Allen turned back to face the cause of the cataclysm taking place before him on Geoff Avenue.

The void stood nearly seven feet tall and four feet wide. It sucked everything into it; everything, that is, but for a man dressed in all white, adorned with a black cloak and a featureless black mask that completed a black circle on the upper half of his body. He stood directly before it, unaffected, with his arms spread wide and his cape billowing madly behind him. He had to duck and weave in order to avoid the large fragments of city life being drawn into the abyss directly behind him.

"Black Hole," Allen muttered under his breath.

He had hard work ahead.

*   *   *

Allen burst into the apartment above Trover's Fine Literature and rushed into his bedroom.

Sophie took cover in the corner of the kitchen with a small television playing on the counter. Franklin busied himself with boarding up the windows facing Geoff Avenue.

"You better take a nap!" Franklin shouted through the apartment.

"I was thinking the same thing!" Allen hollered in return. "Don't disturb me for a few hours, please."

"Not a problem," Franklin muttered to himself as he kept hammering.

*   *   *

Allen tossed his bed aside and lifted up the loose floorboards. He pulled out his black satchel that held the uniform of America's former favorite Colossal. He slid on the red, white, and blue uniform with the large, red, hyper-stylized "F" on the chest, the blue and white cape, and then the red gauntlets and boots. Lastly, he fastened the machination that allowed him to fly, the G-Repulser. He would be killed for its retrieval if he weren't careful. The government gave no mercy to those they considered traitors. But, the danger only existed if caught.

Allen had a grueling battle ahead of him. He realized he'd never beaten Black Hole fair and square. It always seemed to him the villain had given up far too easily for a man with those sorts of powers.

Although he did not command a true black hole, the void Black Hole controlled could lift cars off the ground if he wanted it to, and its range hit up to a half-mile. The only weakness, as Allen saw it, was that the cavity could only devour those things within its perimeter. If a person were to walk right alongside it, they wouldn't feel even a twinge of its power. However, as soon as they crossed its area, they would be sucked in instantaneously.

Because Black Hole always stood directly before the void, it proved difficult to lay a hand on him, shoot him, or even blow him up. Everything—shells, fire, energy of any sort—got diverted right into his personal chasm.

Last time they fought, he and Allen tore up five city blocks in Noir Port before Black Hole's void dissipated and Allen rushed him instantly, knocking him out cold. The battle had lasted about an hour, but he saw no reason why Black Hole's abilities should have a limit. Again, it seemed to Allen almost as though Black Hole had simply called it quits.

"Let's hope he gets tired again," Allen uttered to himself.

In the next moment, Freedom flew out the skylight above Allen Hemmingway's room.

*   *   *

"This is Sydney Attwater with WPUG News, bringing you the live attack of the unstoppable Mega-Mal, Black Hole. It has not yet been determined what the motivation for this onslaught is, but Senator Otto Janus joins me with some strong opinions of his own. It so happens he had granted me an interview in the area prior to this development and has graciously agreed to adapt to the situation at hand. Thank you for that, sir."

Like so many of Old Downtown's denizens, Julie, Nick, Irene, and the patrons of Carmah's Cup took cover from the devastation of Black Hole while watching events play out on the television. They were huddled in the upstairs kitchen of Julie and Nick's apartment. They watched the live newscast set up a block behind the villain, where his powers didn't reach, for the latest developments.

"My pleasure, and thank you, Sydney," Senator Janus responded to Sydney Attwater. I've just called in the only Colossal our nation's government condones—Anthem. He should be here any moment. Let's pray no vigilantes decide to take action upon the monster before he arrives."

"Senator, when you say 'vigilantes,' are you referring to this city's Colossals such as Freedom and the Nocturnal Knight?"

"You're damn right I am!" Senator Janus exclaimed. "We all agree that Freedom is out of control of late, and the Nocturnal Knight has always been a madman, hell-bent on his own agenda. He's plagued this city for decades!"

"But didn't Freedom stop the Nether Man just mere months ago?"

"That's right, Attwater!" Nick screamed at the television. "You give that pencil pusher heck!"

"Shush, Nick!" Irene shot out. "I want to hear this!"

"As I see it," Senator Janus corrected, "Anthem stopped the Nether Man, with the help of a concerned citizen."

"Pastor Irons, I believe it was," Sydney Attwater hissed out with obvious contempt.

"Yes, that's correct. While I am not a member of the Religious Right, it seemed a man of the cloth was integral in the defeat of the rock man. Thank goodness Anthem figured out such a man would be necessary. Freedom simply convoluted the matter. Anthem was doing fine on his own," the senator argued.

"Does this mean the government is not backing Freedom any longer?" Attwater asked.

"That's exactly what that means," Janus clarified.

"Shouldn't this be coming from the president?" Attwater countered.

"In two years, I will be the president," Senator Janus informed.

Sydney Attwater, always doing whatever it took for a scoop, reported, "You heard it here first, ladies and gentlemen! America is no longer sponsoring the

Colossal known as Freedom *and* Senator Janus will throw his hat in for the next presidential election! This has been Sydney Attwater with—"

"Just a moment, Attwater," Senator Janus interrupted. "I want this city to understand something. We have video surveillance taken from one of our satellites of Freedom, the Nocturnal Knight, Turf, as well as Excitor, Silver Streak and two other unknown vigilantes engaging the Shadow Serpent. You remember that, Purgatory Station, don't you? Several innocent civilians were killed that night, and we were ready to deploy Anthem and some other highly trained operatives on the Serpent, ending his vicious murdering spree once and for all. Had those…vigilantes…not interfered, the Serpent would be in our custody at this very moment, and this city could get a good night's sleep once again. I vow, America, when I'm elected president, I will end the reign of these so-called Colossals. Why, don't you see? These Mega-Mals seek out people like Freedom and the Nocturnal Knight for a fight! If you were rid of these grandstanders who take the law into their own hands, you'd also be rid of your Mega-Mals like the Shadow Serpent and Black Hole—"

"I hate to interrupt *you*, Senator, but it seems as though one of your local 'vigilantes' is on the scene!"

Julie, Nick, and Irene watched as the cameraman panned from Senator Janus to Black Hole, just a block ahead of them. Amazingly, the void appeared as nothing more than a haze like that above a fire. The camera then focused tightly on a man flying in at a steep angle.

Freedom had arrived.

"He's going to whip that Meg-Mal just like he did the Nether Man, and it's going to be right outside our apartment again!" Nick cheered.

"That deal with the Nether Man was outside Carmah's Cup?" Irene asked Julie.

"Yeah, what a coincidence, right?" Julie seethed. Senator Janus was right. He was exactly right as far as Julie was concerned. Allen was a magnet for these freaks.

✳   ✳   ✳

Freedom flew right up to the edge of Black Hole's gulf and landed near the villain dressed in black and white.

"What do you want?" Freedom demanded.

"This is just another day at the office," Black Hole responded.

Freedom watched a car lift off and fly toward Black Hole and his void. He stepped back as the car entered the abyss, bursting into a million projectiles while collapsing and folding until completely engulfed.

"Is this going to be like last time?" Freedom interrogated.

"Oh, no," Black Hole answered, turning his head quickly and slightly to glance at the hero. Freedom saw nothing in the mask of total blackness, not even a pair of eyes. Black Hole hurriedly looked back at the objects hurling at him so he could dodge and avoid. "This isn't going to be like last time at all. Today, you don't beat me."

"This is Old Downtown. The Banking District is blocks away. There's nothing of value in this area! What...do...you...want?" Freedom insisted with glaciers in his voice.

"Just to earn an honest day's pay," Black Hole replied musically.

Freedom didn't have time to ponder such an odd statement coming from a Mega-Mal, for he saw several citizens stupidly rush right into the void's parameter two hundred meters away. They instantly jerked into the air, heading for the void.

"Looks like you have work to do as well," Black Hole teased.

Freedom took off, soaring as close to the edges of the void's territory as he dared. He sped toward the two victims and bellowed for them to muscle their hands above their heads.

Luckily, they were near the top of the void's suction, so they were able to extend their hands just beyond its realm. Freedom caught both their hands and yanked them free, though it dislocated the innocents' shoulders in the process. Had he reached in for them, the insurmountable force would have trapped him as well.

He dashed to the nearest storefront and guided the citizens inward, away from the unmerciful gale of Black Hole.

When Freedom turned around, he saw his most dangerous enemy, Anthem, the government sanctioned Colossal who replaced him, launching headlong at Black Hole just above the void's power.

Suddenly, Freedom watched as the cavity inexplicably disappeared and Anthem knocked Black Hole to the ground. It was like an out of body experience for Freedom, for he had gone through the same motions with the villain in the past. Now he understood only too well what Black Hole had meant. He was nothing more than fodder to make the government's agents look good. Like an amateur, he had never thought such blatant deceit possible.

Freedom lifted off and soon landed next to Anthem. Black Hole lay on the ground, his black cloak spread wide beneath him. He cursed under his breath at Anthem for the stiff punch.

"You're nothing but a scrub to make agents look good," Freedom mumbled at the felled victim.

"Hey, gotta put food on the table somehow," Black Hole replied. "Don't you think if the government wanted me gone they'd just nuke wherever I was? That's the only way to get rid of me, and don't think they wouldn't do it."

"They still might do it if you don't shut your damn mouth," Anthem condemned. "Why the hell are you detailing classified information to this traitor?"

"Hey," Black Hole responded, "I might work for you guys, but I ain't one of you. Boss knows I don't give up the info to just anybody. I figure Freedom's going to be taken in with me anyway, right?"

"Right," Anthem said with a grin as he turned and faced his predecessor.

Freedom couldn't see the eyes behind the star-shaped visor of the blonde man in black with a blocked, red "A" on his chest, yet he knew those eyes were full of hatred.

Suddenly, a voice began out of nowhere, "This is Sydney Attwater with WPUG News! Anthem, it looks like you and Freedom have teamed up once again to take down a Mega-Mal! Should we assume you two will be working together regularly?"

Anthem removed his intolerable eyes from Freedom to take in the lovely reporter standing with her usual cameraman and Senator Janus.

"Absolutely not, Ms. Attwater. In fact," Anthem continued, "by order of the president of the United States, I have been called upon to incarcerate Freedom. He must pay for his crimes."

In their kitchen, Sophie and Franklin gasped in shock.

Next door, in the Carmah kitchen, Nick and Irene, as well as the patrons taking shelter, were also astonished.

Julie merely sat tightlipped, resentful of the pain her heart felt.

"So, this is it, huh?" Freedom grumbled at Anthem. "That's what this has all been about?"

"What do you mean?" Attwater asked.

"This whole thing, it's been a set up. Black Hole is no Mega-Mal; he's a hired hand! A lap dog!"

"Are you coming in quietly or not?" Anthem hissed.

"What exactly did Freedom do to warrant such aggression?" Sydney interrogated, sticking the microphone into Anthem's face.

Senator Janus grabbed Sydney Attwater's hand and directed the microphone toward him. "Freedom betrayed the USA several months ago."

"Oh, no," Franklin muttered.

"Oh, no," Julie moaned.

"What?" Sydney Attwater questioned while noticing Freedom's head drop.

"He was given an order, and he defied that order, taking matters into his own hands. He's been fleeing his government ever since that debacle with the Nether Man. Had he not interfered, Anthem could have stopped the Nether Man in record time."

"You've got to be kidding," Freedom groaned. "Anthem was ready to call in an air strike and destroy Old Downtown right along with the Nether Man. If I hadn't smashed his communications link, he would have done just that!"

"Don't be ridiculous!" Senator Janus chastised. "A government Colossal would never do such a thing!"

"What do you take me for?" Anthem feigned.

"Exactly what you are—a cold-blooded killer willing to follow any cold-blooded order you're given."

"The fact is," the senator resumed, "that little piece of equipment you see around Freedom's waist is government property. The taxpayers of this great nation funded that device, and Freedom has taken it upon himself to steal it from those very same people!"

"I use it in the same capacity I always have!" Freedom defended. "I fight for justice in the homeland! I don't go overseas and murder our opponents while they sleep; I protect those who need it here!"

"Really?" Senator Janus countered. "Then why didn't you and the rest of those 'heroes' apprehend the Shadow Serpent? He's been killing the citizens of this fair city for months, yet you've done nothing to stop him!"

Freedom noticed that, with Black Hole still lying on the ground, pretending to be unconscious, the people along Geoff Avenue had started wandering out of the buildings. He looked over and saw Sophie and Franklin standing arm in arm with one another, begging him for a sign to take action. He then saw Irene, Nick, and the patrons of Carmah's Cup emerge.

Julie, however, did not appear.

"Freedom, could you answer the question?" Sydney Attwater asked just above a whisper. He could see the sympathy and understanding in her eyes; after all, she had played a role in the botched capture of the Shadow Serpent as well.[3]

Freedom cleared his throat and said, "The Shadow Serpent was all but captured, but then dove into the waters of the bay in order to escape. We had his victims to tend to, and, with none of us being underwater combatants, thought better of diving in after him."

"So, you were all cowards," Senator Janus mocked.

"Screw you!" Nick yelled from the sidewalk, moving threateningly toward the senator. Just then, a tiny explosion of concrete erupted at Nick's feet, causing him to cry out in alarm and jump back, falling onto his rear.

Irene rushed over to make sure he was unharmed.

"I'm a United States senator, boy," Janus reminded. "Threaten me again and you won't like the results. I have bodyguards everywhere."

Freedom knew better. Yes, Janus had bodyguards, but none of them would have fired upon a high school Colossal-worshipper. Janus had ad-libbed in order to explain the sudden gunfire, but Freedom knew the real deal. He was currently in the sniper scopes of Shootdown, and, considering this seemed to be his grand finale, he sensed Cyber Spy and Hell Hound had guns trained on him as well.

"No bulletproof glass to protect you this time," Anthem chortled so quietly only Freedom heard him.

A large, black transport vehicle arrived without warning. Numerous soldiers of the sort none had before witnessed jettisoned from it and took command of the perimeter. These were the foot soldiers of MAP. They were not genetically engineered like the actual agents themselves, but they had experienced much psychological tinkering. There existed nothing they would not do when given an order by a commanding officer.

They immediately restrained Black Hole with some sort of a sedative and bound his hands with unordinary shackles. They led him, as he stumbled wobbly, into the transport vehicle.

"We've got a nice spot for you in there as well, Freedom," Anthem informed. "So, do we need to clear the people out of here, or are you going to go in quietly?"

Freedom glanced over at the multitudes of people standing along the sidewalks, forced back by the foot soldiers. Franklin and Sophie had expressions on their faces urging him to fight for his sovereignty. Nick and Irene looked horrified that their hero was now considered a villain, though they obviously did

---

3. To find out Sydney's role, read "Knight Writings" from The Imagination's Provocation: Volume II (iUniverse, 2006).

not believe such a thing. And then...then, Julie walked out of Carmah's Cup. Tears were rolling down her cheeks. Freedom could see she was distraught about something—heartbroken.

He had to know.

He left Senator Janus and Anthem so that he could console Julie. No matter how poorly she thought of him, he would always love her. She needed him now; he knew it. And despite what she may think of him, he would not abandon her in her time of need.

"Where are you going?" Anthem interrogated, grabbing Freedom's arm.

Freedom spun in an uncannily fast arc and delivered a thunderous roundhouse to Anthem, sending him bursting into the side of a building twenty feet way.

The next thing Freedom knew, blood blasted from his left shoulder.

"That was a warning shot, traitor," Senator Janus declared. "You give us that G-Repulser and let us take you in and you won't have to suffer more of our artillery designed just for that hide of yours."

"I give you the G-Repulser, right now, you give me two minutes without skirmish. No one gets hurt; none of these civilians get caught in a crossfire. I'll go in quietly, just give me two minutes."

Senator Janus started to laugh, then realized he was still on camera with Sydney Attwater. "In respect to your past good deeds, I'll honor said request. However, remember, one misstep and you will be terminated."

Freedom nodded once, paying no attention to the fire erupting within his shoulder, then unlocked the G-Repulser. His chances at flight were now gone. It fell with a heavy thud. One of those mysterious soldiers instantly gathered it up and ran with it into the transport.

With blood pouring down his arm, Freedom approached Julie. He spoke over the interlocked arms of the foot soldiers who had formed a barrier against the inhabitants of the city.

"What's happened?" he asked her.

"My father..." Julie choked. "He had a stroke a few days ago. I was going to fly out tomorrow to see him. He...he died. There were complications...I just got the call on my cell," she finished before erupting into tears.

Freedom broke through the foot soldiers and took her into his arms, neither minding the smeared blood, and they held one another.

Finally, she stumbled, "You're turning yourself in...j-just so you could find out what's wrong with me?"

Freedom only nodded.

"W-Why?" she asked.

Freedom held her out at arm's length, then said, "Because I love you, Julie. Despite how you feel about me, I love you. I was going to propose to you, you know."

"I know," Julie whimpered.

Freedom felt his eyes water. "What was your answer going to be?"

"Time's up!" Senator Janus yelled from behind.

"Just a minute!" Freedom hollered in return.

At that moment, Freedom's other shoulder spewed blood upon Julie's shirt. He dropped to his knees in horrid pain, staring up at her the entire time.

Horrified at the sight of Freedom's blood all over her and his shoulders ripped apart, Julie began to tremble uncontrollably. "I don't even know your real name," she sobbed. "How can I marry someone when I don't even know his real name?"

The soldiers gathered him up, each taking him by an arm, mindless of the pain it caused, and Freedom answered, "Since my earliest memories, my name has been Agent 0099. But you know my *real* name. You were there for my birth."

They dragged him away.

Freedom, now only Allen Hemmingway, tore his eyes from Julie for just a moment to say good-bye to Franklin and Sophie. He saw both sobbing with sympathetic smiles upon their faces.

"I know a pastor that can help you!" Franklin finally called out.

"No!" Allen yelled in return. "Let me handle this on my own!"

"You're never on your own, son!" Franklin issued in return.

"I know," he responded, gritting his teeth against the pain. "The CEO in the sky, right?"

"Right," Franklin whimpered.

"I love you!" Sophie wailed.

"I love you, too, Miss Sophie," he chuckled through the pain. The old woman couldn't help but choke out a laugh at the old formality that'd become an inside joke for them.

"Be a good boy, Nick. Trent and I are both counting on you now," Allen finally said to his biggest fan as they hoisted him into the transport.

Nick, who had previously been helped up by Irene, fell to his knees once more, covering his face in his hands. Irene dropped to her knees as well and soothed him as best she could. Within the span of one year, the boy had lost his two greatest heroes.

Allen stood, shoulders bloody and torn asunder, just inside the transport as the doors slowly slid shut. He would not remove his eyes from Julie.

"I'm sorry about your father," he yelled. Then, dropping his head, he whispered, "I'm so sorry."

And with that, the transport doors closed, and the mammoth vehicle pulled away.

A clean-up crew arrived and started putting the devastated area back in order. Senator Janus lectured into the camera once more as to why Freedom was a liability who couldn't afford to roam free, just as were all so-called Colossals who were not government approved. Anthem peeled himself from the wall Freedom's blow had driven him into, and then, without making eye contact with any of the citizens, sputtered away. Although no one saw them, Hell Hound, Cyber Spy, and Shootdown gathered their equipment and made for the rendezvous, satisfied at a mission accomplished.

As Irene held an inconsolable Nick, Franklin and Sophie moved to take Julie into their arms. They were comforting her about her father when she lifted up her left hand.

She wore the engagement ring Allen had offered her.

Through a thick wall of tears, she whimpered, "I wanted to say yes."

✳   ✳   ✳

Epilogue One

A conference room existed within the deepest innards of the Meta-Agent Program.

Within this conference room, there was a gargantuan table. At this table, there sat seven men.

One Senator Otto Janus facilitated the meeting.

"And so, the mission was a resounding success. All objectives were satisfied with extreme competence. Well done, Agent 0104," Janus commended.

Agent 0104, Anthem, dressed in standard fatigues, nodded in acknowledgement.

"Well done, also, to Agents 0050, 0073, and 0091. Excellent shooting," Janus said.

"Thank you, sir," Agents Hell Hound, Shootdown, and Cyber Spy replied. Cyber Spy hadn't actually fired a shot, but that was only because he was last to fire if a third shot was needed. He would have been the kill shot. Although he counted Freedom as one of his only friends—if such a word can be used with a member of MAP—he gave an oath to follow orders. No matter what. He would have made that shot to the head if it'd been required.

"Dismissed," Senator Janus, their superior and the Supreme Commander of the Meta-Agent Program, excused.

Anthem, Hell Hound, Shootdown, and Cyber Spy stood, saluted, then left. Now there remained only two men with Janus.

"Well, 'Black Hole,' you delivered perfectly once again," Janus complimented as he tossed a satchel full of hundred-dollar bills the Mega-Mal's way. "Consider this a bonus. The predetermined amount has already been wired to your account. As usual, money impeccably spent."

"I aim to please," the mercenary replied. "You ever need me again, you know where to find me."

"Affirmative," Janus answered. "Take care, Cody."

"Same to you, Otto."

Black Hole stood, garbed in civilian clothing, then took his leave.

Now there remained only one man with Supreme Commander Janus.

He wore black fatigues, from head to toe, and a black mask covered his face as well. A heavily tinted visor allowed the man to see, but other than that, the mask appeared opaque.

This did not prove an unusual sight for other MAP members. Several agents covered their features because, while their abilities were great, some of their appearances were grossly damaged as a result of the experiments making them Meta-Agents to begin with. Hell Hound, for example, appeared to be a wolf-man. Though this wasn't a terribly hideous sight to behold, some members of MAP were changed even more drastically. The man who sat at the table was one such member.

"Agent 0102, now that your bullet wound has healed, you are to resume activities, understood? You didn't need both eyes anyway, right?"

Commander Janus, of course, did not expect a verbal reply, as this agent was incapable of such. Instead, Agent 0102 merely nodded.

Janus stood, leaned upon the table with his hands outstretched, leered at Agent 0102, then said, "It's time Agent Shadow Serpent embarrasses the 'Colossals' of Purgatory Station again. After a few more hundred murders, perhaps the people will finally turn their backs on their 'heroes.' Dismissed."

Agent 0102, the mass murderer known as Shadow Serpent, stood up, silently saluted his commanding officer, then exited the conference room.

*   *   *

Epilogue Two

Prisoner #62618, formerly known as Agent 0099 by MAP, or Freedom by most of the world, or, if preferred, Allen Hemmingway, shuffled through a brightly lit corridor. Shackles constrained him without hope of breaking free. He passed steel door after steel door holding the most nefarious of his country's criminals. He could only assume this was the MAP Mega-Mal prison, located just off the coast of Purgatory Station. No one outside of the program knew of its existence. It was, after all, underwater.

"We got a special treat for you," the prison guard mocked as he poked and prodded Allen along with a taser. "Commander Janus ordered it up just for your cellmate. We usually don't put prisoners in the same hole together, but he knew your new roommate would especially appreciate your company."

"I can't believe Janus is posing as a United States senator," Allen grumbled.

"It's not a sham," the guard informed. "It's the real thing. Remember, no one knows of MAP's existence, not the real MAP, at least. And those who do talk about it, like yourself, well, they don't stay outside these walls for long.

"Here we are," the guard finished, and so Allen came to a stop.

The other guard issued commands through a transmitter for the prisoner inside to face the farthest wall, palms against said wall.

And with that, the solid, steel door whooshed open. Allen's specialty cuffs were removed, and then they flung him into the dark cell the guards lovingly referred to as a "hole." They called it thus because, once the door shut again, as Allen was about to discover, all light dissipated—totally. Utter and complete sensory deprivation.

Who was it in the hole with him?

Some former Mega-Mal? Was he in for a fight right off the bat? So be it. He'd fought in total blackness before and come out the victor.

"Who's there?" he issued forth threateningly, without a hint of fear in his voice.

"I'm just an old man, don't concern yourself with me. I don't know why they gave me a cellmate; it's highly irregular."

"How long have you been in here?" Allen questioned with his fists raised, ready in case the other man put on a ruse.

"How would I ever be able to deduce such a thing? No light, no clocks, no discernable passage of time! I haven't seen myself since the day they locked me up and threw out the key, so to speak."

"When was that?" Allen asked, still not convinced.

"That I know. It was 1988."

"Tell me who you are!" Allen demanded.

"Calm down, young man. I couldn't do you any harm even if I wanted to. My name is Walter Trover."

Had there been any light, the old man would have seen Allen's eyes grow enormous in disbelief.

To be continued…

The Monitor

Adam sat up in bed reading his favorite author, which, of course, was someone most of us would not recognize. The fan wobbled on the ceiling, and the chain hanging from it tapped rhythmically against the globe surrounding the light bulb.

The hour struck one-thirty in the morning, the time when almost anyone without worries would be fast asleep. His father slumbered, but did not sleep soundly. The man from whom Adam had inherited his height hadn't slept well in the last three weeks, but even before that he hadn't had a solid night's rest in almost three years. It's hard to sleep soundly, after all, when someone you love with all your heart is nearing death with every impossibly stagnant second.

He hadn't slept well himself in the last month, for he loved her just as much as his father did, though it was a different sort of love. He'd known tonight was going to come. It was supposed to arrive two and a half years ago, after all. God had granted a reprieve, but it seemed His reprieve would come to an end, at last, any moment.

It tortured him to hear the strained work of her laborious breathing through the baby monitor. No one should have to go through such a thing, especially someone her age. Cancer wasn't supposed to happen to someone so young. Not like this. Not so viciously. So relentlessly.

Actually, he couldn't fool himself into believing that. No, it shouldn't happen to someone so young, but she certainly was not the only one to suffer such a fate. Somehow, it's different when it's someone you love. It's always different when it's someone you love. It's not just a neighbor's friend, or a co-worker's uncle. Now it was theirs. It was in their house, pursuing their loved one.

The last three years had been impossibly hard. The prognosis had been terminal from the beginning. It was as though she had died at that very moment, but no one had bothered to enforce the action upon her, and so she continued on amongst them. She took medicine that helped immensely, though its side effects were less than ideal. However, it had worked, and that was essentially all that mattered. She was originally not to survive more than six months after the diagnosis, but she had. She had made it through both relatively good and painstakingly horrible health for several years since that momentous day.

But now Hospice had entered their home and it appeared her struggle would soon conclude.

She'd virtually been in a coma for the last week. It wasn't a coma per se, because she would sometimes come in and out of consciousness, but for the most part she was unaware of what was happening around her. Most thought it was probably better that way, but Adam would have liked to say his goodbyes under moderately normal conditions. He couldn't be sure she'd know what he was saying anymore.

Unfortunately, Adam's father was all too aware of what was happening. Each week that went by simply delayed the inevitable. He'd made peace with her sickness long ago, but he hadn't made amends with the idea of living without her. Adam could not begrudge his father such a thing, for he hadn't yet accepted her impending absence either, though he knew his faith demanded he do so.

His father, Dan, had asked Adam to stay up and listen to the monitor, just in case. He didn't want her passing without someone knowing. He didn't want her to go alone. Adam had been up since four forty-five that morning. Dan hadn't called him until about eight in the evening, humbly admitting he couldn't go through another night without sleep. Adam fell all over himself to answer his father's rare request of assistance. He'd done all he could prior to this night, but, of course, he felt it wasn't enough. He wanted to do more for his father. He wanted to be a better son.

We all want to be better sons and daughters.

But even after several cups of the strongest coffee ever made, he'd still nod off. After brief excursions into dreamland, he would awake with a start, only to find he hadn't been out more than a few seconds. His book remained perfectly open on his lap.

He listened closely and heard her steady yet overwrought breathing issuing from the baby monitor.

Just inches away from him, through the wall, in the next room, he could feel her presence. Even without the monitor, he'd know if something had changed. His father lay across the hall in the master bedroom, hopefully getting some much needed and greatly deserved sleep.

Adam sat up and shook his head violently, trying to rouse himself. He would not allow himself to fall asleep again. Daniel had told his oldest son to wake him at four so that Adam could get some rest before he had to head off for work. If he could just make it another three and a half hours…

He got up off the bed, standing erect to his full six-foot-four height, then stretched his lanky arms far above his mussed head. His fingertips easily brushed the white stucco ceiling. Had he been a few inches over, they would have gotten caught in the wooden blades of the ceiling fan. He had the window open, and it was unseasonably cool for an October morning. Needless to say, that made it quite chilly in the remodeled room that had once been his years ago. Even with the coffee and bitterly nippy air, he still fought Morpheus with all his might.

He lowered his arms and glanced down at his workbag. There were a pile of papers in there he needed to grade, but those would put him to sleep faster than anything. Instead, he opted for more coffee.

He picked up the baby monitor, as well as his "World's Greatest Dad" coffee mug his own son had given him long before either could be sure such a claim was justified, and then stealthily cracked open his door just enough to allow his thin frame passage.

Adam padded through the hallway, grateful for the lush lavender runner softening his already light footsteps, then entered the country cottage themed kitchen.

There sat Dan, who also held a "World's Greatest Dad" mug that Adam had given him twenty-five years ago.

"Dad, you're supposed to be asleep," Adam mumbled, neither angry nor surprised.

"I know, Son."

"My coffee isn't going to help you get any rest."

"I noticed. I think my Explorer could run off this stuff."

"Well, it's been a long day," Adam mumbled yet again as he filled his mug whose message directly contradicted his father's. After all, is it possible to have *two* world's greatest dads? He then thought about his words and tone, instantly regretting his idiocy. "Dad, I'm sorry, that came out wrong. I'm happy to help you in any way I can; you know that. I'm just tired, that's all. You know I'm not complaining."

"I know, Son. This has been hard on all of us."

Dan said no more and they both suddenly became aware of the tick tock of the cuckoo clock they'd gotten in Germany on vacation back in '95. It sounded like thunder hammering.

"It's been hardest on you," Adam affirmed.

The clock went silent.

"No," Dan replied without a hint of anger in his voice, "it's been hardest on Jane."

Adam stirred in some liquid French vanilla creamer and then took a sip from the potent coffee.

There ensued a long pause, and so the cuckoo's pounding reasserted itself.

Finally, Dan spoke anew, "I think it's going to be tonight."

Spinning on his bare heel, Adam couldn't face his gray-bearded father after such a statement. Instead, he studied the many pictures upon the beige refrigerator. He perceived his own children, Carlton and Amelia, in a shot taken a few months ago at Carlton's second birthday party. Little Amelia had only been around for six months then.

He also saw a picture of Dan and Jane in healthier times, when they'd gone on vacation in Portland, Maine. She loved Maine. If Dan hadn't had such a well-paying job in town, they'd have moved there long ago. They were in the midst of discussing once more an early retirement for Dan and a possible transition when they'd gotten the prognosis. After that, all thought perhaps staying put would be for the best. All things considered, if grandchildren living in the same town couldn't add years to one's life, what could? Dan will be eternally grateful to Carlton and Amelia, for they, along with Jane's faith in God, not to mention the medication, had worked miracles.

Adam next took in a photo of his brother, Leonard, with his then freshly wedded wife, Karla. The picture had only been taken four days ago. Jane had insisted months back that, no matter what, they were to go on their honeymoon. And so, Leonard and Karla were currently trapped in Cancun thanks to Hurricane Wilma, unable to rush home for her final moments.

Then he saw his own wedding picture with his high school sweetheart, Macy, taken five and a half years ago. Thank God for Macy. Adam didn't know if he could have made it this long without Macy and his two children. They, after God, were the rocks that kept him from setting adrift into a sea of despair and hopelessness.

Jane had taught Adam to have faith in God, no matter how terrible the situation, for she said He made all right with the world, even if it didn't seem so. It proved beyond difficult for Adam to believe there was anything good in the present crisis, but he would honor his mother by honoring their God and force worry from his heart.

With a sense of calmness taking hold, he turned back around and faced his father who held the hot cup up to his face with both hands, letting the steam drift into his nostrils. It was a habit he'd had Adam's entire life whenever in deep contemplation.

Adam spoke, "I think you're right, Dad. I think this is her final night."

They both grew silent, and so did the cuckoo clock.

As did the baby monitor.

They stared deeply into each other's wet eyes for what seemed nothing short of a decade, then got up and took one another by the hand, a gesture neither would have ever imagined possible before that moment. They walked down the long hallway, hand in hand, to the second from the last bedroom on the right.

Adam could see Dan needed him to open the door, and so he did.

The blinds were closed, the night moonless.

The room remained pitch dark.

He flipped the switch, throwing light everywhere.

His mother lay, peacefully, in the bed.

The two men approached her, each kneeling on either side. Both took her by a slim hand.

"I love you, Jane."

"Go with God, Mother."

Adam turned off the baby monitor.

I Was In Love With a Pre-Teen Super-Hero

I like to think that even if she hadn't been The Dynamic Damsel, it would have been impossible for me to love Tara Stephens any less.

My name is Leland Guluti. Back then I wished I had been named something with a bit more panache, but mother had apparently insisted I bear her father's name. Dad always told me he thought Leland was a fine name, but I suspect if had he known my mother would leave us when I was nine, he would have lobbied harder for something slightly more…contemporary. In the past I had tried to get the kids to call me Gunsmoke, but it never took. They instead chose Leland the Lightning Head as my nickname early on in my life. I must admit that proved disappointing.

Logically, I can understand how they arrived at such an epithet. I'd been a highly intelligent child since birth. In fact, when I was in the second grade they came to the conclusion that I could probably be moved up to eighth if all involved thought it beneficial. Of course, my mother thought it a tremendous idea. She already had dreams of my destined fame and fortune and how quickly she could partake in it. However, Dad was concerned about my social as well as my intellectual maturation. He thought I should stay put among children my own age. So, when it came down to it, as was most often the case, my parents cancelled each other out and ultimately left the choice up to me.

Well now, by the second grade Tara Stephens had already long been the joy of my existence, and the chances of me leaving her behind were nonexistent. Much to my mother's chagrin, I remained static, firmly entrenched with all the other children. Looking back, I'd have to say it was one of the wiser decisions I'd ever made.

Of course, this isn't supposed to be about me—this is supposed to be about Tara Stephens, a.k.a. The Dynamic Damsel. I capitalize the "T" in "The" because The Dynamic Damsel refused to simply be called "Dynamic Damsel." She insisted the word "The" was as much a part of her name as "Mr." was a part of Mr. Fischer's name. He was our principal, of course. I realized her mistake when using "Mr." as her proof-positive, but who was I to argue with my only love?

She had always operated with that alter ego for as long as I had known her. She'd come to school our kindergarten year with her standard headband keeping her hair from her eyes, her horn-rimmed glasses, and a demeanor that could only be described as mild-mannered. I don't know if she initially caught my eye because of how exquisitely beautiful I found her, or if it was due to the fact that she, like me, seemed somewhat short-handed in the friend department. Perhaps it was a little of both.

Incidentally, I know what you're thinking at this precise moment. You're thinking, "How could a fourth grader be madly in love with a fellow classmate since the time he was in kindergarten?" Well, let me tell you, little boys have crushes on little girls just as little girls have crushes on little boys. Little boys hide their feelings, though, by tugging on the little girls' hair and calling them names; in fact, it's my opinion that some of those little boys grow up to be big men who use the same modus operandi. At any rate, I know what I know, and I assure you, I loved her by the fourth grade as much as any ten-year-old can love anyone.

Within weeks of our first year in school The Dynamic Damsel made her awe-inspiring debut. Believe it or not, a classmate began choking on a cookie one of the kids had brought to celebrate her birthday. The teacher had left for a moment to run an errand, and the class parent there to help out panicked and took on the characteristics of a paraplegic. Within moments, Tara popped out of her desk, ran out of the classroom at full speed, then rushed right back in with a mask on. The mask was actually her headband with two eyeholes cut into it. She always wore a headband, as I've told you, and the part covered by her long blond hair always bore two carefully trimmed eyeholes. It only took a simple rotation for her to assume her more flamboyant identity.

We heard a little booming voice command us to clear the area and Tara quickly administered the Heimlich maneuver. We couldn't believe it when a chunk of snicker-doodle ejaculated from the kid's mouth before he gasped for air no longer in short supply. Once she ascertained the student was fine, Tara galloped from the classroom calling out that The Dynamic Damsel happily served the people. Seconds later, Tara re-entered the room with her headband in place again and acted as though she had no idea how the formerly choking student had been rescued. I think only I noticed that her glasses were broken along the frame from being stuffed into her back pocket.

When the principal heard of the account, he tried to organize a media event honoring Tara for her good deed, but she maintained she had run out of the room to find Mrs. Childers and had no idea who may be The Dynamic Damsel.

Seriously, how could you *not* love a girl like that?

I tried to talk with Tara for the rest of our kindergarten year, then for all of our first grade year, and for most of our second grade year. By and large, I indubitably remained unsuccessful. Quite obviously, she wanted nothing to do with me once we reached third grade. Ordinarily, that would have destroyed me, but she didn't seem to want anything to do with *anyone*. I could handle her cold shoulder as long as it wasn't aimed exclusively at me.

Yes, one could easily argue that Tara Stephens gave new meaning to the term "mousy," but when trouble arrived, we could always count on The Dynamic Damsel to save the day with inimitable bravado. I always found it fascinating that she could be so introverted one moment and then so utterly grandiose the next. At times I wondered if the *student* Tara might have been as much a disguise as the *hero* Tara. I don't know why I would contemplate such a thing; it was simply a hunch. Like I said earlier, her super-heroic identity did not necessarily draw me to her, instead, the feeling we were kindred spirits pulled me like a charged ion.

As you may well imagine, the other kids never understood her. They made fun of her behind her back, and some especially despicable ne'er-do-wells mocked her directly. If I hadn't been such a physical weakling, if I had even one iota of the power of my brain within my biceps, I would have shown those cretins a thing or two. It didn't seem to bother her, however. She maintained the portrait of civility, no matter what identity she operated under. She continuously appeared in complete control of both herself and her emotions, or, perhaps, lack there of.

I like to think I understood her rather eccentric behavior, though. I imagine her father and I were the only two people on the planet who comprehended her actions. For this reason, her father refused the psychological counseling urged by school officials. The fact he knew, even then, why Tara did what she did was quite astute. And admirable. Next to my own father, and Tara of course, Mr. Stephens was my hero.

I say I understood her because during a brief moment of euphoric conversation, I got a peek into the psyche of Tara Stephens. Mother's Day quickly approached, and our second grade teacher had given us a project consisting of both designing and producing a card for our mothers. I was less than thrilled with the project due to my mother having little interest in me beyond what sort of inventions I mulled over and how lucrative they may prove for her purse. I noticed during my lackadaisical manufacturing that Tara simply drew a picture. Perhaps she too did not feel an urgency to create something nice for one's mother. Her sketch displayed a mom, a dad, a little girl, a cat, a house with a picket fence, a bright sun, and a car nowhere near accurate enough to determine a make and model.

The teacher walked by us, glanced first at the emaciated effort before me and nodded in understanding, then looked in interest at Tara's picture. She squeezed Tara's shoulder compassionately, and then moved on.

I'll never forget the one, brief conversation we had that year.

"Why aren't you making a card for your mother?" I timidly asked her.

Astonishingly, she actually answered me! It was rare indeed to hear Tara's little, squeaky voice. She replied, "Why are you slacking off on your mommy's card?"

"If I tell you, will you tell me?" I bargained.

Tara only nodded without looking away from her drawing.

"My mother only stays with Dad for financial reasons. She doesn't love us; she loves Mr. Cuhneeng down the street. That's where she goes during the day when Dad's at the laboratory. Therefore, I feel this card would be an exercise in futility and would have little effect upon her immorality or her misgivings about Dad and me."

She looked up at me, perfectly serious, and said, "I think I get what you're saying. Do you want a friend of mine to do something about your mommy?"

I smiled a semi-toothless grin to her and chuckled, "No, that won't be necessary." That was a bad year for my teeth. I wish I'd been silly enough to believe in the tooth fairy. I knew Dad just put money under my pillow. I saved the money he gave me and used it to get him a subscription to his favorite sports magazine. I did this more out of logic than a sense of doing something nice for him. It was his money, after all, and I thought it ludicrous to reward me for something that most every carnivorous animal on the planet does automatically.

Tara went back to her drawing.

"Aren't you forgetting something?" I prodded.

She looked very uncomfortable and then stated, "I was hoping you forgot."

"I know every element's atomic number on the periodic table and every country's capital on the planet; I'm not going to forget a deal made less than three minutes ago."

"You're smart," she said with her head down.

"Thanks," I replied with my sunken chest out.

"I'm not saying smart's always a good thing."

"Oh," I muttered in disappointment.

"Doctors are smart," she whispered.

"Yes, they're supposed to be smart."

"Are you as smart as a doctor?" she asked.

"I will be," I answered.

Once again, she looked up at me with complete seriousness, "The doctors weren't smart enough to save Mommy when I was born."

That turned out to be the last thing she said to me until the fourth grade.

I persisted as a total enigma to most of my classmates even as we reached fourth grade, hence the charming nickname they chose as my moniker. Although I refused higher level placement, Dad and I determined that a bit more stimulating material may actually behoove my aspirations, so he hired a collegiate tutor to visit me three nights out of the school week. Dad repeatedly told me he completely agreed with my choice to stay at my own age level. He felt I learned invaluable lessons from my classmates. I actually believed most of my classmates were Neanderthals, and it turns out most grew up not far off, but I couldn't imagine being away from Tara for any serious length of time.

So, by fourth grade, The Dynamic Damsel made regular appearances at the school. During fire drills she ushered students out. At tornado drills she shoved heads down into the proper position. She constantly solved minor mysteries taking place in the elementary classrooms. Oh, yes, she was quite famous at the school. However, I'm guessing her father kept a pretty close eye on her at the house because The Dynamic Damsel never made the newspaper. I unabashedly maintain if he'd been less of a monitor, the town's crime levels would have dropped significantly.

I finally decided about half way through fourth grade that conventional methods would prove useless in capturing the heart of such a heroine. I started placing myself in predicament after predicament in the hopes she would arrive to save the day. I suspended myself by the foot from the monkey bars. I purposefully locked myself in the cafeteria storage freezer. I climbed maintenance ladders in the gym and pretended to be too scared to come down. I would even stand in front of the parked busses after school with my back to them, feigning ignorance of their existence. In all cases, some meddling grownup interceded before The Dynamic Damsel could come to my rescue, and my efforts were for naught. Oh, and I would be grounded and lectured by Dad, but not in that order.

On a warm April afternoon I found myself in a very dire situation indeed, but this one, unfortunately for my posterior, and I'm being quite literal, was completely unplanned.

I was walking home after school when Chris Haeffering and Jerome Weatherspoon, a couple of sixth grade bullies, stopped me on the sidewalk.

"What's up, freak?" Chris hissed at me. Apparently, he was unaware of the charming soubriquet my fellow classmates had given me. I suppose that's why he used the rather bland "freak" in place of my first name.

"I'm Leland, actually," I informed while trying to maintain my composure. Honestly, I was scared to death. My contemporaries tended to regard me in a sort of begrudging toleration. Most of them were either too threatened or too frightened by my intelligence to do more than speak poorly of me behind my back. Until that afternoon, none had ever decided to take physical action against me for simply being different.

"You think we give a crap what your name is, brainiac?" Jerome yelled in a voice completely too loud.

I refused to make eye contact with them. Looking back, I think I was rather like those people on the wildlife shows who happen across a bear in the woods and fear for their lives. I slowly tried to walk around them, but Jerome grabbed me by the shoulders and threw me to the ground. My rear end hit a lift of concrete where a root had forced it uneven and my tailbone instantly cried out in torture. My eyes leaked.

"I knew he'd be a crybaby," Chris said gleefully while shoving his elbow playfully into Jerome's ribs. "All these geeks are always crybabies. My uncle told me they're nothing but a bunch of wusses."

I forced my tears away through sheer will power, but I knew I had bruised or perhaps even broken my coccyx. Such an injury could take months to heal properly. I've studied anatomy rather ambitiously.

"What's your deal, anyway?" Jerome questioned.

"In what regard?" I responded sincerely while fighting to block out the pain. He seemingly felt I scorned him because when I started to stand up, he roughly shoved me right back down. Upon the second impact, my bladder very nearly surrendered to the pain of my tailbone. I was tortured.

"You think you're pretty smart, huh?" Chris harassed.

I knew better than to answer his rhetorical question.

Chris towered over me; he was easily five-five. Jerome stood even taller, at least five-eight. Compared to my five-one, I felt a bit disadvantaged.

"Is there anything I can do for you gentlemen?" I asked them as politely as I could. I thought perhaps if I buddied up to them, they would let me off easy.

"Ha!" Jerome laughed. "Listen to this kid, will ya! How smart are you, anyway?"

Unsure as to whether this was also a rhetorical question, I gulped hard and replied, "I've tested at 146, but I was nervous and maintain I could do better given another opportunity."

They both looked at me blankly.

I decided to put it in terms they could more easily understand, "Think of the smartest person you know and triple that. That's me."

I'm guessing they correctly took this as an affront because they began yelling it was people like me who fired their daddies, and then they started kicking me. For the record, I've never fired anyone. Never have and never will. I'll admit, I can be more than arrogant at times, but it's not in my nature to fire people. I'd have no stomach for it.

As I desperately tried to cover my face from their assaulting tennis shoes, I heard a strange battle cry, and then they both shot over my head. I sat up instantly, and there postured The Dynamic Damsel in all her glory.

Her garb had altered a bit in the years since her debut. She still wore the trusted headband/mask, but now she also wore a pair of, I'm hoping, her father's yellow bikini brief swim trunks over her jeans. To top it all off, she currently sported a pink shawl that doubled as a cape. I later learned it had belonged to her mother.

Jerome and Chris both got up menacingly off the ground. I scurried behind her on all fours. I'm afraid I was not the most courageous of sorts back then. Come to think of it, I still wouldn't describe myself as surpassingly valiant.

I can still remember every word of that afternoon's exchange as though it happened only a few short days ago. Of course, I have a photographic memory, which also lends itself to recalling auditory events, so I remember most everything I encounter. Anyway, you get the point.

"If you think you being a girl's gonna save you from a smack-down, you're wrong," Chris threatened with hatred in his voice.

"My daddy beats up on girls all the time," Jerome added rather unsophisticatedly.

The Dynamic Damsel merely stood stoically with her hands on her hips while I peered from between her legs.

"Ain't you got nothin' to say?" Chris demanded with his cold eyes narrowed.

"Cowards talk plenty enough to suit me," The Dynamic Damsel responded.

"Jerome, my man, we're gettin' a two fer one today," Chris growled as he cracked his knuckles.

"You said it, man. The two biggest freaks in the school and we get to beat on 'em at the same time."

"It's like Christmas," Chris laughed.

"You boys sure are talkers. Is this going to be a verbal assault, or am I going to get some exercise?" The Dynamic Damsel questioned with a lopsided grin. My mouth dropped at the completion of her query. She must have sensed my apprehension because she looked down at me from over her shoulder and winked through her homemade mask.

"Don't worry," she whispered confidently as Jerome and Chris darted toward her at full speed. "Master Hiachi taught me to bend like the sapling."

I had no idea what that meant, but at the last possible moment The Dynamic Damsel looked back to the bullies, grabbed each by the wrist, rolled backwards, planted her foot rather firmly in both their groins, and then proceeded to propel them headlong to the hard cement below.

As an intellectual prodigy at that age, I thought I was the only one at our school who significantly excelled at anything. During the next two minutes, I quickly realized my uniqueness did not exist singularly. For as smart as I was with the books, I saw that Tara, or rather, The Dynamic Damsel, moved as though she had been born, bred, and fed from Bruce Lee movies. I literally could not believe my sight. I can only describe it as a whirlwind of pink shawl with feet and fists flying every which way. She was a savant in the art of hand-to-hand combat. Now more than ever, she was my hero.

And I loved her.

She hastily finished up with Jerome and Chris, gave them a stern warning that they evidently took very seriously considering I never had another moment's problem with them, and then walked over to me.

"Are you okay?"

I remember staring at her with nothing to say; I found myself dumbstruck. She reached her hand out to me and lifted me up.

"Why do you wear a black turtleneck everyday?" she asked nonchalantly.

"That's what geniuses do," I answered without a hint of humility. "Why do you wear a cape?"

"That's what heroes do," she informed just as matter-of-factly.

We stood and looked at one another for several moments. Her mask didn't strike me as odd at all, and I'm certain my unruly red hair couldn't have bothered her less.

"I better get going…crime to fight and all that."

She turned and assumed a dramatic and impending position as though she were about to lift off when I stopped her with a cry, "Hey, don't go yet!"

She stood up straight, evidently postponing her takeoff, and faced me again. "Yes?" she spoke with intense interest.

"How did you know those guys were going to bully me today?"

"I didn't. This is just part of my regular patrol route," she quickly replied. "I just happened to be in the right place at the right time."

I knew better than to let on I realized she was really Tara Stephens and lived in the complete opposite direction than I did, so instead I tried to play it safe while still attempting to get my answer.

"I've always heard you patrolled the north side of town."

She grinned at me. I saw her gray eyes flash with liveliness. "Well, you got me there. I guess that is public knowledge."

"So…how did you know I needed help?" I pried relentlessly.

She put her hands on her hips and stood proudly before me. She then said, "Leland, it is against my moral code to lie, even when I'm uncomfortable telling the truth. Therefore, you leave me no choice. I follow you home everyday. I worry about your safety."

"You do!" I was shocked! I'd never once seen her following me home, and believe me, when you're the school nerd, you spend a lot of time looking over your shoulder. "Why are you worried about me?"

She refused to break her gaze from mine as she responded, "You're special, Leland. You can do a lot of good in this world with your gift. I just want to make sure nothing happens to you."

"But, you haven't spoken to me in years." I instantly regretted the slip. I'd been trying so hard to maintain the charade Tara put on as The Dynamic Damsel; I couldn't believe I had taken a misstep.

Although I saw no change in body language, I did not hear the hyper-authoritative voice of The Dynamic Damsel or the voice of the reclusive Tara issue forth. Instead, I guessed I probably heard the voice her father listened to on a regular basis. I always knew there was a third voice lurking within that little body. I felt honored to have been chosen worthy. The new voice, the *real* voice of Tara, said, "I know I haven't talked with you a lot since that day you told me about your mommy. I just really like you and I worry about people I really like. Sometimes I worry if I get to know people better that I really like, I'll like them even more, and then…"

"They might go away," I finished for her.

"Yeah," she replied steadily.

"It hurts when people go away," I mumbled.

"I know," she said while biting her lip.

We stood in silence with one another for several more moments, and then Tara did the unthinkable. She removed her mask.

"You're revealing your secret identity to me!" I shrieked in disbelief.

She just giggled as she fixed the headband into place and straightened her hair. Then she said, "You're pretty smart, Leland. I think you've known for a long time."

I grinned. She removed her father's trunks and stuffed them into her back pocket. She then pulled her glasses out from behind her and put them back on. The shawl remained unaltered.

"Does this mean you need a sidekick?" I asked her.

She smiled widely at me and then took me by the hand. For the first time, she allowed me to know she walked me home.

Seven Devils' Hills of Thrills

Warren Potthoff trudged into Prufrock's Café and quickly surveyed the grimy little diner, which also happened to be the only place in Austerburg to eat a meal that wasn't pizza or fast food. Upon finding a booth sufficiently isolated from the majority of the little café's patrons, he reluctantly took a seat with his back to the entrance.

He removed the light, tan GAP jacket he wore, careful to drape it over his khaki clad legs so as not to get any grease or crumbs on them. If said particles attacked his pants…well, he couldn't stand at a table and eat to avoid such a thing, could he? But, he was determined to keep the damage to a minimum.

Warren pulled the laminated menu out from between the napkin dispenser and the salt and pepper shakers with only the tips of his forefinger and thumb, fighting the urge to retch at the filth of the plastic encased paper.

The sounds of the Austerburg denizens slurping and chomping away on their lunch irritated him to no end. He knew if he turned and saw the bits of food dribbling down their faces he would scream in tortured torment and bolt out of the restaurant, leaving Austerburg once more, but this time forever.

He faced one problem, however.

He had nowhere else to go.

Life had dealt Warren a heavy blow, and, ironically, returned him to the one place he never wished to visit permanently again. Austerburg, his hometown, a primarily blue-collar community of no more than twenty-five hundred people, had treated him well enough growing up, but he had developed some bias against the town and its people that defied all rationale. He saw it as a place of failure, despite the fact both his parents had made a very good living during his lifetime. Perhaps it was that so many of his friends never escaped Austerburg, or perhaps it was that so many of his friends had never had any desire to escape Austerburg. Life could not be any more unfair, in Warren's opinion, because all he had ever wanted to do was leave this town, and now he was back, completely against his will, and without a single other option to lead him elsewhere.

"What can I get you...Warren?"

Looking up, Warren's heart skipped a beat when he saw one of the last people he ever wanted to encounter again—Alexa Greer. He never had the nerve to ask his parents what had become of her, for that would have tipped his hat and they would have realized he still thought of her from time to time. Had he ever asked, however, it's rather likely they would have informed him she now worked at Prufrock's Café, and he would have made sure never to step foot in that place in order to avoid the woman whose heart he had broken twelve years ago.

"Um, hi, Alexa. It's, uh, it's nice to see you."

There were even odds who was more embarrassed between the two. Alexa had been known in high school as something of an intellectual, certainly smarter than Warren ever hoped to be, and how she had wound up as a hometown waitress proved beyond Warren's imaginings. Of course, the same could be said for Alexa because she couldn't begin to conceive what in the world brought the big city boy back to Austerburg.

Her freckled face a crimson shade, Alexa stammered, "It's good to see you." A long awkward pause transpired between them before she choked out, "What brings you home?"

Home? Warren thought she presumed too much. Nonetheless, he answered, lying through his straight, white teeth, "Oh, just visiting Mom and Dad, you know."

"Right," Alexa nodded uncomfortably. "I heard about Cheryl. I'm so glad she's okay; back at work and everything, right?"

"Yep," Warren answered, also quite flushed. "Can't believe she broke her ankle just two and a half weeks ago and she's already up and moving around. Amazing."

"Sure is," Alexa agreed without making eye contact. The truth was, she had never dreamed the man sitting in her booth with his back to her could have been Warren Potthoff. She would have asked Sara Whitree to take her table if she'd known he sat there.

"Well, what can I get for you?" she asked.

Within his racing mind, Warren cursed his parents for locking the doors to their house when they knew he was coming back to live with them. Granted, he arrived six hours earlier than planned, and he'd known his retired father was helping his mother with her senior citizens until she completely convalesced. He *had* told them not to bother leaving a key under the welcome mat because there was no way he'd be there before five or six that night, but he cursed them anyway for his current misfortune.

Warren looked at the hazel-eyed woman, still with her wavy, red hair and realized she had remained quite stunning over the years. They had been quite the item through most of high school until their senior year when he had broken it off with her before he went to college. He'd told her he needed to be his own person for the next stage of his life, and he didn't see how he could do that when he wanted to go to the University of Chicago and she wanted to go to the University of Illinois. He had told her this as she stood on the steps of her house, and that had been the last time they spoke face-to-face.

"Biscuits and gravy," he whimpered.

"Got it. I'll bring you some coffee in a minute."

She turned quickly and raced away from him. Warren dropped his head, his mop-top strawberry-blonde hair falling just a little into his field of vision. His heart thumped like a card in the spokes of a madly ridden bicycle and he felt a sheen of sweat seep out over his body, especially his back.

Although not a particularly poetic man, he couldn't help but wonder if he ruined both his and Alexa's lives by breaking up with her. After all, what had "being his own person" gotten him in the last twelve years but a lot of grief and heartache? He nearly entertained the notion of karma, but he had trouble imagining a once pre-med hopeful working now in a greasy spoon as karma.

Could it get any worse?

A loud, abusive voice reverberated throughout the café, "I'll be damned! Is that War Potthoff?"

Warren, without turning around, suddenly became aware of the entire diner putting down their spotted silverware and staring at his moist back.

"It is!" he heard before Cameron Piefer burst into his sight, taking a seat directly across from him at his table. Not surprisingly, Doyle Dilpazo, or, as he'd been known since preschool, Double Dee, accompanied him. Both men wore filthy flannel shirts and work jeans. Warren could only guess at their line of work, but he surmised it involved a great deal of menial labor and the outdoors.

"Hey guys," Warren uttered, further mortified.

"What the hell do you sound so down about?" Cam attacked. He'd never been one to beat around the bush. "You ain't seen your old pals since the day we graduated and you look like you're at a funeral! What's up your corn hole, son?"

Doyle, as usual, said nothing. While totally alert, and far smarter than any gave him credit for, he compulsively remained content to merely watch life pass him by.

Warren found himself at a loss. What was up his "corn hole?" Could he put into words all that had gone wrong in a matter of days? Could he possibly explain how his life had come toppling down? Did he even want to?

No, he did not.

"Hey, boy, I asked you a question," the big, muscular blonde repeated. He had a smile on his face, but Warren knew to defy Cam for too long would arouse an anger that often turned violent. Did Warren really want to end his wonderful lunch with a trip to the parking lot, trading blows with a man he hadn't thought about in over a decade?

"Here's your coffee," Alexa interrupted. "Your b and g will be ready soon." She made a concerted effort to avoid the eyes of Cam and Doyle. "Get you guys something?" she asked them as her job dictated.

"Oh, now I see what's got you so worked up," Cam huffed. "I guess having lunch served by the gal you hung out to dry will do that to you, huh?"

"C'mon, Cam, don't do that," Alexa pleaded, looking directly at Cameron with a stare that could freeze an erupting volcano.

Doyle, not irregularly, seemed quite interested as to how this would play out.

Warren looked out the big window next to him, trying not to notice the dead flies along its ledge mere inches from his coffee, and studied the many oversized trucks in the parking lot.

"Hey, I don't want to stir it all up if you two don't," Cameron said, raising his palms up to Alexa in passivity. Amidst his goatee, a sudden flash of yellowed teeth erupted.

"What can I get you guys?" Alexa repeated.

"I'll take the barbeque and a ice tea," Cameron ordered, fixing his gaze on Warren, who still stared out the window, wishing he could be anywhere but at that table.

Doyle simply pointed to the cheeseburger on the menu he had pulled out, then at Warren's coffee.

"Got it," Alexa mumbled after she finished writing it down. Though she could still recite the entire Declaration of Independence from memory, the owner of Prufrock's Café insisted her waitresses write down all orders. She felt it would save trouble in the long run, and so Alexa complied. "Try not to be a jerk, Cam, okay?" she requested before taking her leave.

"Well, this is a real fun place to have lunch, huh, Double Dee?"

Double Dee grinned in accordance.

"You two sound like you got some unfinished business, War."

Warren broke his gaze from the lot now that Alexa had departed and looked at Cameron. "Call me 'Warren,' would you, please?"

"Didn't bother you none in high school," Cam informed.

"We're not in high school anymore, Cameron."

"Man, you've really turned into some kind of jerk, you know that?"

"Yeah, to you I probably have."

"What's that supposed to mean?"

"It means that anybody who ever got out of this town and made something of themselves probably seems like a jerk to you, so I'm not going to get too upset by your summation." Warren felt his hands shake.

"If you made something of yourself, why's your car filled to the top with what looks like a houseful of stuff? Looks to me like you're back for good."

This made Warren more than angry, and he slammed his fist down on the table, rattling the silverware and ejecting a bit of coffee from its cup. "How the hell do you know what I drive?"

Cameron flashed those yellow chompers of his again, always delighted at instigating anger, and said, "Your dad and me talk cars all the time. He keeps me up to date on what everyone's driving, including you. I'm not as dumb as you always thought I was, you know."

Warren said nothing as he fought to calm himself. How much further could he be pushed before he cracked? He knew not, but he realized nothing would give Cameron more pleasure than seeing Warren Potthoff, the man who had once told his gang of buddies who were staying in Austerburg that they were visionless clouts who were happy to amount to nothing, make a fool of himself in front of those he obviously considered fools.

So, Warren did nothing more and said nothing more.

"You know, I thought maybe you'd grow up a little, War," Cameron criticized. "I thought that silver spoon you self-inserted would tarnish a bit over time, but even now, when you got nothing more going for you than us 'losers,' you still act like you're God's gift. Where'd all your high and mightiness get you, War? Looks to me like you got no woman and you got no job, so, if you ask me, Double Dee and me here have taken the lead on you, even without your fancy college degree and city living."

Setting his jaw and boring a hole through the massive man across the table from him with his eyes, Warren refused to lose his temper.

"You know, War, me and Double Dee were happy to see your car. We thought our old buddy had come home and we could forget about the ugly things you said in the past and start over, but you're more of a punk now than you ever been, and I think you're going to find yourself mighty lonely in Austerburg. Corey would be spittin' fire if he saw you now."

"Corey's dead, so he can't," Warren hissed.

Cameron nudged Doyle on the elbow, signaling that they were going to sit elsewhere in the diner, leaving Warren alone at his table with his back to the rest of the Austerburg people.

Alexa, once the love of his life, returned, dropped his biscuits and gravy down in front of him, said nothing, then walked away. She had overheard Warren's callous reminder of his only brother's status.

Warren had never been more alone, and he had no one to blame but himself.

✳   ✳   ✳

Faced with several hours to kill, Warren found himself driving his Accord all over Austerburg, and then even out into the country surrounding the small town. He soon discovered himself at the stretch of road they called Seven Devils' Hills of Thrills, otherwise known as Rural Route 13, which was rather ironic. Since 1931, twenty-seven people had died on this particular stretch of road, specifically on a one and one-quarter mile of softly rolling hills. For decades, daredevils had attempted and failed to drive their vehicles in excess of seventy-five miles per hour over all seven of the hills, none of which were any higher than the top of an average sized car. Twenty-seven had tried, and twenty-seven had died.

Of course, anyone with any sense knew it was impossible to drive a car that fast over hills that small and abrupt while maintaining a speed of seventy-five. To attempt such a thing resulted in suicide. Sure, some had made it further than others, but no one had made it past the seventh hill…ever.

Consequently, this being a small town and not without its share of superstitions, most subscribed to the local legend of the evil spirits trapped on those hills as the true cause of death for the speed racers. Supposedly, hundreds of years ago, long before Pierre Auster founded Austerburg, there existed a tribe of Native Americans who lived quite resourcefully in the area. Lore argues that seven devils from a realm unknown attacked the tribe, but their shaman defeated them all, one by one, and imprisoned them each in a tree at the top of those seven consecutive hills along what is now Rural Route 13.

Those with irrational minds will drive slowly along the hills and witness demonic faces in the gnarled bark of the trees, but this could have been nothing more than people seeing what they wanted to see. The mind plays terrible tricks among the weak willed.

Warren remembered vividly the horrid faces he would make out in the inconsistent grain of the wood panels that made up the walls of his bedroom as a child. Many a sleepless night he spent convinced one of those fiends would leap out and drag him fighting futilely to the depths of Hell.

The statistic that people who attempted the run at seventy-five always suffered a fatal accident, one tree at a time, proved uncontestable. That is, if the last person died on the fourth hill, then the next person died on the fifth hill. If one person died near the seventh tree atop the seventh hill, then the next person that tempted fate would meet their maker near the first tree, starting the cycle all over again. Even Warren couldn't argue with this fact.

Corey, Warren's brother, had spent the better part of his late teens and early twenties working on a hot rod that would be able to keep up the necessary speed and still remain manageable. His ultimate goal became to defeat the Seven Devils' Hills of Thrills, but he finally came to his senses when he impregnated his girlfriend. With no skills to speak of other than car maintenance—a talent not found lacking in Austerburg—he joined the Army. He eventually married the chubby young lady named Iris Butler after she gave birth to their daughter, Violet, and lived on an Army base together in Virginia. After Corey's untimely death at the youthful age of twenty-eight, the muscle car passed down to his younger brother, Warren.

In the three years since Corey's death, Warren had not so much as even thought about visiting the car out in the old garage his father rented on the other side of town. Gerald had all but claimed the car for his own after Warren's severe disinterest, and Warren had no problem with that. His work at the Chicago Board of Trade kept him far too busy to have Corey's ticket-waiting-to-happen stored in the city. He would have left it to rust away to nothing, but Gerald did just the opposite. Warren always secretly suspected Corey may have been the favorite son of Gerald and Cheryl Potthoff, and it seemed Corey's car had managed to fill in that empty position since Corey's demise.

Warren drove his Accord at nearly ten miles per hour as he studied each and every tree, fighting the urge to scream as the demon faces taunted him with imagined curses and hexes. The last death reported on the Seven Devils' Hills of Thrills had been a forty-nine-year-old woman trying to convince her teenage children that she was, indeed, "cool." The sixth tree waited next to taste blood, everyone in Austerburg knew that much, and the sixth devil did not go disappointed. The woman lost control and rolled six times. Against all odds, her seatbelt decapitated her during the topsy-turvy of the 1979 Camaro she drove.

Rolling to a stop at the top of the seventh hill, Warren stared at the imagined face of the seventh devil's horrid countenance. It seemed to challenge him. It ridiculed his termination from the Board of Trade; it mocked his fiancée, Megan Tomasino, leaving him for another man, a richer man; it scorned his decision to show his face in the town where everyone thought he was now nothing more than just another loser. He'd become the worst kind of loser, the tree hissed, he was the loser who insulted all others before leaving, only to return with his tail tucked between his legs.

Before he could stop himself, Warren threw his middle finger into the air and shouted at the devil, "You bastard! We'll see who's laughing at me a week from now! You wait; I'll prove you wrong! I'll prove this whole damn town wrong!"

Warren shoved the accelerator down and sped off, beyond the seventh devil cresting the seventh hill. He took an alternate route to get back to town.

*   *   *

That night, Warren sat at the dinner table with his mother, his father, and, though not at the table, nearby sprawled the family cat, Leonardo da Kitty. Yes, that was his real name.

As they chewed and tugged on Gerald's flank steak, they spoke little. Of course, Cheryl's walker was nearby, and although it was a freak accident that led to the sixty-three-year-old woman severely breaking her ankle, it still rattled Warren immensely to see the tool of an ancient at hand. He felt as though things had been very much beyond his control of late.

"Sorry you had to kill so much time, Son; we weren't expecting you so early," Gerald informed more than apologized. Although sixty-six, his hair had not thinned out in the least and still appeared as dark as it had when he was twenty years old. His eyebrows, however, had turned a solid line of white, and he now had a lone white hair growing off the tip of his nose that he plucked religiously. This endured as a matter no one spoke of, for Gerald did not like discussing developments signaling his body's aging.

"Yeah, well," Warren started, "things didn't go as planned. I left a little early."

"What happened?" Cheryl asked without looking up. Warren secretly suspected his mother was delighted things hadn't worked out with Megan. His former fiancée had very much been a person concerned with materialism, and this had always rubbed Cheryl the wrong way. Megan, the one time she came to Austerburg during her and Warren's two-year engagement, had done nothing but criticize the little town for all its inadequacies, and Warren, never a fan of the community himself, took this as encouragement to berate his parents' choice of society more boldly than ever before. Cheryl and Gerald had no idea how they had brought up such a snot of a boy, and they were not surprised at all when they learned Megan acted even more abrasive than Warren.

"She didn't want to talk with me, that's all," Warren dismissed. He had thought perhaps he could reason with her. He accepted the fact she found a new lover, but he couldn't believe she kicked him out of their apartment when he had just lost his job the week before. He had nowhere to go, and without any job prospects after his rather flamboyant dismissal from his trading company at the Board, he realized no one would take him in at their business. Needing time to form a plan and gather himself, he returned to the only place that had never charged rent—his parents' house.

"Are you disappointed?" Cheryl asked.

"What's it matter, Mom? It wouldn't change anything one way or the other. She's with someone else now. The apartment is in her name and given to her by Daddy-richer-than-dirt. Nothing I could say justified me sticking around."

"You've had some rough luck of late, Son," Gerald said before taking a swig from his Diet Mr. Pibb.

"Yes, Dad, I realize that," Warren returned, rolling his eyes as he did so.

"What did you do for lunch?" Cheryl questioned.

Chewing his food before he replied, Warren finally answered, "I ate at Prufrock's."

"*Really?*" Gerald blurted out with a hopeful smile upon his face. It was no secret he had wanted Warren and Alexa to marry; some thought he was more distraught about their breakup than Alexa herself.

"Yes, Dad, she was working."

"*What?*" Gerald asked, feigning innocence.

"What. Don't 'what' me."

"Well, you never once asked us anything about Alexa Greer. How were we to know you'd walk right into where she works?"

"I didn't even know she was back in town!"

"Oh, we learned long ago to avoid brining up Alexa Greer's name around you, Son," Cheryl reminded. "How were we to know you'd come home six hours early and eat lunch at Prufrock's?"

"She looks good, doesn't she?"

"Daaaad," Warren moaned.

Gerald grinned at his wife, and she grinned in return. Out of all the girls Warren had dated, Alexa wasn't her favorite, but Cheryl thought she was light years better than Megan Tomasino.

They sat in silence for several long moments, Warren and his parents. They knew he was dying to ask how a U of I graduate wound up working at a local café, but his pride demanded he not ask and they were *not* going to give him another reason to scold them for bringing up her name.

Instead, they said nothing more about Alexa Greer.

"Dad?" Warren initiated.

"Hm."

"Can I have the keys to the garage?"

"Why?"

"I want to look at Corey's car."

"What for?"

"I just…do."

"Sure, I'll take you out there on Saturday."

"Why can't you just give me the keys so I can go by myself tomorrow?"

Gerald shifted uncomfortably in his wooden chair. Though he weighed no more than a hundred and fifty pounds, the chair creaked and groaned with each fidget. "Son, I don't know why you're suddenly so interested in Corey's Mach I, but if I go with you, I can give you the grand tour. I mean, if you go look at it, you'll just see a car. If you wait for me to take you, I can explain all the little details making it great."

Gerald actually feared Warren would do something stupid with the Mustang, like try to drive it, and cause hundreds of dollars of damage to the pristine vehicle. It was not a car simply to be taken out for a stroll, and he highly doubted his second son drove skillfully enough to handle a high performance vehicle such as Corey's.

"Saturday?" Warren complained.

"That's just the day after tomorrow," Cheryl lectured between bites of her peas. She had the strangest habit of eating them one at a time, and when she saw an episode of *Seinfeld* making fun of a woman who did just that, she avoided peas for years. She'd finally brought herself to eat them again in the last few months, still one at a time.

"What am I supposed to do until Saturday?" Warren whined.

"What's that supposed to mean?" Gerald asked.

Warren had formed a plan in order to gain the respect and admiration of a town for which he had no love, but he would need that car in order for it to reach fruition. He would beat the Seven Devils' Hills of Thrills, and then he could get any job in Austerburg he wanted, tiding him over until Chicago took him back. Who knows, maybe he and Alexa were meant to find themselves down on their luck at the same moment. Perhaps the universe was trying to right a wrong made over a decade ago. But, again, that thinking was a bit too poetic for someone like Warren, and he immediately dismissed it.

However, the thought of winning Alexa back with his triumph over the devils did not disparage him.

"Nothing," Warren finally responded to Gerald. "Nothing. We'll go out Saturday. Saturday's fine."

They finished their meal, and there existed barely enough left over for someone's lunch. Gerald, as he had been retired for some time now, assumed it would be his for the taking, but Cheryl gently reminded him that perhaps Warren would want it.

"No, that's fine," Warren said. "I'll find something to eat around town."

Cheryl and Gerald did not have enough nerve to make eye contact, though they both knew very well where their son intended to have tomorrow's lunch.

The next day, Warren walked into Prufrock's Café, but he was terribly disappointed when he did not see Alexa anywhere. He approached the register, for this was one of those places where you pay by the door, not by giving the money to the waitress, and asked if Alexa was working today. He learned she had left only a moment ago if he wanted to try to catch her out back.

Warren sprinted out the front door and raced around the building. As he turned the corner, a red Chevette driven by the very person he sought slammed on the brakes to avoid running him down.

He stood, dumbfounded, as he realized he had been caught in a truly idiotic moment by the person he had wronged the most in his entire life. And by the way, that was no short list.

"Warren, are you out of your mind?" Alexa yelled, popping out of her ancient vehicle.

"Yes" seemed the only reasonable answer, but he would never concede such a thing to another human being. Instead, he straightened out his Express for Men black jacket, took a deep breath, then sauntered around the hood of her car.

"I thought we could talk."

"Talk?" she repeated.

"Yeah, you know, catch up."

"Are you serious?"

"Very."

"Warren," she began incredulously, "I'm not still upset with you for dumping me; we were kids, after all. But, you haven't spoken to me in twelve years! I tried forever to get in touch with you, and you never so much as acknowledged my existence. Why in the world would you want to talk *now*?"

"Well, you know, I just want to know how you've been."

"I've been fine."

"Oh." Warren did not miss the finality in her update. "Well, could I get you a cup of coffee or something?"

"Why, Warren? And don't tell me you want to catch up."

"I just…I could use someone to talk to, someone who doesn't hate me."

"Who said I was one of those people?" Alexa asked in visible pain. She jumped back into her car, slammed the door, then drove madly past her one-time boyfriend.

The truth was, Warren didn't *need* to talk with anyone. He knew in a matter of days he'd be the talk of the town, the first person to ever conquer all seven hills on Rural Route 13. He really wanted to know what had gone wrong in her life. He needed to know what unfortunate events had brought her back to town.

✳   ✳   ✳

Saturday finally rolled around after spending Friday night reading Michael Chabon's short story collection, *Werewolves in Their Youth*. He and his father rode out together to the garage on Joe Mitchell's property. Although it looked shoddy on the outside, Joe had converted the old building into a twenty-stall garage for people who owned high-end vehicles. After Corey's untimely death, Gerald rented out one of the last available spaces and kept the Mustang Mach I in it, moving it out of his own, obviously much smaller, garage.

They walked in and Gerald switched on the fluorescent lights. Warren saw it parked in the middle of the floor in a space big enough for two cars. It had a blue cloth tarp covering it.

"Help me out," Gerald muttered as he pointed to the left front bumper while he approached the right. He took up the cloth and began peeling it back, and so Warren followed suit.

Beneath waited an orange 1970 Mustang Mach I with black stripes. It took Warren's breath away, not because it was testament to his brother's life, but because he saw it as the only means of gaining the celebrity status he thought Austerburg owed him.

"She's a beauty, huh?" Gerald complimented gleefully. "That boy, he sure had talent. This thing was a bucket of trouble when he first got hold of it…I still can't believe he died defending our country."

"He died in a truck accident transporting fatigues, Dad. I'd hardly call that 'defending the country.'"

Gerald's face contorted into a mixture of disgust and outrage. "How dare you disrespect your brother like that, Warren?" his father seethed. "What is your problem, anyway? Just because your life hit a few bumps, you're making everyone else's life a living Hell, is that it?"

"I've hit more than a 'few bumps,' Dad! For God's sake, I set my boss's car on fire!"

"And you're damn lucky he didn't press charges!"

"He didn't have to. He knew I'd never get a decent job again, and the fines alone took every cent I'd managed to save. As a final insult to injury, he's probably bonking my Megan even as we speak."

"Well, Son, he'd been doing *that* before you set his car on fire, right?"

Warren looked away and mumbled, "Why do you think I set his car on fire?"

"I thought you said that was an accident."

"It was; I was trying to ruin his paint. I didn't realize that stuff would keep burning."

"Well, what's done is done," his father muttered, looking down pensively and shaking his head. Then, as though ready for something more positive, he said, "Let me tell you about this car of Corey's."

"Well, technically, it's mine now, right?"

His father squinted at him from over the top of the vehicle, not sure where Warren was going with such a statement, but, the truth was the truth, and technically, yes, the Mustang belonged to Warren.

"Yes, Son. It's yours. If you try to sell this car, though, I will—"

"I'm not going to sell his car, Dad," Warren interrupted. "You don't really think I'm *that* bad, do you?"

Gerald seemed distracted by his shirt buttons after Warren's question.

Warren, still standing on the opposite side of the car and peering at his father, finally requested, "Tell me everything you know about this car."

Gerald's head snapped up with a smile upon his face. "First of all, this car's worth thirty thousand dollars, so *whatever* you have planned, be good to it. This baby is not any normal Mustang. It's a Cobra Jet four speed. We're talking high performance, Son. She's got a 428 cubic inch engine, a heavy-duty transmission, a 3.91 traction loc rear end, heavy-duty suspension, heavy-duty Koni shocks, and she has 390-horse power. You know what that means?"

After waiting for his son to reply, which he did not, Gerald finally answered his own question with, "That means this gem will hit ninety miles per hour in about eleven seconds, depending on road conditions."

"He custom built this car, didn't he?" Warren asked.

"Most of it. Some of it came stock, but Corey insisted on fitting it so it could take a lot of wear and tear and keep going. I don't know what he had in mind, but he built this baby to withstand some rough roads. If you ask me, I think he wanted to start some drag racing racket. Thank goodness he got that out of his system."

That's all Warren needed to hear. He knew his brother had intended to use this car to take on the Seven Devils; he had simply never followed through. His father all but guaranteed the car could make the run, but Warren knew it would take more than car muscle to successfully defeat the Hills of Thrills. He'd need skill—ability he didn't yet wield.

"Dad?"

"Yeah?"

"Would you teach me to drive this car?"

"Why?"

Warren pontificated for a moment, searching for the most believable answer, and finally came up with, "Well, what else do I have to do around here? It's not like I've got a lot of friends, is it?"

✳   ✳   ✳

Over the next few days, Warren and Gerald took the Mach I out in the country, father teaching son how to speed shift and maintain control of such a powerful automobile. Much to both men's surprise, Warren seemed to have a knack for that sort of driving, and Gerald became relatively comfortable with Warren's high-speed maneuvering within just a few practice sessions. He trusted his younger son so much, in fact, he agreed to allow Warren to hold onto the keys and take it out on drives without him. It was obvious to the older man that Corey's Mach I filled a hole that had formed in Warren's existence, and he wasn't going to be the one to risk his still living son's life getting any worse.

✳   ✳   ✳

The following Wednesday finally arrived, and Warren was brimming with confidence. Tomorrow he would prove victorious over the undefeated Seven Devils; he would do that which no one had ever done in the history of Austerburg. He would be a hero, the stuff of legend, and a man whom everyone would worship.

But in order for all that to happen, he would need witnesses.

He knew just who could provide them.

After much searching for Cameron Piefer's number in the Austerburg phonebook, he found himself unsuccessful. So, on a lark, emboldened with the power of the three hundred and ninety horses he now controlled within one engine, he dialed Cam's mother, a once attractive woman who had been dealt far too many hard blows in life. Each line in her face represented a man who'd left her; each dark circle under her eyes a child she had to raise alone.

Fully expecting Cam's mother's baritone, he was quite surprised when he heard his quarry's voice instead. Part of him started to jeer at the fact his old friend still lived with his mother, but a quick inventory of his own living conditions negated such a thing.

"Cam?"

"Yeah, who's this?" an inebriated voice replied.

"It's me; it's War."

"What do *you* want?"

"Hey, do you and Doyle work tomorrow?"

"Yeah, moron. We work six days a week. That's the way it is for people who have to earn their money."

"Any chance you could take the day off; you know, call in sick or something?"

"Why would I waste one of my sick days?" Cam slobbered out through his phone.

Warren couldn't help but grin to himself as he said, "I'm using Corey's car to take down the Seven Devils."

A long pause resulted, followed by a tremendous belch. Then, "What time you want me and Dee to meet you there?"

"I knew you couldn't pass up the possible death of one of your best friends."

"Former best friend. But you're right; if you're gonna die, I don't wanna miss it. Now what time're you doing this thing?"

"Meet me at the first tree around noon. Dad'll be gone by then to help with Mom's patients."

"Consider it done, boy."

Just before Warren flipped his cell shut, he quickly asked, "Hey, Cam! You still there?"

"Yeah?"

"One more thing."

"What's that?"

"Where's Alexa live? I couldn't find her in the book."

✳   ✳   ✳

Easing his Accord into the driveway, Warren couldn't believe he hadn't assumed Alexa lived in her parents' old place. Unlike Cam's abode, Alexa's had existed for over a century and survived as an indigenous home along Wolff Avenue, one of Austerberg's original streets. It was a big, two-story affair with a wrap-around porch and several gables. Although dark out, Warren's headlights told him nonetheless that the old home still direly needed a fresh painting.

Only one vehicle sat at the end of the driveway leading directly to an alley, and that was Alexa's Chevette. Her father's old, beat-up green station wagon was nowhere to be seen, nor her mother's sedan. He had no way of knowing what Alexa's mother currently drove—it'd been twelve years after all—but he had no doubt it would be a silver sedan of some sort. The green station wagon belonging to her father, well, that was as eternal as the sun rising each day.

Warren got out of his car and strode along the little cement walk leading to the cement stairs, which, in turn, led to the porch. As soon as he stepped upon the porch, its old wooden planks groaned beneath his weight.

He had two doors as options for entering the ancient home at opposite ends of the porch. One of them was the official doorway to the foyer where there was a piano and an elaborate wooden staircase leading to the bedrooms. The extra door, on the other side of the porch, gave entry directly into the living room where they used to sit and watch television.

Many lights were on throughout the house as he chose the more formal of the two entrances. They never had a doorbell installed, so he knocked against the glass, careful not to put his hand through it, as he had always feared he would.

A bustle arose above him in the room he knew to be Alexa's, and then he heard her footsteps take the back staircase emptying out into the kitchen at the rear of the house. Several more steps, though they fought to remain noiseless, approached the door Warren stood before, but Alexa remained out of sight.

"Who is it?" he heard her voice shout. He imagined it was meant to sound threatening, but it came up woefully short. Knowing the inside of the Greer's home as well as his own, he placed Alexa exactly. She stood right beside the piano, careful to remain unseen, but close enough to hear and be heard.

"It's Warren!" he called through the glass, grinning immensely as he did so.

Quite a strung out moment of silence occurred.

"Warren Potthoff?" she finally questioned.

"None other!" Warren returned with more jovial drama than he believed himself capable.

Slowly, ever so slowly, he saw one of her hazel eyes peek past the edge of the glass. She must have been sitting on the piano in order to do such a thing, for the instrument ran flush against the doorframe.

Once confident it was her old high school sweetheart, she unfastened many bolts and allowed him in, admonishing him as she did so with, "Are you crazy or just rude? Can't you call ahead before you go scaring me to death like that?"

"You're unlisted," Warren answered as he entered the house, removing the tan GAP jacket he chose to wear once more.

"Oh...well, you should have asked me for my number at the café if you wanted it," she lectured as she closed the door behind him. His eyes grew just a little wider in disbelief as he watched her refasten no less than six deadbolts.

"I don't remember all those..."

She finished at last, turned around, narrowed her eyes hatefully, then uttered, "Well, a lot's changed, hasn't it?"

She brushed past him and Warren couldn't help but detect the old perfume she'd worn in high school effervescing. He watched her walk away in her pink pajama pants and pink, long-sleeved shirt before she disappeared.

He guessed where she headed and followed her. He entered the living room and saw her flipping through channels, not really interested in anything television had to offer. She never had been.

"Where are your folks?" Warren inquired while he moved past the other door that emptied onto the porch and sat upon a loveseat cattycorner to the couch she rested rigidly upon.

"They moved."

"Where?"

"Kithlessville."

"You bought their house?"

"They gave it to me."

Warren simply nodded, protruding his lips so that they nearly made a kissing face. He often did this, even in high school, when keenly interested in asking a multitude of questions but dared not, for whatever reason.

Sensing his tenacious curiosity, Alexa informed, "I didn't want to move to Kithlessville."

"Well," Warren replied, "who *would*? Pretty weird town from what I've heard."

Alexa finally seemed to settle upon an episode of *Lost*.

"Good show. Megan and I used to watch…" Warren suddenly felt very awkward and let his sentence trail off into oblivion."

Noticing his discomfort, Alexa spoke, "You can talk about the tramp if you want to, Warren. We're both adults…now."

Sitting up straight, taking a deep breath, pursing his lips this time in an inverted fashion, he finally mumbled, "So Dad's told you all about her, huh?"

With one leg propped up to her chest and her remote control wielding arm resting upon it, she asked, "What's this show about?"

"Kind of hard to explain—"

"Then don't," she interrupted brashly. "I don't really watch the tube other than news channels or *Arrested Development*."

"Yeah, I heard they might cancel it," Warren informed.

"That happens to most of the good shows."

She flipped through the many channels again, finally settling on CNN. There seemed to be some story about an infamous terrorist being captured. Warren was far too distracted with Alexa to pay much attention to it.

"What happened, Alexa?"

Without looking at him as she sat upon the red wine colored couch, she whispered, "I told you I don't want to talk about this stuff. Why don't you just leave?"

"I don't get it," Warren continued on. "You were an A student in high school, one of the best of your class. For crying out loud, you had a scholarship to U of I! I don't want to knock you or anything, but what are you doing back in Austerburg working at freakin' Prufrock's Café?"

Her narrow jaw visibly clenched beneath her pale skin. Alexa retorted with, "Well, at least I'm working and I've got a place of my own. More than can be said for you, isn't it?"

The anticipation of tomorrow's glory was too strong for Warren to take offense at her comments, and, in essence, he knew she spoke the truth. She had every right to be furious with him. She had a clear vision of her future at the age of seventeen, and he had obliterated everything she had foretold and dreamt.

"I'm sorry," she blurted out.

"Don't be, I had it coming."

"You're right, you had it coming and more, but I pride myself on being civil, even to jerks like you, and I'm not going to lower myself."

"Did you get pregnant or something?"

Alexa sprung from the couch like she had been shot from a canon and flung the remote at Warren with such velocity that he didn't have time to even think about reacting. Before he knew it, he had blood trickling down his forehead, running right between his eyes. He felt it form an upside down Y as it streamed along both sides of his nose, only to collect in his agape mouth.

"Oh!" Alexa gasped. She ran over to him and forced his head back, causing the blood to choose new and interesting routes down his face as it obeyed gravity's uncompromising laws. She grabbed a wad of tissue from the end table and pushed it hard against the wound. She then yanked roughly on his arm, bringing him to his feet, and led him to the bathroom connected to the kitchen, an admittedly odd choice by the architect of this home.

She thrust him down upon the toilet and then rifled through the medicine cabinets, searching desperately for band-aids.

"Was that a yes or a no?" Warren interrogated.

"That was a no, you sanctimonious idiot!" she cried. She finally found a band-aid that had surely expired if such a thing were possible and applied it rather roughly to the wound she had inflicted.

"If you have to know," she growled as she next wiped away the blood all over his face, "I was lucky enough to obtain a stalker my last year at U of I. He broke into our apartment and raped my roommate in the dark, thinking it was me. After that, I had a hard time concentrating, you know?"

Warren was shocked! The thought of someone potentially violating her aroused many feelings he hadn't experienced for anyone else—ever. He took her by her long, slender hand and whispered, "I'm so sorry, Alexa; I had no idea!"

She wrenched her hand free from him and hissed, "That's because you refused to answer my e-mails, my calls, and my letters! The whole damn town knows; it was *only* eight years ago! You weren't perfect in high school, Warren, but you were nowhere near this monstrosity you've become."

"You don't mean that," he said as he stood up from the toilet, feeling a bit wobbly and light-headed as he obviously stood too fast after sustaining such an injury to the head.

He reached for her, and it was not in order to steady himself.

She withdrew from him, pressing against the sink.

"I think you should leave."

Warren lowered his head, shook it once, then walked through the kitchen, approaching the back door.

He stopped after he unfastened the many deadbolts of this door as well, turned his head to her so she could only see his profile, then said, "Tomorrow I'm using my brother's car to make the run at the Seven Devils' Hills of Thrills. I'd like you to be there."

"I have to work."

"Can't you take off—a sick day, maybe?"

"No."

"I could die."

"I won't be there."

And with that, Warren left Alexa's home, careful to pull the door shut as he did so.

✳   ✳   ✳

The next morning, Warren eased the Mustang to a halt on the shoulder of the road about one hundred yards before the first hill. The devil of that perfunctory tree sneered at him, as though admitting he posed no danger to Warren, but his friend on down the road certainly did.

Warren left Corey's muscle car running as he got out and greeted the several men having a little tailgate party at Doyle Dilpazo's old Ford truck. He noticed gleefully that Doyle and Cameron had brought along some other detainees of Austerburg.

There stood his old friends Debert Whaley, Ethan Harrison, Calvin Jach, and Joyce Keys. They all worked some blue-collar job or another, none of which would suffer without them on this day of glorious reckoning.

"Thanks everyone, for coming," Warren stammered. "I appreciate you taking the day off to see this, it really means a great deal to m—"

"We just came to see you bite it, bud," Debert informed.

"Don't act like we're still pals, Warren, 'cause we ain't," Calvin chimed in.

"Now, come on guys, these could be the last words you ever say to old Warren here; you don't want to leave off on a sour note, do ya?" Cameron asked sarcastically.

The other five Austerburg High School alumni laughed heartily at the simple joke.

Standing inertly, unsure of what to say, Warren chose to usher forth no words at all.

"Tell you what we're gonna do, War," Cameron commenced. "We're gonna all hop in the back of Double Dee's truck here and drive about a quarter mile past devil siete. He's up, you know; it's his due."

"I know," Warren replied.

"Well, okay then. So, we'll either see you make it or see you…well, not make it, you know?"

"I know," Warren reiterated.

"Let's go, y'all," Cameron commanded.

Warren watched as people he cared nothing about tumbled onto the bed of Doyle's truck. They knocked Pabst Blue Ribbon beer cans and laughed at Warren remorselessly as they pulled away, kicking loose gravel up into his face and the grille of his brother's Mustang.

Although he had no doubt he would make it out of this undertaking alive, Warren still felt a slight chill as he fastened his seat belt and turned off the radio. He wanted no distractions.

If he wanted to keep the car and himself in one piece, he had to drive straight down the middle of the road. He couldn't allow even a fraction of his tires to hit the loose stuff on the shoulders at the speed he'd be going or else he'd be thrown into a fatal roll. This would be a magnificent blend of mechanics and instinct, and, after all the practice he'd had over the last few days, he felt confident he could pull it off without a hitch. So long as, of course, the legends weren't true. If they were real, however, the greatest amount of skill in the world would not help him against the devils.

Pushing against the accelerator while holding the brake, he got the car up to tremendous speed before he allowed it to jettison forward. His father had been right, within seconds he reached seventy-five miles per hour.

Over the first hill he went, propelling through the air. He landed and fishtailed, but he let his gut take over and got the car under control.

He looked ahead to the right and saw the upcoming second devil mocking him. He set his teeth and jumped over the second hill.

Next came the third, the face in the tree snarled, over the hill he went, sparks burst out from the car as its wheels rubbed the fender wells. Those heavy-duty shocks were proving essential for this feat.

The fourth devil posed no threat at all, nor the fifth, nor the sixth.

The seventh, however, was quite different.

Warren knew if anything were going to happen beyond simple pilot error, it would happen while he crested the seventh hill.

In a wild, unalterable path up the hill, he glanced at the seventh devil.

Warren swore its eyes were on fire, boring through him just as they had several days ago.

He came over the top of the hill, and there, a few hundred meters off, he saw Alexa's Chevette next to Doyle's Ford. She must have come the back way at the last minute. Warren saw she had made a church steeple with her hands as her fingertips touched the tip of her nose. Her eyebrows were arched in a series of concerned waves, and the Mustang's driver detected tears rolling down her cheeks.

She worried about him.

…He'd made a terrible mistake.

In less than a hundredth of a second, Warren saw himself for what he was, and that was nothing more than a shallow, stuck up, thankless ingrate. But it was not too late to change.

It was never too late.

He would apologize to Alexa, to his friends, to his family, and he would make a life in Austerburg, never to demean the hard working people of the unassuming town ever again.

He understood all this in the tears of one of the only people who cared about him any longer.

It was enough.

He undid his seatbelt as the car propelled through the air, then pulled on the handle and pushed against the door.

His instincts now told him if he stayed in that car he would not survive the seventh hill. Warren, with this newfound sense of benevolent passion, refused to let everyone go on thinking of him so poorly, as he knew he deserved. He would make amends with everyone. He didn't care if he became a hero; he now only wanted to be a good man.

The door stuck.

Eyes bulging in terror, Warren, still suspended above the ground as he went over the seventh hill, watched as his view of Alexa, Cam, Double Dee and the others dissipated into a scene of pure fire and brimstone. Rocks melting into lava surrounded him with sparks and embers flying everywhere. The noxious smell clogged his throat and his eyes watered, and when he saw a horned creature made of scorching flames emerge from a pool of lava, he knew the legend to be true.

It sprung from the lava, lifted a flaming tomahawk into the air as it rushed at him, leaving a trail of fire behind it, and then slammed the weapon onto the hood of his Mustang Mach I.

*   *   *

"No!" Alexa screamed.

She immediately broke into a sprint, running toward Warren and his car. Before she did so, she vaguely noted Cam pulling his cell phone from his belt and dialing for an ambulance.

As she ran, Doyle pulled up alongside her, thrusting open his passenger door and yelling, "Jump in!" It'd been the most she'd heard from him in months.

As Doyle pushed his Ford truck to its limits, Alexa replayed the image she had just witnessed within her mind.

Warren had seemed to try to bail out of the car as it flew through the air, then, impossibly, the front of the hood inexplicably caved in. Even more incredibly, the Mustang, still in midair, made a ninety-degree turn and then landed, hood now afire, and drove straight into the seventh tree, bursting into flame.

When Doyle and Alexa finally made it to the scene, the Mustang blazed too severely to approach. They could see a hunched silhouette within the flames of the wreckage, and, just above the flicks of fire, the face of the seventh devil appeared to be smiling coldly, eyes glowing hot from the inferno beneath it.

"No, he's still trapped in the car!" Cameron yelled into his cell as he ran up beside Alexa and Doyle. Alexa glanced around and saw her Chevette parked next to Doyle's Ford. Ethan stood next to Cameron, as did Debert, Calvin and Joyce.

"Hurry!" Cameron screamed at the 911 dispatcher. "Yeah, Rural Route 13; we're on the seventh hill! Come as fast as you can!"

Then, as an immediate afterthought, Cameron warned, "But if I were you, I'd keep it under seventy-five over that first hill!"

Sitting Silently In the Back Pew

Alice Goddard had been attending St. Mark Lutheran for her entire life. Pastor Stone, who had long since left and later died, rest his soul, had baptized her in the eloquent old church twenty-nine years ago. She attended Sunday school without falter, took part in catechism, and was confirmed in the eighth grade, when she vowed her allegiance to Jesus Christ. She later married a man named Richard, whom everyone called Dick, when she was twenty-one. They gave birth to two children, Clive and Anthony, during the four years of their marriage, and then they divorced. Somehow, Richard, again, known by all as Dick, got custody of the children only to move to Madison, Wisconsin, immediately thereafter in pursuit of a girl he'd gone out with in junior high school. Since then Alice had not even gone on a date with a man, and she had never missed a church service.

Oh, and she gave up believing in God around the time the State granted Dick her children.

So why does she continue to attend church? Great question. Perhaps, with both her parents gone, no brothers or sisters, and her own children several hours away, church granted the only stability in her life. Perhaps she knew that, as much as things may unexpectedly change, every Sunday there would be church.

Alice was once, about ten years ago, quite attractive. She had long, blonde hair, green eyes, a tall, thin frame, and a perkiness that always brought a smile to her fellow Lutherans' faces. She'd won countless popularity awards throughout her private school experience, and while at Augustana College, she had been all the rage. That's where she met Dick, by the way.

Now, sadly, her features were no longer pleasant, despite her young age. She had large, black bags under her eyes, her hair had become an entity unto itself, refusing to form any sort of truce with its home base whatsoever, and her skin had turned a sort of colorless hue, somewhere between gray and ashen.

Of course, these new qualities did nothing to bolster her self-confidence, and with each year that passed, her bags got a little darker, her skin a bit more colorless, and her hair even more rebellious.

Long ago, she had friends who would have come to her rescue and taken her mind off her many problems, but they had all left town for various reasons or become so busy with their own children that they didn't have time enough to use the bathroom, let alone tend to her desperate needs.

The current pastors—Hadden, Byus, and Scholfield—had each visited her empty home on several occasions, quoting Scripture and inviting her to church functions, but Alice always had some reason or other why she didn't have time for such things. She did, however, sit and listen quietly as they reiterated the Scripture and reminded her of the wonderful Christian she had been, once upon a time. They vowed to her God waited for her to come back to Him, she just had to open her heart once more.

Not surprisingly, only one of them had been divorced, and he quickly remarried. All of them were still allowed to see their children, and except for the oldest, Pastor Schofield, their parents were still living.

In other words, Alice thought God had been pretty good to them.

She had long ago decided that if God was going to turn His back on her, she would do the same.

But, a lifetime habit of being in a certain room at a certain time could not easily be broken, so she continued to attend St. Mark, sitting silently in the back pew, usually all alone. As though she had yellow police tape surrounding her, forbidding anyone to approach and cross a threshold that would bring them within her parameters, she always sat utterly alone. She remembered a time in sunnier days when she wished people would leave her alone so she could have a moment to herself in God's house.

How had she fallen so far?

One Sunday, near the end of January, a young man sat directly in front of her, breaking the self-imposed boundary the congregation had unconsciously established around Alice Goddard. He apparently visited their church for the first time because Alice had never seen him before. He wore a dark brown sports coat, the kind you could get for under thirty dollars at Old Navy, a pair of dark jeans, and a plain white dress shirt. He wore it undone at the collar. His hair was a dark oatmeal, unkempt and somewhat greasy. If Alice had seen more than just his profile as he sat down in front of her, she thought for sure she might have found him handsome.

She nearly got up to leave at such a hated contemplation, but Pastor Byus began the morning announcements before she could do so, and then the opening hymn dutifully followed. She could hear the man singing, but it wasn't nearly loud enough to appoint as a tenor or baritone. In fact, he seemed to be one of those singers who sang just above a whisper only so that no one could accuse him of not praising God.

She once had a beautiful voice to go along with all her other nearly perfect aspects, but she had quit making sound of any sort while at church, and, frankly, outside of church as well.

Then came the time she had dreaded the entire service, the moment when all were supposed to take a minute and say, "Peace be with you," to their pew neighbors. Fortunately for Alice, as already established, no one ever sat closely enough for such a thing to be an issue, and none made an effort to come to her, nor did she make any attempt to go to them. However, with this man sitting directly before her, in the second from the last pew, she might be forced to interact with him somehow or other. Perhaps she would be most fortuitous on this day and he would bypass a salutation to her, as rude as doing such a thing may have been.

"Now take a moment to share peace with those around you," Pastor Byus prompted.

Alice immediately lowered her eyes and hoped against hope that this man would be a shy person, unwilling to make the first effort in a place where he was the stranger.

No such luck.

He turned to face her, his brown eyes catching the winter sunlight peeking in from between clouds though the windows. She lifted her eyes involuntarily, she had been known in the past to simply ignore someone trying to fraternize with her by keeping her eyes staring directly downward, even closing them on occasion, but the lure of an attractive man tempted her too much, though he wasn't particularly all that handsome. She noticed he had a light beard about him.

"Peace be with you?" he asked more than stated, extending his hand. She noticed they were quite ragged and calloused.

He raised an interested eyebrow when she said nothing in return, but instead literally turned her entire body so her back was to him. He clenched his outstretched hand into a confused, passive fist, flattened out his modest sports coat, then turned back around to shake hands with the people in front of him.

Alice slowly rotated until she faced the man's back again when the service resumed. Had she really turned her back to a man who had extended his hand to her? Had she been that crass? Why did she behave in such a ludicrous manner? Sitting with her chin down to her chest for the duration of the service, Alice was shocked when everyone but the man before her exited the church while she sat inertly.

Again, he turned around slowly, cautiously, and faced her once more. She lifted her eyes until they met his own, but she said nothing, not an apology, not an excuse—nothing.

"Are you okay?" he asked her with a voice somewhere between that of a child and an old man.

She nodded her ashen face once as a reply.

"Do you need to talk?"

This time he perceived a quick shake of the face as the separate entity on the top of her head moved in unison, deciding, for once, that it would act cooperatively with the being below it.

"You sure?"

Before Alice could answer, some congregation members stood at the end of the man's pew, welcoming him to their church. He nodded politely to Alice, then walked down the length of the pew to converse with those actually willing to verbally communicate with him.

It would be an acute lie to say that Alice did not experience disappointment.

She followed the visitor with her eyes as he approached those who had turned their backs on her and had a nice conversation with them, laughing and smiling, doing all the things that humans are supposed to do when they take joy in being a Christian and living a Christian life. She'd been one of them, once, before everything she loved about her life was taken from her and she was made into a farcical reproduction of her former self.

The next week, like clockwork, she sat silently in the last pew at the ten-fifteen traditional service. It was Communion Sunday, and this would mark the fifty-fifth consecutive Communion she chose not to take. She had ceased to believe it was really Jesus' body and blood up there. Instead, she thought it was just cheap wine and some bread chips.

Long ago, about four missed Communions in, some then-friends in the congregation attempted to persuade her to reintroduce Christ into her system, both spiritually and physically, but she had instead insulted them and their idealistic, utopian lives, and then sent them away from her rage quite beside themselves. Those people in question never made contact with her again. Alice thought they were total failures as Christians. She didn't consider herself a disappointment, her disdain for God and Christ had been a conscious decision, not some accidental shortcoming due to lack of character.

At any rate, for the second straight Sunday, there sat the mysterious man with the light beard before her. He wore the same outfit, though it appeared the dress shirt might have been a slightly different shade of white. As he sat down, he looked just over his shoulder and nodded slightly at Alice with a sincere but wary smile upon his face. She looked away from his kindness, finding it pretentious and awkward.

There they sat, one in front of the other, without any sort of communiqué at all until the greetings stage arose. Once more, he turned to her, held out his chapped hands, smiled truthfully, and said, "Peace be with you." This time he uttered it as though it were an order, not a hope. His voice was solid, like she could have done chin-ups from it if she'd so desired, and because of his sureness, she couldn't help but reach for him. She took his hand and found it was indeed quite coarse, a layman's, possibly that of a construction worker or a farmer. While she shook his hand, still unable to make eye contact, she glanced about the church and noticed the entire congregation had paused to take in the irregular sight of Alice Goddard making human contact with a fellow church attendee!

Her hand shot out of his as though it had been suddenly held over an open flame. Her ashen face turned a bright crimson, which was a welcome sight compared to the usual gray devoid of any sort of emotion other than indifferent apathy.

"I'm Josh," the dark haired man notified.

Alice said nothing in return to the first man she had touched out of choice rather than necessity since Richard, whom all addressed as Dick.

"Alice," she mumbled suddenly and indirectly.

"Nice to meet you, Alice."

Josh found himself pulled away from her by the people in front of him. They did not realize what a pivotal moment this was in Alice's life, for she nearly returned the sentiment to the stranger, making more progress than she had in years, but alas, it was not to be this Sunday, for Josh had no choice but to turn and greet those before him and grant them peace as well. He did not have the luxury of turning anyone away, even those who were nowhere near as tormented as Alice.

When it came time to rise and take Communion, Alice despised herself when she realized she would take it if only Josh invited her to walk up with him. Upon reflecting for no more than a nanosecond, she thought perhaps she did need to physically take Christ into her being. Perhaps the Savior did reside in that cheap wine and bread. Had Christ himself not told them as such?

But, Josh did not invite her up, because he also did not rise to take Christ into his body.

At the end of the service, he stood and faced Alice, who wore a dingy purple mock turtleneck and khakis. He stared at her for just a moment with a pleasant look upon his face, then said, "It's good to see you again."

She lifted her eyes from the strange streaks always left upon the pews where people sat and met the gaze of the thirty-something standing over her. "It's nice to see you, too," she muttered. She had forgotten how to talk civilly with someone after years of everyone treating her like a broken toy. However, she told the truth. It was nice to see him again.

"Why do you sit in the back pew?" he asked.

Although terribly straining for her to maintain the conversation, she pressed on for some unknown reason, "I don't believe in God anymore."

She expected him to shoot her a dirty look, say something disparaging, then take his leave, but he proved himself even more a mystery by emitting the following, "Yeah, it can be hard, can't it? I mean, He used to talk to people directly all the time, like it was going on every other day, whereas now, well, not many of us have that sort of familiarity with Him. And His Son, wow, that's a hard one to swallow, too, isn't it?"

"What do you mean?" she asked, her eyes becoming suddenly alert.

"Well, they want us to believe that, what, two thousand years ago some guy who was supposed to be God in human form died for our sins? Where's the proof? I mean, the Bible? That's the proof? That's not much for today's information age, is it? Seeing is believing, and no one's seen Jesus in person in quite some time, have they?"

Beyond belief, Alice found herself growing aroused and argumentative, countering with, "Well, maybe we see him more often than we think. Maybe he just doesn't walk up to us and say, 'Hey, I'm Jesus, how's it going?'"

As she spoke with Josh, the congregation exited, shaking hands with Pastors Schofield and Hadden—Pastor Byus currently presided over the contemporary service that met at the same time—and everyone stared at the bearded man as he roused more flair from their former princess than anyone had in years. Most had to tear themselves away from the sight in order to make way for the next set of people wishing to shake hands with their pastors before they began their Sunday afternoons.

"Oh, come on, Alice," Joshua laughed, "you don't *really* think Jesus physically walks among us, do you?"

Although she started to answer yes, because, indeed, before she had met Richard, the man many called Dick, she had fervently believed such a thing possible, that it was even a fact. Finally, she whispered, "I think he could; maybe he doesn't, but I think he could."

Josh walked around his edge of the wooden pew, then sat down next to Alice and the wild tenant positioned upon her head. "Alice, you either think he does or he doesn't; you can't take a 'maybe' position on this one."

Meeting his brown eyes with her own green ones, Alice thought a moment, bit down on her bare lip, then confessed, "When I was younger, all the way back to when I was a little girl, I swore I saw Jesus sitting in this back pew, right where you're sitting now."

"That's ridiculous!" Josh laughed with a wink.

That wink confounded Alice; she had not one iota how to respond to such a thing. All she knew was that this man had gotten more conversation out of her than any man or woman had in a long, long time, and that included her doctor, accountant, and therapist.

"It's not ridiculous," she disagreed. "He sat back here all the time. Even at my wedding; I told the ushers not to seat anyone in the spot you're sitting in, and, lo and behold, he walked in just as the service began."

"What'd he wear?" Josh asked, seemingly without entertaining the notion what she said could be the truth in any way, shape, or form.

"He wore a suit, what do you think?" Alice burst out in her normal voice, even approaching some tone of playful sarcasm. It refreshed her ears to hear the voice of the woman she once was.

"Seriously?"

"Of course," Alice replied. "He always wore nice clothes, I mean, nice enough. Just nice enough to show respect in his Father's house, but never showy, never too glamorous. A lot like you dress, actually," she said, narrowing her eyes.

"I dress like this because I'm poor," Josh answered with a grin, "not because I choose to."

"What do you do for a living?" she asked.

"Wood worker."

Although she knew that for a current atheist, her impending reaction bordered upon the utterly preposterous, she couldn't help but feel a wave of euphoria wash over her heart, something she used to believe with the strongest conviction was the Holy Spirit, and she cried. Inexplicably, the bags under her eyes lessened. They did not disappear, mind you, but they did lessen, and her flesh grew slightly more healthy in hue, not much beyond the color of burnt leaves it had been, but just a little. As for her hair, well, that was a battle only a bottle of conditioner would win.

"Why are you crying?" Josh questioned, reaching out and taking her hand as he did so.

She did not retract hers from his.

"I've been telling myself and everyone that would listen that I reject God," she sobbed. "But I'm not mad at God, I'm mad at Richard!"

"Don't most people call him 'Dick?'"

With laughter mixing in with her tears, Alice both giggled and sobbed, "Rightly so."

"I want you to make me a promise," Josh demanded, squeezing her hand tightly with his while placing the other upon her narrow, scrawny shoulder.

"What?" she asked, paying no heed to the tears rolling down her cheeks, which now had a rosy pallor.

"I want you to sit with your pastors and talk things out. Talk them out for real, no holding back due to pride or resentment. Tell them the truth, even if you think you shouldn't. Trust me, pastors have made mistakes in their past, that's just part of being human, right? That's why he died for us, so when you make mistakes you'll still be forgiven, correct?"

"Yeah," Alice choked out.

"Good. It's okay to be mad at God, Alice. Everyone gets mad at God at some point in their lives, that's part of believing in Him. But, you can't stay mad at Him, not if you truly believe. He's given far more than He will ever take, and you know that."

"He took my sons," Alice cried.

"No. Dick took your sons, and that's because the judge presiding over the case owed him a favor. Everyone knows that. You were supposed to appeal his decision, remember? But you didn't; you immediately lost heart, stopped praying, turned your back on the Church and God, and descended into this strange doppelganger. You came to rely on Dick more than your Creator, and when Dick turned his back on you, you turned your back on your entire foundation.

But God is always willing to take you back, no matter how long you've been away. He's always waiting for you, isn't He?"

"Yes," Alice responded, nodding her head, smiling joyfully.

Josh stood up, flattened out his humble sports jacket, nodded at the pastors who remained, watching incredulously along with the church elders and some of the congregation, and then called out to them, "She's going to be fine." He smiled down at Alice, then looked back to the pastors and asked, "Hey, do you guys think you could whip up an impromptu Communion for her; it's been awhile."

The pastors all but fell over themselves as they rushed back to the front of the church while the elders sprinted as fast as their knobby old legs would allow for the materials they would need.

"Will you take it with me?" Alice requested, standing up but still holding the tradesman's rough hand.

"Me?" he asked with a smile. "Oh, I don't think so."

"Of course," Alice nodded, closing her eyes in humility. "I should have known better."

"Well, for all you know, I could be Missouri Synod; you know they don't let outsiders take Communion with them or vice versa." Josh let go of Alice's hand, removed his from her shoulder, then reminded, "You keep your promise, because God will keep His, okay?"

"We're ready," Pastors Hadden and Schofield called out as they stood before the alter at the front of St. Mark Lutheran Church. They had joy in their hearts, for a member had finally reclaimed the Holy Spirit all had known still resided within her.

There would be many apologies over the coming weeks, both from Alice and to her as well. For all were in the wrong, and it took only the reminder of their purpose to bring them back together.

"I'll keep my promise, Josh," Alice pledged.

"Say 'hi' to the kids for me, and even to Richard, too," Josh said before he started to walk away.

Before she approached the alter, Alice reminded, "Most people call him 'Dick.'"

Josh flashed a smile accompanied by a short chuckle, and then went on his way.

978-0-595-40590-9
0-595-40590-8

Printed in the United States
57651LVS00005B/373-474

9 780595 405909